I0556010

Relics of the Underworld

The Sage's Legacy, Volume 3

Alexa Whitewolf

Published by Alexa Whitewolf, 2018.

This is a work of fiction. Similarities to real people, places, or events are entirely coincidental.

RELICS OF THE UNDERWORLD

First Edition. August 21, 2018.

Copyright c 2018 Alexa Whitewolf.

ISBN 978-1-9993839-7-8

Written by Alexa Whitewolf.

To hope, to strength, to overcoming destiny.

"Leave all else to the gods."

— Horace, Roman poet —

Acknowledgements

This series, that I started when I was only 14, has been a huge part of my evolution as a person, from a former teenager to a now-woman. In many ways, Freya has characteristics of mine, and I think that's a given when you're a writer – you leave a bit of yourself behind with each character created.

I would not have been able to finish this series without the support of my husband and furry canines! To Mom, who encouraged those first pages from years and years ago, thank you.

And to my friends, my editor, and everyone that worked in the background to bring this to fruition, a huge HUGE thanks!!

To Y. Nikolova at Ammonia Book Covers, an IMMENSE hug for bringing my vision to life in the covers of this series, I couldn't be happier!!!

And to my readers, I hope you enjoy this last installment in *The Sage's Legacy* ☺

Prologue

T *welve years earlier...*
    "Evelyn!" a male voice shouted through the fire. "Mark!" it called again.

There was a huge explosion and fire burst everywhere. Aside from the roar of the blaze, the silence was deafening, only adding to the eerie sensation the smoke created.

Through the flames, a shape appeared. It was Seamus, but a younger version with dirty clothing, barely in his mid-twenties. His blonde hair was glued to his face, and sweat dripped off his brow. He searched around frantically, his grey eyes widened with anguish and panic.

"Mark! Evie!" he yelled. "Freya!"

Shouts answered him, and he paused to listen, trying to pinpoint their location. Once he found what he needed, he purposefully strode through the fire. She had to run to keep up with him, taking in the tension in him, the way his breath was coming panting.

Seamus reached a burning car, his eyes glistening more than before. The smoke was thick, and he coughed. Despite his discomfort, he stepped closer to the people within.

He placed his palms on the burning metal of the hood and gritted his teeth. Freya's eyes widened at the power emanating from his palms, a surge so strong it rippled across the metal, trying to leash in the fire.

"Stop!" Seamus growled, and the blaze seemed to diminish for a moment. Before he even had a chance to speak, it burst higher, and he backwards with the force.

The Sage recoiled back in shock. "Impossible..." he whispered.

"Very much possible," a voice came from behind him.

He turned towards it and staggered back. "You! *You* are the cause of this!"

The shapes were dark, obscured by the smog, only a faint outline visible. Freya could not discern them any better than Seamus could, but she sensed his wrath as if it was a living thing.

He clasped his hands together, snarling and trying to grasp the air around and use it to his advantage. He struck forward, and energy escaped towards the attackers.

"You scum!" he yelled as they disappeared.

Seamus turned back to the car, and a female voice called from within. "Seamus! Save her!"

Pale hands streaked with cuts and smoke held a bundle wrapped in a dirty rag. Seamus rushed closer, and they handed the child to him. A raven-haired grey-eyed four-year-old baby.

Seamus held the baby in his arms, wrapping his coat around tiny Freya's face to shield her from the fire.

"Evie! Where's Mark?"

A weaker someone answered from within. "I'm here. Run, Seamus... Run before they come back."

"You know... You know who they were, don't you?" O'Keeffe whispered, and there was so much emotion in his tone, it seemed to strangle him.

"Yes. *He* sent them. And they'll come back for Freya. Get her out of here, please," Mark pleaded. "Leave us, just...make sure she's safe."

"No!" Seamus' eyes filled with tears as he choked out, "I can save you too!"

"There's no time," Evie's voice was wistful, but firm. "They will return, make no mistake. Save Freya!"

"*Go!*" Mark croaked from within, and the sound tore through the air. "Run, Seamus. Do it for our friendship!"

Seamus shook his head, but another plea from them both was his undoing. He nodded past the lump in his throat and, biting back tears, hugged the child closer.

"I'm sorry... Mark... Evie..." he whispered to the air.

Seamus turned and ran through the smoke until his chest was ablaze and he dropped to his knees. He had reached the end of the road when he turned and looked back. He witnessed the same two shapes coming out of the fire and raising their hands, blasting energy at the car simultaneously.

Sobs burst past his lips, soon followed by the anguished groan of a hurt beast. "No..."

Seamus watched, powerless, as the flames consumed Freya's parents. Movement in his arms drew his gaze to the tiny baby, and the ache in his heart eased ever so.

"Farewell, my friends. I will protect her as my own."

&&&

Moments after dying, Evie opened her eyes to a bright blue sky. A warm hand in hers tightened its grip, and she turned her head to the side. Mark was blinking awake, and taking in their surroundings.

As they both go to their feet, Evie gasped. Clear, blue water surrounded them, so clear in fact she could see fish swimming. If she didn't know better, she would've thought they were in the Caribbean.

"Mark..."

Her husband squeezed her hand in reply, his body taut with tension as he did a slow turn. When he froze, Evie turned in the direction he was staring.

A gilded palace shone as if carved out of the landscape. It had not been there mere moments earlier. But now it stood tall, proud, a majestic reminder of a forgotten past, from the times of Pharaohs and long lost dynasties.

Evie let go of Mark and stepped closer, ignoring his soft pleas to not move any nearer. She recognized the architecture of the sphinxes which guarded its entrance. *It cannot be...*

As if on cue, the doors to the palace opened and out stepped a woman. Dressed in a long, white robe, she was adorned with a lapis-lazuli necklace and a throne crown. Her olive-skin and high cheeks spoke of blue blood, as did the way she held herself – like a queen.

Evie stopped dead in her tracks. Eyes wide, she dropped to her knees, pressing her forehead to the ground. "Goddess..."

Mark was by her side in an instant. "Evie, are you hurt? What's wrong?"

She knew not how to explain the urge to salute the goddess, nor how to answer the need within her. Fearful of attracting her ire, Evie lifted her head off the ground, and chanced a glance upwards.

"Rise, daughter."

The woman was only a few feet away now, smiling down at the couple. Mark's frown did nothing to shatter her confidence, nor did it affect the kindness in her eyes.

"Evie, talk to me."

As if in a dream, she turned her gaze from the goddess to Mark, and swallowed hard. She owed him so much, and yet she had always kept this away from him, even through her pregnancy, even through them being hunted... Would he be able to forgive her?

Mark dropped his forehead to hers, his eyes never once leaving hers. "You trusted me in life, darling. There is no reason to stop now."

"It is not a matter of distrust, Mark," the woman intervened, "rather of fear. What Evelyn needs to tell you may shatter certain illusions you have... Are you prepared for that?"

Mark broke eye contact with his wife to glare at the stranger. "Who the hell are you?"

"Watch your tone with my wife, human." The booming voice appeared first, followed by a man. He crossed the entrance to the palace and joined the woman in front of them. "I am Osiris, god of the Underworld, and you stand before Isis, goddess of magic, wisdom, and mother of pharaohs."

Mark's jaw slacked from surprise, and he glanced between the two deities, then back to Evie. His background in archaeology had educated him enough to recognize the names, but his wife's own in Egyptology much surpassed it.

"The gods of Ancient Egypt?"

Evie nodded to his question and stood. "I... need to tell you something, Mark. It has to do with everything we've been through."

Her tone predicted nothing good, but Mark forced himself to relax his tense muscles. "I am listening."

"One night, when I was a young girl, a book appeared in my backyard. It told me I may have to use it in the future, but until such a time, to forget about it. And I did..."

"A book *told* you?" Mark repeated, frowning.

Evie placed a calming hand on Mark and met his gaze head-on. "I know this sounds crazy, but is it any crazier than us being killed by a pack of demons?"

"You've got a point there, darling. Keep going."

"I forgot about the book until shortly before meeting you. When I visited Scotland on my own, and you found me at Stonehenge, it was not by luck. The book led me there, and many other places across Scotland. I found out I was its guardian, and what I was protecting..." Evie trailed off at that and glanced to Isis and Osiris for help in explaining.

"She guarded, unknowingly, the relics of power for us," Osiris said. "They are two powerful objects that, together, can render one master of the undead. They can also release my vengeful brother, Set, from the cage I have imprisoned him in the Underworld."

Mark crossed his arms over his chest. "Go on," he nodded to Evie.

"Well, I wasn't the only one who had such a responsibility. When you introduced me to Seamus, I found out one of his friends, Thomas, protected a similar artifact... A medallion."

"How did you know something related them?"

Evie bit her lip. "Do you remember at our wedding, when you asked me if something was wrong?"

Mark frowned, thinking back that long-ago memory. "Yeah, you were white as a ghost after taking a walk with Seamus, and I couldn't figure out what happened."

"That's because I met Thomas."

A growl from Osiris silenced her, but Isis glared at her husband. She motioned for Evie to continue.

"When I saw the medallion around his neck, I panicked. Also, something seemed to happen to us, like the book and the medallion were trying to keep us apart, at opposite corners of the Earth..."

"It is part of the spell we set upon them," Isis revealed. "They are only to be in the same vicinity with the two chosen to be their guardians, in order to lead to the relics."

"Now why would you do that?" Mark scowled.

"Because long ago, the entity who helped us hide the relics said the time will come when someone will have to step up. And that brings us to now, and your untimely demise."

"What do you mean?" Evie's question was a whisper, and Mark moved closer to hold her.

"We had hoped you would raise Freya into someone powerful enough to follow in your footsteps." Osiris' expression sobered. "As the greatest two Sages in the world, you were fit to protect the artifact. Unfortunately, the book is now being protected by a man who lost the quasi-totality of his powers."

"Who?"

"Seamus O'Keeffe."

Evie inhaled sharply in Mark's arms. "No! *How*? What happened?"

"He tried to save you two and faced off against demons much too powerful for one man."

Mark tightened his grip on his wife. "What are we to do, in that case? How do we help?"

"And what does this all have to do with Freya?"

"She will be one of the chosen," Isis said softly. "And you, too, have a choice."

Osiris stepped forward. "I can allow you to continue to the Underworld, where you shall receive the eternity of peace owed to you. Or, you remain a guardian to your little one... Spiritually, if nothing else."

"Meaning what, exactly? That we'd be ghosts?" Mark's brow creased in frustration.

"Yes." The confirmation came from Isis, who stepped closer to her husband. "If you release your identities, you would have some, if not much, combined spiritual strength. It would be enough to cross into the physical world Freya lives in, from time to time..."

"But you cannot tell her who you are, and you have to swear to act unbiased."

"She is our daughter! Do you realize what you ask?"

Osiris only stared, unfazed "Yes."

Evie and Mark shared a look, communicating without words. In the end, Evie nodded for both of them. "We accept."

Isis sighed and lifted a palm. A soft, golden fog rose around the two, and they became orbs. As their souls fused to become one, she turned to Osiris. "What of Thomas?"

The god growled once more, his jaw clenching at the name. "He has done enough. I cannot risk the medallion falling in the wrong hands."

"You believe it is time to change guardians? But the artifact..."

"Perhaps it chose wrong."

Their conversation was interrupted as the orb took shape, and in front of them appeared a white tiger, its green-golden eyes shining fiercely.

"Welcome into the world, Tyr," Isis spoke softly.

Chapter 1

P*resent time....*
  In the palace of the gods, Evie and Mark rushed into each other's arms. Osiris smiled at Isis, recalling more than one such reunion between them. For those memories, he allowed them a moment of peace, before clearing his throat. They pulled away, seeking the gods.

"Why bring us back?" Was Mark's first question.

Osiris narrowed his eyes, recalling the countless times Tyr had disobeyed. It was apparent now where that streak of rebellion came from. When they had merged the souls, Isis had assured him both Mark and Evie's personalities would survive. In practice, one side would take prevalence, depending on the situation.

His wife had not been wrong then. And it was still Isis' touch on his arm that calmed him enough not to spit out fire. Instead, the god took a deep breath.

"Years ago, you both helped us out, unlike your companion."

"He's wasn't our companion." Mark's jaw clenched, his eyes darkening with fury. "He was an acquaintance. A mutual friend of someone we both respect."

Osiris threw him a look, but Mark was not done speaking. "And if I recall correctly, you scared him into hiding."

Isis sighed by her husband's side and took a step towards the couple. "It was not our intent, but Thomas did take it rather....hard."

"*Hard?*" Evie's eyes narrowed. Though her tone remained soft, there was a steely quality to her gaze that surprised the gods. "A demon killed him and he has not seen his grandson grow up. We can relate to his pain, believe it or not. What you did, forcing him to give up a lifetime of peace, was cruel."

"We tried to rectify it, Evelyn."

"You should have tried harder." Mark wrapped an arm around his wife, pulling her into him. She buried her head in his chest and let out a loud sigh, as though releasing tension.

When she stepped out, her expression was calmer. "If we are to help in whatever this is that you needed our human forms for, our price is Thomas' freedom. Let him get his peaceful slumber, with no consequence for crossing you."

Isis turned to her husband, expecting him to deny the request. To her surprise, Osiris' attention was on Mark, not Evie. "Do you agree to this?"

"Yes."

"Then I swear it will be done," Osiris said. "Thomas will be free to choose his soul's path, as soon as we handle the latest mess."

Mark nodded and intertwined his fingers with his wife's. "Which is?"

"We brought you back to human form because it was the only way to save you," Osiris said. "After your fight with the demon, Raksh killed some of my guards and saw Set. We believe it was to bring him the dragon artefacts."

"But they were empty," Isis finished. "Freya and Brennan absorbed the two halves of the map."

Evie gasped, taking a step out of Mark's arms and towards the gods. "If they did, that means she and Brennan....they've truly connected?"

Isis inclined her head, barely hiding the smile that threatened to emerge. "Yes."

"When?" The curt question came from Mark, whose darkening expression hinted he was none too happy about his daughter's proximity to a certain Wiseman.

"Before they fought Cortés," Osiris said, tilting his head to the side. "Why the attitude, Mark? You should be happy – the bond protects your daughter."

Evie squeezed his hand before Mark could answer, calming him down. "He's being a wary father, is all. But if they did connect, how deep does their connection go?"

"Enough that they can tell each other's location and strengthen each other's powers when needed. Their spiritual potential has grown, and will continue to rise the more they are together. But we are not the only ones who know that."

"Raksh."

Mark's growl drew Osiris' attention once more. "Yes, and my brother by default. But let us not forget what this map absorption means."

When the couple seemed confused, Isis smiled. "The power of the artefacts will push them to find the relics. And they will need help, someone to protect them."

"You're asking us to play guardian to my daughter and her boyfriend?"

"I suppose so," Isis murmured wryly.

Evie shook her head in amusement at her husband of-fended tone. Mark stepped towards Osiris, his demeanor much too calm.

"You know, I've had a while to ponder what you told us, long ago."

"Mm." The god only arched an eyebrow, nowhere threat-ened.

"Twelve years ago, you mentioned an entity that helped you hide the relics. What did you mean?"

Isis' shoulders rose in a delicate shrug. "Did you never wonder why the powers of Sages and Wisemen come from the same dragon?"

"Or why you two were so successful safeguarding the book?" Osiris added.

Mark and Evie shared a look, but in the end seemed more confused than ever. Evie spoke first. "I was chosen when I was young, as was Thomas. That's where my connec-tion ends."

"And Mark was the strongest in his class of Sages, bested only by Seamus." Isis smiled at their surprised exchange. "We did not choose you by chance, when you died. Your creden-tials spoke for themselves."

"And exactly what does this background have to do with anything?"

"Your strengths and your powerful auras showed you were descendants of the greats. It also meant you had in your veins the strongest potency of the powers gifted by a certain dragon upon a maiden."

A stunned silence followed Isis' explanation, interrupted by Osiris. "At the risk of repeating myself, were you never curious about the source of your spiritual strength?" When he smiled this time, the skin at the corners of his eyes crinkled. "Only a creature of the Underworld could gift such a thing."

"Are you saying... The dragon in the story with Estella, he's... from the *Underworld*?" Evie's voice squeaked at the end, betraying her surprise – and awe.

"Yes. He was guardian to my palace, but when I got wind of Set trying to overthrow kingdoms through the influence of humans, I sent him to the surface. When he was injured, Draykho acted of his own accord."

"Draykho..." After a stunned silence, Mark spoke. "Is that... Does that mean he's also the guardian of the relics?"

Osiris did not answer, instead stared back. Mark turned to Evie, noticing her stricken expression. *So she also hadn't known.*

He focused his attention back on the deity. "Then if Freya and Brennan search for the relics...."

"They will be driven to Draykho, and wherever he lies in wait."

"I don't understand. Did you lose him or something?"

A flash of annoyance crossed Osiris' face at Mark's question. "No, I did not *lose* my dragon. But when we realized the threat Set still poses, I and Isis asked him to go into hiding. He was to keep the location a secret, known only to him. The artefacts were his only clue to us, and we made sure they found someone worthy."

Mark recalled Evie's story. She'd always thought the book from her childhood had been normal. At least until they'd met, and the tome revealed itself to be more than a page-turner.

He wrenched his gaze from his wife, turning to the gods once more. "So if Raksh follows Freya and Brennan..."

"He would have the opportunity to steal the relics, and kill Draykho. If the ancient being ceases to exist, what he has bestowed upon your kind will also flounder out of existence."

"You mean Sages and Wisemen..."

"Would become mortal again." Osiris' words were like a death sentence.

Mark and Evie shared a look. "How much of this can we tell Freya and Brennan?"

"Whatever you think is right," Isis confirmed. "We put no restrictions on you, not this time. You were brought back as separate entities because it was our only option. We cannot enter the earthly realm, thus you will be our only link."

"And the youths' only hope at success. You alone can protect them."

The two adults nodded and morphed into their tiger shapes. *Time to see Seamus.*

&&&

"Ow!" Brennan hit the ground with a groan of pain, then rolled to his back in time to avoid his opponent.

Hair up in a ponytail, dressed in shorts and a simple t-shirt, Freya was flying with her leg extended. It was aiming straight for him, unless he planned to move out of the way and concede the win.

With a muffled sound of pain, Brennan stood and grabbed her leg mid-air, circling around and releasing her towards a tree. Undeterred, Freya rolled over her back and landed in a crouch.

She flashed a grin. "Giving up?"

Brennan snorted and held up his hands. "Keep it coming, girlfriend."

Freya shook her head, then stood and faced him. They continued sparring for long hours, until they both landed on the grass, unable to move a muscle.

"Remind me never to lose a bet with you again." Brennan's mutter was strained, as were his muscles.

He turned to Freya, noticing her intent expression as she started at the sky. "Frey? All good?"

When she remained quiet, Brennan interlaced their fingers in the grass. The action had her turn to him, smiling. "Yeah, I'm good. Was just thinking."

"What about?" Freya bit her lip, and it was enough answer. "Tyr?"

She avoided his too-perceptive stare, until he reached with his free hand and grabbed her chin. "Talk to me, Frey. That's what we do, remember?"

Freya met his gaze then, blinking hard against the tears that threatened. "I know it's stupid, and there could be a million reasons that explain it... But I haven't been able to find Artemis, and I can't help thinking something bad happened to Tyr. And I miss..."

Brennan pulled her in his arms, hugging her as she cried. "I know, love. I know."

After a few long moments, Freya calmed down enough to sit upright. "We need to find Raksh, Bren. He's the only one we can get answers from."

"Only problem is, that's *all* we've been trying to do for the last weeks."

"Maybe we need more than studying sessions in the middle of night," Freya said. "There's nothing in Seamus' library, and you can't recall there being anything in your grandfather's. We've tried everything we can think of, but maybe we just haven't thought outside the box."

Something about the way she said it had Brennan's attention. "And what more can we try?"

Freya hesitated. "We could try bait."

Brennan hated the sound of it, and he had a feeling Freya's idea would be much worse than what it implied. "Meaning?"

"The map is in our heads. If we try, we could get it to reveal enough clues to start us on our journey. No matter what Raksh is doing, he'll jump on the chance."

"And if he catches us? We haven't exactly been able to replicate our feat from defeating Cortés."

"I know that." Freya looked away, resting her head on her knees. "Didn't think that far ahead, to be honest. I know that if we find him, we can put an end to this crap."

"And if that route really takes us by the relics, what then?"

"We destroy them, plain and simple. No relics, no weapons for Set."

Brennan mulled the matter over. "But what if it affects the ghosts? Or worse, our abilities?"

Defeat coated Freya's voice when she spoke again. "You may be right."

"I'm more than willing to look into it with you, Frey, but keep in mind how my grandfather died." He squeezed her hand, dragging her attention from the grass to him. "I don't want anything to happen to you, not when you mean so much to me."

Freya smiled at that and leaned closer, pressing her lips against his. "Same here. It was a stupid idea."

Brennan opened his mouth to add more, then closed it. He'd learned long ago that Freya's mind worked in intricate ways, and sometimes it was better to be delicate than outright blunt. "Plus, I doubt Seamus would approve of such a plan."

Freya sighed. "I know, I figured as much. It was worth a shot."

The Wiseman peered at his partner, trying to figure out if she was truly letting go of the idea or if it was a ploy. Before he could conclude either way, Freya got to her feet and held out her hand. "I'm starving. Let's hunt for something to eat."

&&&

Freya ducked the Wiseman, dancing away and shaking her head. Already half-falling apart, her ponytail came undone and her raven hair fell in straight locks around her shoulder. "Bite me, Bren. This one's mine."

Eyes on him, she took a big bite of the chocolate cake, making a show of enjoying it while he scowled. "You're *mean*."

Freya only shrugged, taking another bite. Brennan chose that moment to lunge for her, making her shriek and try to run away, only to trip over herself and fall down.

Brennan wrapped one arm around her waist while his free hand caught the plate with the treasure. He tossed Freya on the couch, then repositioned himself at the head of the table.

"Like I said – never get between a man and his stomach."

Freya scowled, but laughter trickled through her expression while Brennan stuffed his mouth. "You're such a child sometimes!"

As if to make a point, Brennan turned his back to her, covering the plate with his upper body. He gulped down the remnants of the cake.

Their playful banter was interrupted when Sam walked through the wall. Freya grinned his way, but it soon fell when she noticed his serious expression. "Sam, what's wrong?"

"I need your help."

Brennan dropped his plate, joining his partner. "What happened?"

"It's not for me," Sam explained, shaking his head. "It's for her."

He turned and a young girl about his age floated inside. Dressed in something akin to rags, she looked frightfully pale and malnourished. Brown hair fell in limp threads, framing a heart-shaped face. Her huge chocolate eyes stared at them as a doe would a hunter, and she appeared ready to bolt.

"Who's your friend, Sam?" Freya kept her tone soft, unwilling to scare the young girl.

Sam took a step closer to the newcomer, pulling her small hand in his. "This is Anya, and she needs our help." He turned to Anya, whispering in her ear.

Freya noticed Brennan's intense expression. Eyes narrowed, he stepped closer. Despite Freya straining her ears, she only heard the word "countess". Something about their hushed conversation was enough to raise her hackles.

After long moments of whispering back and forth, Sam faced them once more and pushed Anya gently forward.

Anya looked between her and Brennan. "You have to help... Please." A thick accent lined her every word, and it took Freya a moment to clue in to its origin. "The Countess won't let us go, and I'm afraid... She'll ruin the whole town, our families, our souls – forever."

"Countess?" Brennan's tone was full of confusion, but Freya staggered back.

She had placed the accent to an area she had seldom visited, and the implication was enough to stun her into silence.

It can't be...

Freya searched Anya's expression, looking for deceit. But all she could read was the terror in her eyes, and the pure fear in her aura. *She's not lying.*

The Sage cleared her throat, but still her voice came out shaky. "She means the Bloody Countess.... Elizabeth Báthory."

Chapter 2

At first, Seamus thought he was dreaming. The air in the room chilled, and he half-opened his eyes to see a light shining. With a groan, he turned over in bed, trying to catch a few more hours of sleep.

Yet the brilliance only intensified, enough so to raise the hairs at the back of his neck. Now fully awake, he flipped over and faced it, only to blink in astonishment. "What...?"

Freya's tiger guardian was in his room, its green-golden eyes as startling as before. Before his bemused gaze, however, another tiger appeared. Its fur was also white with black stripes, but it was a grey stare he met instead.

Goosebumps rose across Seamus' entire body, even as his mind tried to comprehend. "You... Tyr?" There was confusion in his tone, but also hope.

The tigers shared a look, then the green-eyed one stepped closer. *You knew us under that name, yes, but do you truly not recognize us now?* The voice was inherently male, no longer neutral as it had been.

His companion nudged him, and this time it was a female resonating in Seamus' mind. *How could he, in these forms?*

O'Keeffe gaped at them for a long moment before voicing what he still couldn't believe. "Mark... Evelyn? Is it really you?"

The grey-eyed tiger nodded, moving close enough to rub her muzzle over his hand. *It's us, Seamus.*

"But... You're dead."

Another shared glance, and this time Mark spoke. *That, we are. But the gods called upon us to help them and gave us powers of Dreamwalkers. We live between the realms of spirits and humans, watching over Freya... and you.*

"The gods?"

Isis and Osiris.

Seamus' face lost all color. "Then it's true... What Thomas told me. It really is a match between gods, and we're all pieces on a chessboard."

I am afraid so, Seamus.

"But how..."

Mark went on to explain what happened twelve years earlier, finishing with, *They thought it was time to split us and allow us back here in a proper and due form.*

"Are you saying Thomas is also a Dreamwalker?"

Evie nodded. *Yes, but he refused to help the gods and partake in their games... He disappeared after.*

Seamus ran a hand over his face, trying to gather his thoughts. Eventually, he kept coming back to the same question. "What is it that brought you back *here*, specifically, to Scotland?"

Freya and Brennan... They are no longer safe.

&&&

"Countess *who*?" Brennan frowned, his gaze shifting from Freya to Sam, then Anya. The young girl cowered under his severe expression and shied back next to Sam.

"Báthory. She's the first documented vampire in history."

Freya's statement drew Brennan's attention to her. "The first *what*!?"

The Sage rolled her eyes at him and stepped towards Anya, kneeling on the floor. In that position, the girl barely reached shoulder height, yet even her frail appearance couldn't take away the haunted gleam in her eyes.

"Anya, I need you to tell me everything."

She looked up, biting on her lip. Her glowing form was unmoving, responding to Freya's innate strength. "Long ago, my village in Čachtice was quiet. Until a woman married our lord, the count in charge of the area. He left on many a trip, but she stayed behind. She was....*evil*. Pure evil."

A shudder ran through the girl's slight form, and Freya reached out to hold her hand. "You're safe here with us."

Anya hesitated for a beat before saying, "She wanted to stay young, and keep her beauty. Girls in my village started disappearing... At first it was the ones without homes, like my sister. But then the richer ones started, too. She's been... Ever since we've been back on Earth, she's been collecting her dead victims and forcing them to obey. The Countess wants to use us to ensnare men..." Anya trailed off, looking scared to continue.

"Ensnare how?"

Rather than answering directly, Anya whispered, "The Countess is different. Men follow her, listen to her. Alive or dead, they do her bidding... Like the virgin girls she once killed."

Freya's stricken expression matched Brennan's. She gulped and said, "Do you know what she is searching for?"

Anya lifted her gaze and looked at both teenagers though she seemed not to see them. "Immortality."

A deafening silence fell in the room, so at odds with the laughter that had existed there before. After a few moments, Freya let go of Anya's hand and joined Brennan.

"Immortality?" he asked. "But she's already a ghost. How much more immortal can she get?"

Freya shrugged, glancing back at Anya. "I have a feeling our understanding of immortality is vastly different than Elizabeth's."

"So?" Sam gloated closer, looking between them eagerly. "We can help, right?"

The couple shared a look, and Freya nodded. "Yeah, of course. But Bren and I need to research this. How about we meet here in the morning?"

Sam offered them a small smile. "Thanks, guys." He took Anya's hand in his and disappeared through the wall.

Freya watched Sam leave with Anya, lost in her thoughts. When Brennan touched her shoulder, she turned to face him. "We have to stop that woman, there's no choice about it."

"What of the demon?"

Freya's expression darkened. "I want nothing more than to hunt Raksh down, but these are innocent lives we're talking about."

Brennan nodded. "I know, and I agree. So, up for a late night studying?"

Freya grinned and leaned in for a lingering kiss.

&&&

Seamus stared between the two tigers, uncomprehending. Brow creased, he asked, "What did you mean about Freya and Brennan's safety?"

Mark sat down, bowing his head. *The demon is after them again.*

"That's nothing new, and they fought him off well last time."

Perhaps. But the difference is, now they protect what I and Thomas did, long ago.

Of unspoken accord, the tigers had decided it would be counter effective to tell Seamus everything. The more he knew of Freya and Brennan's abilities, the more he would worry.

"The map? So I heard." The elder Sage sighed and pinched the bridge of his nose. He seemed exhausted, at the end of his wits.

Why are you so tired, Seamus?

Evie's nudge had tears rising to his eyes. "You have no idea how good it is to see you two once more. Freya... We have to tell her, too."

He stood to go meet his protégée, but Mark called out. *Wait.*

Before we tell our daughter anything, there is something we must share with you. Evie moved in Seamus' path, blocking him from leaving the room. *We made a bargain with the gods for Thomas' peaceful ever after. If we stop Raksh and save the relics, they will allow Thomas to have his forever sleep.*

"So he was right..." Seamus whispered, almost to himself. "They were after him?"

Yes. The gods don't take too kindly to being refused, and Osiris is no different.

Evie shook her head at Mark's statement, then met Seamus' gaze once more. *We can only be in this form on Earth, but in the spiritual realm we have regained our physical appearance. I tell you this because Thomas may be the same...*

"You think he's watching over Brennan, same as you two were over Freya?"

Perhaps.

Seamus nodded, rubbing his chin. "I could see it. But what is it you wished to tell me?"

More like a question. Did you know the dragon from the Sage tales is linked to the Underworld?

The elder Sage gaped at his friends, then made his over to the edge of the bed and dropped down. "You... No, I did not."

Evie told him what Osiris had revealed. When she finished, Seamus could only shake his head. "While that is amazing to hear of, what is the link with your daughter?"

Don't you see, Seamus? If she goes after the relics, she'll meet with the dragon. And he's a trickster like those of his kind. How can my daughter survive, especially if she and Brennan only connected once?

Seamus' gaze shifted between the tigers. "But why would Freya go after the relics? Only destruction lies on that path."

Evie and Mark stared at their friend, waiting for the realization to dawn on him. When Seamus made no move, Mark said, *You know they hold the map now, absorbed within them.*

And Raksh knows this, as does Set. It was the demon who nearly killed us... If nothing else, Freya wants revenge. For Tyr, and for the parents she believes are dead.

Seamus felt as if the floor was splitting under him, and before he knew it, everything went black.

Evie stepped near him, sniffing him. *He is but unconscious, tired.* She lifted her muzzle in the air. *But I smell another presence in this castle...*

Mark joined her by the door, growling low. *I know that scent.*

&&&

Freya got up from Seamus' desk and headed to the wall-to-wall library. Her eyes perused the hundreds of books until they settled on a single beige tome, high up. She lifted her hand and felt for air, commanding it to bring the book down.

It fell in her outstretched hands, and she turned to Brennan's amused expression. "Show off."

Freya laughed, walking over to the couch he was lounging on. "Don't get jealous because I can use my power without passing out."

The Wiseman snorted into the book he was reading. "As if."

Freya settled by the foot of the couch, half-sitting on the edge. She flipped through the book, looking for a passage she'd read a while back. Brennan watched her for a moment, then reached out and tucked a strand of hair behind her ear.

"What are you looking for?"

Freya took a moment to answer, lost as she was in the search. When she found the spot, her face relaxed into a smile. "This! It says here that according to the lore, a stake killed the Countess through the heart. They buried her with a necklace rumored to hold the will of the girls killed."

Freya snapped the book shut and raised her excited gaze to Brennan's. "Don't you see? All we need to do is get to Slovakia, find the necklace and destroy it. It'll nullify her power over the girls, and she'll have no leverage."

"Wait, Slovakia?" Brennan arched an eyebrow. "I thought Elizabeth was Hungarian."

"She is," Freya slid on the couch cushion next to him. "Or, was. Whichever way you want to look at it. She was a noblewoman in the Kingdom of Hungary." She poked Brennan. "But that kingdom was split into Hungary and Slovakia. Čachtice Castle, where she lived – and has returned to, if we're to believe Anya – is located in Slovakia."

Brennan rolled his eyes. "Show off," he chuckled under his breath.

"Blame it on Seamus' history lessons," Freya grinned. "Anyway, what do you think of my plan? Fancy sending an evil Countess to the hell she belongs in?"

"I do believe you've got yourself a winner there, Frey. Simple, but effective plan. I like it." When his girlfriend beamed in pride, Brennan lifted his index. "Only one problem, gorgeous. What about her so-called vampiric strength?"

Freya snorted and took the book out of his hands. "What have you been reading?" A full-blown snort escaped her at the title, and she tossed the volume onto the coffee table, before leaning against Brennan. "She's no vampire, they don't exist. A bloodthirsty psychopath, maybe."

"And how is that any better?"

Freya stretched her neck, now inches away from Brennan's face. "Don't worry, I'll protect you."

His brown eyes twinkled with amusement, and he tapped the tip of her nose. "Cockiness doesn't suit you, love."

"Says you!" Before Freya could continue, Brennan's mouth descended on hers.

She melted against him, wrapping her arms around his neck and pulling herself closer. Brennan's hands came around her waist, holding her tight as he continued to kiss her.

Long moments later, Freya pulled back and lay her head down on his chest. "So, we tell Seamus tomorrow that we're going on another mission?"

"Maybe. Let's do some more research, then we can tell him."

"And while we're there, we can search for the relics? If anything strikes us, like a vision?"

Brennan stopped drawing circles on her back, hesitating. Could he promise the girl he cared for that he would be a willing accomplice in her crazy stunt?

"Wouldn't hurt to try," he whispered.

I must be crazier than she is.

&&&

In the dark of the night, the demon paced restlessly. His red gaze scanned the nearly empty mountain, waiting...

She appeared out of thin air, dressed in a robe reminiscent of mediaeval times. Her beautiful face was wrinkle-free, perfect in symmetry, with shaped brows and a pouty mouth. Her eyes were more startling by their iciness than the unnatural hue of blue.

"You are late," Raksh admonished.

Lightning crossed her gaze, and a smile as cold as the rest of her graced her lips. "You were early, demon. What is it you wish?"

"A bargain, Countess. Nothing but a bargain..."

The spark of interest in her expression confirmed he had her attention.

Chapter 3

F reya set the book down and stretched, stifling a yawn. A quick glance around showed Brennan had disappeared, and she stood from the sofa to go find him.

They had been researching Elizabeth's history for the last few hours, and it was now well past two in the morning. As she stepped out of the library, Freya realized they hadn't seen Seamus at all in the evening.

Her feet carried her up the stairs, and she headed to Seamus' wing. With each step closer, she could hear murmurs of voices. When she got by his door, Freya frowned, her hand half-raised to knock.

Seamus was talking inside, but no one answered. "This can't be happening." There was a pause, as if he was listening for an explanation. "And if I don't?"

More than worried for him, Freya knocked on the door. After some hushed whispers, Seamus opened it a crack.

"Freya... Bit late for a walk, no?"

She tried to peer past his shoulder, but Seamus shifted to block her view. "What's going on?"

Her mentor had always been a bad liar. But in that moment, O'Keeffe's features were a complete blank. "Nothing. I was sleeping, and you woke me up."

Freya's frown deepened. "I heard you talk to someone."

Seamus ran a hand over his face and sighed. "Freya, I'm tired. I must have been dreaming or when you came up here." His voice took on more irritation with each word. "Now, was there a purpose to your visit, or are we done here?"

Freya opened her mouth, then closed it. "No, I'll... It can wait until morning."

"Good. Great. Have a swell night." He nodded and, before she could stop him, practically slammed the door in her face.

Freya stood there in shock for a few moments before ambling away. She threw a few glances over her shoulder, but no further sounds escaped from her mentor's room.

As she turned a corner, she ran smack into Brennan. He dropped two apples on the floor and held his arms instead to stop her from tumbling to the ground. "Where did you go?"

"Where did *I* go? Funny. You're the one who disappeared without a word."

Brennan arched an eyebrow at her tone, then shrugged with a sheepish smile. "I was hungry, love."

Freya rolled her eyes, pointing to the floor and the apples. "And you were eating fruits?"

"Nah," Brennan laughed and picked up his bounty, holding one out to her. "Brought these for you. I was eating the leftover pie in the fridge. And some mashed potatoes and meat I found."

Freya snorted, then wiped the apple and bit into it. "Of course you did. Let's go back to the library."

As they walked through the silent castle, Brennan threw her a side look. "What were you doing up there, anyway?"

"Went to see Seamus, make sure he's okay."

Brennan tilted his head at Freya's distracted tone. "And?"

"Um... He seemed okay, I guess."

"You guess?" Brennan stopped dead in his tracks, reaching a hand to pull Freya back. "What's that supposed to mean?"

Freya sighed and told him what she'd heard, and her theory.

"So you think he was talking to someone?"

"Either that, or he's losing it. Neither is good news for us." Freya took another bite of her apple, then shrugged and moved towards the library once more. "Whatever's going on with him, what we need to do is focus on the Countess. There's only so much my brain can take right now."

She stepped into the cozy room and reprised her seat on the couch. Brennan remained standing, jumping from one foot to the other.

"What's up with you?" Freya frowned, assessing his mood.

"I might've found something... But you're not going to believe this." He pulled a book off the table and joined her, opening it at a bookmarked page.

Freya started at the picture, not understanding. It depicted a river, and some kind of underground body of water. It passed through a cavern, lighted by candles. And on the other edge was a large portal.

She glanced at Brennan, shrugging. "What am I looking at?"

Brennan pointed to the portal, near the top. "Do you recognize that?"

Freya peered closer and gasped. "Dragon runes! Brennan, where did you find this?"

The Wiseman pulled the book in his lap, grinning. "You're not the only good researcher around here. But you want to see the weirdest part?"

Freya nodded, eyeing the tome as if it held all the secrets of the universe. To her confusion, rather than flip to another page, Brennan simply closed it and showed her the front cover.

At first, Freya didn't register what it said. Then it sank in, and she raised wide eyes to her boyfriend. "How is that possible?"

"The better question is, what the hell are dragon runes doing in a book about the death rites of Ancient Egyptians?"

Freya bit on her bottom lip and stood, pacing the length of the library. "Does it say anything about Set in there?"

Brennan flipped through a few pages and she watched his expression closely. "Yeah, but only the basics of his jealousy, the fight with Osiris, Horus..." The Wiseman trailed off, frowning as he read.

"Brennan?" Freya stopped her pacing and rushed to peek over his shoulder.

A lesser known fact about the thunder god is that Set escaped his first prison. As punishment for attempting to kill his son more than once, and for cut-

ting his body in pieces and throwing them into the Nile, Osiris called Set to the Underworld. The nefarious god was not prepared to surrender. With the stolen relics of the Underworld, he tried to rouse the spirits of the dead against their lord. Draykho, Osiris' protector, stepped in. With his flames, Osiris regained power over his domain, and imprisoned Set.

Freya met Brennan's equally stunned gaze. "A *dragon*?"

"It's too much of a coincidence, Frey. Think about it. Why would we be protecting relics made by gods... Unless the way we came to be has something to do with the gods themselves?"

She bit on her bottom lip, trying to reason it through. "Are you saying this Draykho is the same one who created Sages and Wisemen?"

Brennan tapped his chin, then nodded. "Yeah, I suppose I am."

Freya plopped down on the sofa next to him and stared into space for long moments. When Brennan nudged her, she sighed. "It wouldn't be any more surprising than all that's happened so far. So the ghosts have weapons through a demon. And our strength comes from a dragon that may or may not have protected the lord of the Underworld."

Brennan nodded and closed the book, before pulling her against him. "So if we take all that into account, do you still want to try out the map, and see where it leads?"

"Absolutely."

His heart sank, but he forced a smile on his face.

&&&

Sam watched Anya settle in a corner of the room. Her sad gaze looked out the window, and her shoulders curved inwards.

"What is it?"

"Your friends... It is nice of them to help. But can they fight? She... The Countess...." She started trembling, and Sam inched closer.

"If anyone can defeat Elizabeth, it's Freya and Brennan."

"And if they don't?"

Sam bit his lip, unsure how to answer. He settled for the truth as he believed it. "They *will*."

Anya's silence clued him on something else going on, aside from her worry. Much as he liked her, Sam knew it was his duty to his friends to find out more.

"Anya... Is there more? Something you're not telling me?"

When tears continued to slide down her cheeks, Sam floated closer. "Please tell me."

&&&

The desert air was cold, and stars glittered across the nightly sky. Freya shivered. *Am I alone?* She took in her surroundings and her eyes fell on Brennan.

We've been here before... It was all too easy to recognize the sandy environment they were in. After all, they'd been dreaming of it enough times.

She was about to call out to Brennan when a bird's cry distracted her. Freya glanced up and saw the hawk, its beady stare fixed on them.

Light in the distance caught her eye. A ragged cliff in the shape on a beak stood in contrast to the horizon. The moon shone on it as if pulling their attention there on purpose.

In two long strides, Brennan joined her and stared at it. "What the hell is that?"

Freya shrugged and reached for his hand. The minute they touched, a jolt of electricity passed through them. Freya's muscles felt like fire, and she shuddered against the force. Behind her lids, scenes moved.

As quickly as it came, they were jolted back to reality, and more cries from above. The hawk zoomed down to them, aiming straight for their heads with claws stretched out.

Brennan heard a voice shout his name, but it wasn't Freya. She was still trying to catch her breath after the vision. He looked around and his eyes fell in the distance, on a shadowed figure. He lifted a hand, and the hawk changed directions, heading for him.

When the bird attacked, the man's cloak fell on the sand and Brennan caught sight of his face. "*Grandpa?*"

"Guys!" Sam burst in, and Freya and Brennan tumbled off the sofa, to the floor underneath. In mirrored crouched positions, their breaths panting, they stared at each other, then at Sam.

"What... Did I interrupt something?"

Freya stood straighter, dusting herself off and trying to school her expression. "Nope, just a bad shared nightmare. What's up, Sam?"

He wasted no time in explaining his rush. "Anya told me something else, about the Countess. She's been meeting a guy...with red, glowing eyes."

"Raksh." Freya near-spit the word, then waved Sam off. "We have more research to do, but we'll take care of this, don't worry."

After a slight hesitation, Sam nodded and left. Once he was gone, Freya relaxed and flew into Brennan's arms. "Are you okay?"

He was unresponsive to her, his gaze lost in the distance. It took some coaxing, but finally he focused on her face. "What was that? Did I hear you call out for your grandfather?"

"He was there, Freya. I don't know how, but he was there." When she opened her mouth to say something, he shook his head. "I'm *not* crazy."

"Did I say that? On the contrary, there must be an explanation." She gestured to their surroundings. "And we're in a library. So, what better place to find a clue?"

She shrugged off his grateful look and moved to the nearest shelf. Seamus organized his books by subject, then in alphabetical order. It took them a few minutes to pull enough reference materials on dreams, before settling back on the couch.

After an hour or so of reading, Freya came across a passage.

> *It was frowned of powerful beings to do so, but they could evade death's door. Rather than pass on as*

rested souls, they would keep roaming the Earth and become Dreamwalkers.

"Brennan..."

Freya heard a shuffle, and a second later he'd moved to read over her shoulder. His entire body froze, and she leaned against him in comfort. His face tensed, devoid of emotion, but his eyes shone brighter – filling with tears.

"So he *is* dead."

Freya nodded. "But not gone."

&&&

Brennan stood watch over Freya as she went back to sleep, wrapping an arm around her shoulders to tug her closer. Though he wanted nothing more than the sweet oblivion of rest, his mind raced.

If the map could take them to the relics, perhaps there was still a chance to find out what happened with his grandfather. And if they could defeat Set...

What then? He peered at Freya's peaceful face. *Will I stay in Scotland? Is this where I belong now?*

His eyelids grew heavy, and finally sleep claimed him, though it was not to be as restful as he wished. Not even a few minutes after dozing off, fog filled his dream.

In its depths, a shadow came forward. Brennan braced himself, fearing another hawk attack. But it was a woman who stepped from the mist, and she was beautiful.

Pale, creamy skin. Eyes the color of a thunderstorm. Lips as red as roses. Dark hair that fell down her back in waves, reaching her waist. She was wearing a burgundy mid-century gown, off the shoulders and with large sleeves.

Her long neck sported a ruby necklace, its pendant falling between her ample breasts. Its bloody hue sparkled with each step she took, almost pulsing with a life of its own.

When she smiled, Brennan's entire body froze, like a snake mesmerized by a charmer.

"My, you really are something," she whispered.

Chapter 4

The Countess moved among the silent trees, relishing the power in her hands. No one dared come out of their houses at night, even less let their unwed young daughters out of their sights.

I have missed this... Too long have I been without their terror. She laughed under her breath. *Nothing beats fear. Nothing.*

"You sssseem mighty sssatisssfied."

Elizabeth stopped in her tracks and threw a careless sneer over her shoulder. The demon stepped out of the shadows, his white teeth glinting even in the pitch darkness. The red eyes glowed like a fire's embers, and she shivered.

Yet she was not intimidated, far be it from it. They had a deal, and as long as she kept her end of the bargain, it would mean unlimited power.

"Well?"

The Countess met his gaze and smirked. "You have nothing to worry about. The boy will be too easy, as most men are."

"I will need more than your reassurance, Countesss. He essscaped my clutchesss many timesss before."

"Perhaps you were not fit to catch him." When she registered his glare, Elizabeth shrugged and amended her statement. "He is strong, yes. But mightier men than him have failed. I have only contacted him once, but he shall be mine within a fortnight."

"Very well. You had bessst not make me need an alternative way."

"And where is my reward?"

Raksh produced his chains of fire, an equally cold smirk on his lips. "Ssshow me proof he isss becoming yoursss, then you ssshall receive your reward. Your victimsss' blood will be all the sssweeter for it."

Once the Countess left, Raksh walked out into the night. *It will not be long now...* It was time to head to a slightly further destination.

&&&

Isis turned from the fire to Osiris, biting her lip. They had followed the demon from place to place, as much as they could, without being able to see past his next move. "What is he doing?"

"I cannot predict his intentions, they are ever-changing. We have no choice but to wait, my sweet."

"Perhaps we should consider waking Horus...."

"Darling, no."

Isis frowned. "But he faced Set once...."

"When Horus went to sleep, it was with the certitude we would not disturb him until the end of the world. This is not such a time."

"Unless Set makes it so."

"My brother may be ambitious, but no world would mean nothing left for him either."

Isis allowed her husband to gather her in his arms, quieting her own discomfort. If only he could see Set for what he truly was – god of Chaos.

&&&

Seamus walked into the kitchen to find Freya and Brennan already wide awake, and in an argument. He bypassed their tense selves and headed straight for the coffee machine.

After he poured himself a cup, he turned and met their stunned expressions.

"What has you both so stupefied?"

Freya shared a look with Brennan, then faced her mentor. "Since when do you drink caffeine?"

Seamus ran a hand over his face and shrugged. "Since today."

Brennan took a step closer, peering at Seamus. "What has you so agitated? Your emotions are all over the place."

O'Keeffe held back a scowl. *I forgot how perceptive Wisemen could be, especially this one.* He sensed a probe mentally and turned his glare to Freya. Her innocent air didn't fool him.

"I would thank you both to stay the *bloody hell* out of my head. Is that clear?"

Freya opened her mouth to argue, but Brennan gave a faint shake of the head. She fell silent, pursing her lips.

"Our apologies, professor. There is something we need your help with."

Seamus took a larger sip of the coffee, grimacing as the bitter beverage went down his throat. "Go on."

"Bren..." Freya rolled her eyes at her boyfriend's description and got off the chair. "What he means is, Sam came back last night with a friend."

Seamus looked between the two. "I am afraid I don't quite catch on. A human?"

"No...." Freya glanced at Brennan. "A ghost. A young girl, about Sam's age. From Slovakia."

Seamus stopped with the cup near his lips. "Slovakia?" His eyes shifted from one teenager to the other. "Why is that significant?"

Brennan beat her to answer. "Some vampire missus from the past is back, terrorizing an entire village. Anya, the young girl, needs help, before history repeats itself."

The cup slipped out of Seamus' hand and dropped to the ground, shattering into large chunks of porcelain. He stared at the mess, then slowly raised his gaze to Freya. "Elizabeth Báthory?"

Freya nodded, frowning at his behavior. Seamus had turned ashen, his hand trembling. Disregarding the broken pieces, he dragged himself to the closest chair and plopped down on it.

Freya and Brennan shared another glance, though this time the Wiseman picked up on his girlfriend's agitation.

"Seamus?" She stepped closer to him, kneeling and reaching for his hand. "What is it?"

"I met Elizabeth a long time ago, when I was but an arrogant Sage and in my youth. We were on a mission, your father and I, and we ran into her." When he met her eyes, his expression was haunted, and the questions got stuck in her throat.

"What happened?" Brennan asked what Freya couldn't get herself to.

"We failed. It is the only reason that siren is still around... We almost had her, too. But she ensnared me in her trap, and Mark would not leave me to die. I would have imagined the damage we did was enough to keep her off the charts for years, but it seems not."

Freya glanced from her kneeling position to Brennan, curious to see what he thought of the confession. Instead of his open expression, her boyfriend was frowning.

The Sage tapped into their connection. *What is it?*

I feel something else within him... O'Keeffe isn't telling us everything.

Freya had learned to trust his instincts, so she reached for her mentor's hand. "What else do we have to know?"

His shoulders slumped and he wouldn't meet her gaze. It was the most shameful Freya had ever seen him, and her next question confirmed the truth. "Seamus, did you... Fall in love with her?"

O'Keeffe looked at her then, his blue eyes sad. "Aye, I did. Enough so I was willing to kill for her."

Freya gasped, but Brennan moved closer and placed a calming hand on her shoulder. "Tell us everything, Seamus. We need to know this, if we're going to win."

O'Keeffe sighed, then stood and walked to the window. The story came out while he overlooked the grounds. "Mark and I were in Eastern Europe hunting down a group of radical ghosts, when we fell upon the Countess. I had less practice than Mark, and was a year younger, but hailed to be more powerful. Elizabeth picked up on that and moved on me like a shark would its prey. I was... helpless. I only had to take one look at those blue eyes and fell so fast I could not fathom what had happened. Over the course of the next weeks, I grew irritable. In the end, I betrayed Mark and caused his imprisonment... All so I could be with the woman I love."

"And, were you?"

Seamus turned to face Brennan and nodded. "I was. For a brief time, anyway. Mark escaped and came to rescue me. I... almost killed him."

Freya straightened up at the confession, watching her mentor like it was the first time she was seeing him. And, in a way, she was. It took all her will to bite back impulsive emotions before touching Seamus' shoulder.

"What happened?"

Seamus smiled wryly. "Your mother showed up. She was alerted her that we had gone off grid, and came after us. Somehow, she used the power of the dragon manuscript to tap deeper into her spiritual energy than ever before, and saved our hides."

Freya's eyes shined with tears, but she fought them back. "And Elizabeth?"

"We did not know back then that ghosts could die, thus we did not try anything. Elizabeth disappeared, and we thought the threat ended... until now."

Freya glanced to Brennan, silently communicating, then nodded. "Yeah, we're still going."

"Freya—" Seamus stopped, as if understanding he no longer had the right to advise otherwise.

To his surprise, Freya stepped closer and pulled him in a hug. "You're only human, Seamus, and I don't hold you responsible. But... It pains me, this story you told me. If nothing else, it further enhances my belief that need to eradicate this Countess once and for all."

Brennan watched his girlfriend, but said nothing of his own dreams lately. "Professor, the more you tell us, the easier it will be to vanquish her. So, what else is there to know?"

Seamus paced back and forth. "Elizabeth is vain, if nothing else. Her girls are her downfall. Those ghosts hate her with all their being, as you must imagine."

When Freya nodded, he continued. "She also has a necklace, the source of her enthralling power. Destroy that, and you have a chance."

A heavy silence followed, until Freya moved to the door. "I'm going to check on Anya, see if there's anything more she could tell us. We can leave in three days, tops."

Brennan watched the Sage leave, but made no move to follow. After she disappeared around the corner, he turned to Seamus, who was watching him. "Was there no way to fight off Elizabeth's influence?"

Seamus sighed and pinched the bridge of his nose. "None. Elizabeth was in my dreams, in my lungs... She was an obsession."

When he looked up again, Brennan had vanished.

&&&

Seamus stepped in his room, only to find two tigers by his bedside. He jumped, then closed the door behind him. "You need to be more careful. What if Freya had followed?"

She didn't, old friend. We would have felt her presence. A pause, then, *There is another's aura we sense.*

"Are you referring to Elizabeth's young ghost?" Seamus shook his head. "This is such a mess."

What do you mean?

"You both remember what happened with me and Elizabeth. What do you think she will do with an untested Wiseman?"

Are you saying my daughter's boyfriend is already in that witch's clutches?

Seamus thought back to Brennan's question before answering Mark. "He may well be. Powerless as I am, my intuition has never steered me wrong."

Mark lay on the ground, and Evie moved to his side. *Then it shall be our duty to undo it, like before.*

Seamus sighed, then said, "You need to talk to Freya. She is worried about this mission, and there are other things they do not tell me. It is about time she knew you are back."

Evie rested her head on her husband's flank. *Soon.*

Chapter 5

Freya jumped awake in her bed, panting. *That damn hawk...*

It had been a dream, only a nightmare, but her heart thudded wildly, and she felt the pain of its claws on her back. Absentmindedly, she reached behind to touch the skin – and her eyes widened in shock.

Brennan!

She slid out of bed and ran to the bathroom. Turning her back to the larger than life mirror, Freya had to bite her lip to stop from screaming.

The door to her bedroom opened and footsteps headed her way. "What is it?" Brennan's voice, still groggy from sleep, reached her before he entered the en suite.

He took in what she was wearing – a top and shorts – and grinned. "Is this all for me?"

When Freya didn't respond, he met her teary gaze. Stricken, his eyes flicked to the mirror. He could see three large scratches peeking from the top of her tank top, and blood permeated the rest of the material across her back.

The grin slipped off his face, and he moved closer. "What the *hell*?"

"I don't know, Bren," Freya whispered. "That...I had the nightmare again, with the hawk, and in it the stupid thing hurt me. When I woke up, the pain was *real*!"

"This is impossible," the Wiseman murmured, passing his hand over the wounds to see if he could pick up anything.

Images of a bird of prey, coal dark eyes and feelings of ruthlessness passed through him. He gasped, and his stunned golden-brown gaze met Freya's.

"We need Seamus. He'll know what to do."

Freya tore her eyes from the mirror, biting her lip. "If we go to Seamus, we have to tell him everything, Bren – even about Tyr."

His hand moved from her shoulder to her back, a muscle ticking in his jaw. "Then we do so. I'm not taking chances with this, Frey. Not now."

Reading the determination in his expression, Freya nodded and returned to the bedroom. She pulled a sweater over her tank top, then faced Brennan. He was holding his hand out, and she took it gratefully, drawing some comfort from the small contact.

Careful of her injured back, Brennan pulled her against his side and they walked together towards Seamus' room.

&&&

Seamus heard the knock to the door and dragged himself out of bed to answer it. Freya's fearful expression and the seriousness in Brennan's eyes had him on high alert.

"What happened?"

Brennan scowled, then pushed Freya past inside. "Not what – *who*."

He grabbed the hem of her sweatshirt and pulled it up, showcasing the scratches on her back. A sharp intake from Seamus drew both the teenagers' attention, even as the elder professor moved closer.

He passed a hand over the wound, but the light touch caused Freya to hiss in pain. Brennan tightened his arm around her, and Seamus backed away.

"What happened?"

Freya pulled her shirt back down and turned to her mentor. "I've been having these nightmares... They got worse in the last two weeks."

Seamus' gaze shifted to Brennan, asking a silent question. The Wiseman only shook his head.

"What are they about?"

Freya sighed, then admitted, "Always with a hawk, in the desert. He seems to be looking for something, and Brennan's there too. Whenever we try to move, he attacks. It never hurt, but tonight..."

"I don't understand," Seamus shook his head. "Why not come to me sooner? With the artefacts gone, you must have known there is nothing normal about this."

The glance shared by the two teenagers had him concerned. It was Brennan who spoke, breaking his silence. "We haven't been able to contact Tyr since beating Cortés. No research we did helped, and we didn't want to drag you into this, if it meant danger."

Seamus rubbed the side of his head, gritting his teeth. "Because, what, Raksh removed the remnant of my powers?" He scowled at the teenagers. "Freya is under *my* roof, Brennan, and that means she is *my* responsibility."

The Wiseman clenched his jaw. Something sparked in his eyes, but Seamus was too far gone to care. *Evie and Mark were right, they have been playing with things they do not understand.*

"What research did you dig your noses into?" His demanding tone left no room for questioning.

Freya shifted under Brennan's arm and whispered, "Just about Set, and the relics. We found out there's a dragon from the Underworld that could be tied to this and..." She hesitated, chewing on her bottom lip. "It looks like there might be a clue in Slovakia."

Seamus pursed his lips. "It is not a good idea for you two to leave here, not any longer."

At that, the Sage moved away from Brennan. Her grey eyes shone with determination. "That's not right, Seamus. Punish me if you will, but we can't just let the people of Čachtice village suffer!"

When the elder Sage said nothing, Brennan intervened. "You'd really allow Elizabeth to best you, again?"

Seamus' piercing glare settled on the Wiseman, and he took two steps closer, towering over him. "Watch your tone, young man."

They stared at each other, upset for different reasons. Freya stepped between them, pushing them apart. "Enough, both of you! Seamus, we *can't* stay behind. Please. Don't try to stop us."

After a beat, he sighed. "There is nothing I can do to hold you back. But this injury.... Turn around."

Freya did as she was told, and Seamus peered down at it. "If the hawk did this, it was at the behest of Set. And nothing the god does is without reason, remember that."

Brennan frowned at Seamus. "What are you saying?"

Freya, however, had caught on. She bit her lip as she turned around, hugging her middle. "You mean, this is a mark?"

Seamus nodded. "Yes. Quite possibly, some kind of tracking spell." His eyes settled on both. "You will not be safe out there. Not alone."

"And who do you propose we get to help us out?" Brennan scowled. "It's not like we have a catalogue to pick from."

Seamus hesitated, unable to tell them what he wanted to. Not yet, at least. He blew out a breath and stepped away, pacing and running a hand through his hair.

Brennan tried to be patient, but with Freya's scratched back ingrained in his mind and his own uneasiness, he couldn't last past a few seconds.

He moved closer, towering over the elder man. "We don't have time for this. If Set can track us, then it's even more important to unlock this map and figure out how to get the relics before Raksh can." He paused. "Help us, please."

Seamus dropped his head in his hands, and his voice came out muffled. "Do you realize what you ask? This is a demon that has been after you since we fought the Vikings. He has resources at his disposal, and a god backing him up."

"As do we," Freya said. "Please, Seamus. We were chosen for a reason, you said so yourself."

O'Keeffe looked up at them, and nodded. "Very well. To access the map, do what you did the first time you got to it – allow yourselves to connect on a deeper level. That is what opened the objects to you."

"And then?"

"The map should be accessible in your minds. It is alive, and will give you clues leading to the relics." He sighed. "We can talk more in the morning." To Brennan, he said, "For now, clean up Freya's back and get some rest, as will I. We have a long day ahead of us tomorrow."

&&&

Seamus waited until the two teenagers left his room, then slid to the floor, resting his head on his bent forearm. "Did you hear all that?"

As if on cue, the tigers slipped out from his bathroom. Evie came close to him, resting her massive head on his knee, while Mark kept a distance.

We did, she said.

How did that young punk connect with Freya?

Seamus rolled his eyes. "Do you not think it a tad late to lay on the overprotectiveness?"

She's my daughter. Mark's emerald gaze flashed. *And you haven't answered the question.*

"You know who he is, he's Thomas' grandson. There was always a possibility..." O'Keeffe shook his head. "And to think we thought the gods had chosen you two." He turned to Evie. "We were wrong."

Perhaps. Or perhaps the gods always intended it to end this way. Even you have to admit, Freya has much more power at her command than I did at her age.

Seamus grimaced, loath to agree. "She does, but that does not mean she knows how to control it."

You have another problem, Mark said. He waited until he had their attention. *If they use the map, it will lead them directly on Set's path. And there is no way I'm allowing my daughter to fight a god.*

"Which is why I tried to get them to ask for help." Seamus sighed. "All due respect, old friend, Freya has your stubborn gene. Good luck explaining that to her."

Mark said nothing, but Evie nudged Seamus. *There is one more thing. We've been meaning to tell you. The barriers around this place are soft.*

"What?" He hadn't thought about them in ages, not since he'd used the last of his powers to ensure it hid them well.

Have you checked them lately?

A flash of annoyance built in Seamus. "No, I have not. You may not have noticed, but I have been too busy raising your daughter."

Mark rose to his paws, growling. *Watch yourself.* His sharp canines came into evidence with the curl of his lips. Seamus scowled at him, but Evie nudged his hand.

He didn't mean it that way, Seamus. We're worried, because it looks like this place is barely protected.

He deflated at her soft tone. "I'll handle it in the morning, all right? But for now, I need sleep."

Evie moved back, joining her husband. *Rest. We will stand guard.*

Seamus dozed off to dreamland the moment his head hit the pillow.

&&&

Isis stepped out onto the balcony. Her hair was loose over her bare shoulders, and she wore a simple white cotton dress, cinched at the waist with a golden belt.

Her eyes lingered on the night sky, and the stars above. Where most mortals saw only bright lights, she read destiny in the making. And the story imprinted there was enough to make her shiver.

Warm arms wrapped around her waist, pulling her against a firm, heated chest. "What troubles you, beloved?"

Isis relaxed against her husband, though her gaze remained pensive. "The stars tonight..."

"What of them?"

"Something is coming, Osiris." Isis turned in his arms, her pleading eyes on his. "Something bad that will wreck with the balance."

He kissed her forehead, then pulled her into another embrace. Isis rested her cheek on his shoulder, wishing she could unsee the future.

"It will work out."

Not even his quiet reassurance was enough that night.

Chapter 6

A blast to the side distracted Freya and instead of focusing on her kick mid-air, she hurtled into Brennan with all the grace of a rock. They both tumbled to the ground.

Since early morning, they'd been practicing fighting moves while waiting to speak to Seamus. Unable to sleep, it had kept them entertained. They'd intended to meet with the elder Sage after lunch, but got lost in the intensity of their workout.

A rumble in the distance tugged at her attention. Freya straightened from her crouch, turning towards the castle. Wisps of smoke carried into the sky, and she paled. Everything narrowed around her, and she was all too aware of her shaky breath.

"Freya!"

Screams of her name escaped through the fog, and she turned a bemused gaze to Brennan, who was equally shocked. "We have to go, *now!*"

He grabbed her hand and dragged her after him, dispensing energy where needed to propel them past Freya's defenses and back onto the castle grounds. The minute they exited the forest's shelter, Freya stumbled to a stop.

Half of the ancient château stood proud, but the other was a mess of ruins. Smoke and fire were everywhere, and a choked sob escaped her. "Seamus!"

She moved towards it, but Brennan tried to stop her. "He's here." He lowered his palm, shuddering at the energy he'd picked up.

"What?"

"Raksh. This is *his* doing." Brennan's brown eyes, gentle most days, were cold and glinting with anger. His jaw was clenched, body taut with tension.

Freya's own being responded in kind, and a wave of rage overwhelmed her. The sky above gathered with clouds, and Brennan's gaze shifted upwards. "Frey…"

"*Don't.*" Her expression radiated determination, and she glared at the heavens. "It's my turn now."

From soft grey, the clouds grew heavy, obscuring what was left of the light. Thunder rolled across the land, and a strike of lightning hit far in the distance. Freya squared her shoulders, then took off towards the castle, Brennan on her heels.

&&&

Isis and Osiris were casting protective spells throughout their domain. It was a ritual they had to redo every few weeks. Since they had broken their own rules by helping Evie and Mark, it was time to replenish, earlier than usual.

They circled the palace, hands outstretched. Rays of light escaped them – pale pink for Isis, dark blue for Osiris. A translucent dome encompassed their home, and the spell clicked into place.

Before they could relax, the palace shook, and the gods peered around, trying to find the source.

"What is the meaning of this?" Isis' soft question spurred Osiris into action. He ran inside, striding across the long hallway.

He burst into the lounge area where the two tigers relaxed near the fireplace. They'd returned early morning to recharge their forces, before heading back out.

Osiris paid them no mind, heading straight to the fire.

The tigers rose to meet him, hackles up. They shifted to their human forms, and Mark was first to speak. "What is it?"

"I am unsure..." Osiris waved his palm over the blazing element, and the flames soon showed them a mirror image.

Rubble and debris were scattered around what had been a majestic castle. Now, it stood forlorn, covered by dust. No one moved within the darkness, but flames rose higher with each passing second.

"Freya!" Evie lunged towards the reflection, held back by her husband. "What are we waiting for? Mark, the entire castle is up in flames!"

Contrary to his nature, Mark looked to Osiris for confirmation. The god, lost in his perusal of the flames, didn't answer.

Isis stepped forward then, deciding in his stead. "Yes. Go."

While they shifted to tiger form, Osiris' expression revived and morphed into one of panic. "Be very careful. The demon Raksh is there, no doubt at my brother's bidding."

The tigers disappeared through a portal, leaving Osiris to stare at his wife. "I need to see Set, there is no choice left. This has to stop, before he tears both our worlds apart."

Isis stepped to her consort and kissed his lips, then rested her head against his chest. "Do as you think is necessary, beloved. But be wary of his treacherous ways."

&&&

Away from the gods' palace and Scotland, Sam floated down a street, Anya by his side. Since they were not around the Sages, their forms were as intangible as ever, but it didn't stop the boy from throwing a longing look to Anya.

"Are you sure about this?" His words were whispered to avoid an echo.

"Yes," Anya said. There was a determined expression on her face, at odds with the fear shining in her eyes. "The Countess needs to be stopped, and any information we can gather for your friends will help."

Sam nodded and turned his attention back to their surroundings. The houses on each side of the dusty road were disheveled, some with doors hanging off their hinges. The windows were dark, with no lights shining inside.

"Is everyone asleep?"

"Or gone," Anya said, but didn't stop to look around. "They fear her as much as the devil himself. More, probably."

They continued in silence until they reached the bottom of a hill. Metal gates stood wide open with spiky tops. Sam's gaze went past them and landed on the castle at the top of the hill. Set against a backdrop of amber sky, it loomed over the town. A few windows flickered, as if someone burned fire within.

"This way."

Sam snapped out of his daze and followed Anya towards some bushes off to the side. Beyond lay a narrow path that winded upwards, towards Elizabeth's home. "This leads us there?"

"Yes," she threw nervous glances around. "We need to speak to someone."

They continued further into the woods, floating out of sight.

"Why not just appear there?" Sam asked halfway.

"She will know. She *always* knows." Anya's tone was foreboding, but he tried not to let it get to him.

When they reached the back entrance, another glowing shape appeared. Anya stopped, and Sam followed suit. "Friend or foe?"

Anya shushed him and advanced forward. Sam lingered behind, but within earshot.

"Elena..."

The older girl was taller than Anya, but just as thin. Ragged clothes hung off her bony shoulders, and her cheeks were sunken. Tears shone in her dark eyes, and she spoke in a stronger accent than Anya. "You came back."

"I promised I would," Anya said. "Does she know?"

"No, she..." Elena glanced over her shoulder to Sam and stopped.

"You can talk in front of him." A string of Hungarian followed, which Sam didn't understand. From the way the young girl kept looking to him, he guessed Anya was summarizing the last few days.

"He helps?" The hope in Elena's voice had Sam advance.

"Yes," he said softly. "But we need to bring more information back to my friends. Where is the Countess now?"

"She returned from meeting that cursed demon."

"Again?" Anya frowned, and her pale form trembled. "Why?"

"A gift. He gave her..." Elena gestured with her hands, circling her wrist.

"A bracelet?" Sam asked.

"No, *lánc*." She turned to Anya, her wide eyes asking for a translation.

"Chains," she said. "What use are chains for a ghost?"

"Not regular..." More Hungarian followed, and whatever was said left Anya gaping.

A light turned on in the windows closest to them and Elena jumped, glancing over her shoulder. "Go," Anya said. "And keep hope."

Elena scurried away, and Anya floated into the darkness of the forest, gesturing for Sam to follow her. Once they were under cover, she advanced towards the bottom of the hill.

"What was that about?" Sam asked.

Anya faced him, biting her lip. "She says the Countess did a deal with the devil. He promised her chains of fire for her help. Elena doesn't know what the Countess has to do."

"What would a ghost do with chains?"

Anya's expression was filled with worry. "That is the problem. Since she is dead, she takes no joy in the victims' blood. But with the chains, she could torture the girls as she did when alive. It would give her immense pleasure to be the reigning queen once more."

Sam glanced towards the castle, then back to the young woman. "Then we need to warn Freya and Brennan, now."

Anya nodded, and they got away before they risked capture.

&&&

Freya burst through the smog, coughing and looking around. She waved her hand and cast air to clear up the surroundings. In the distance, she saw Raksh's dark form facing off against Seamus. Her mentor was bent over as if in pain, but hadn't fallen down. His shoulder-length hair had escaped out of his ponytail and obscured his features.

"Raksh!" The Sage's yell echoed across the grounds, causing both men to face her.

Seamus' left side was full of soot, as if he'd been lying in ashes for the better part of the day. A ragged scar cut his right cheek, bleeding profusely, and he was holding his arm folded to his chest, at an odd angle.

"Freya, no!"

Raksh looked the picture of the entitled demon, smirking and motioning for her to join them. "Do not keep your distance, little girl. You have something I need."

Freya bit back a cry of rage, instead clenching her hand. Lightning struck near Raksh, enough to make him stumble away. He hadn't been expecting her attack, by the looks of it.

When Freya moved closer, she smirked. "What's the matter? Did you expect we'd give up so easily?"

The demon frowned. "We?"

Brennan stepped from the rubbles behind the wraith, his palms facing him. "Yeah, mate. *We.*"

Raksh turned to face him, only to be cast backwards by an energy field. He flew and landed into a wall. Its already crumbling mass toppled down, covering him.

Freya rushed to Seamus, ducking under his shoulder to support his weight. "Are you okay?" She placed a hand on his chest, reassured by his steady heartbeat.

Seamus coughed, then offered a feeble smile. "I will survive, yes. The injuries are more from the castle blowing apart than anything else."

"Seamus, how did the bastard get past your defenses?" Brennan glanced to the pile of rocks, but nothing moved. *Could it really be that easy?* The professor's next words caught his attention.

"His blasted chains – or so the demon claims. When Raksh used the weapon on me in Spain, it created some kind of link. Because I didn't die, he could follow us here. As for how he got through, I would guess a good deal of godly support."

Freya bit her lip, thinking back to the mark on her back. "Why would he wait so long, then?"

"Because I had to be sssure you have what I have come sssseeking." Raksh's voice took them all by surprise, and Seamus' arm tightened around Freya, as if to protect her.

The ruins still lay undisturbed. Yet Raksh was now standing mere feet away, with no scratches on his body.

"And what is that, you think?" Brennan inched towards to Freya, preparing his energy.

"The map, of course."

Freya slipped from Seamus' hold. "Then come get it."

She pulled lightning from the sky and shot it to Raksh, only to have him block it. Brennan followed suit with another attack, catching Raksh by the ear. With each strike, they stalked him, forcing Raksh to back away.

Then he materialized the chains of fire, morphing them into a sword of fire. He launched it towards Freya, but Brennan pushed her out of the way in time. They heard a choked gurgle from behind, and rolled off the ground.

The sword was embedded in Seamus' stomach, and he stood with a shocked expression on his face. His free hand gripped the hilt of the weapon, as if to dislodge it, but already he was stumbling, unable to remain standing.

"Seamus!" Freya's raw cry shattered Brennan, and she jumped up and ran towards her mentor, catching him as he fell.

"I got you," Freya sobbed, pulling Seamus and hugging him. "Please don't leave me, Seamus. Not you too, *please*!"

Grime and soot streaked her mentor's face, and his breathing was slow and erratic. A cackle in the distance drew her attention, but Brennan was already standing and placing his body between her and the threat.

"I aimed for you, foolsss. But the old man will do, I ss-suppose."

Freya's closed her eyes, inhaling to pull herself together, then wiped at her tears. She lowered Seamus back down little by little, then joined Brennan's side. She clenched one hand, while the other pulled on the elements.

"You demonic *bastard*!" Her hiss only made the wraith smirk, and Freya felt Brennan react next to her. A wave of anger blew off him, enhancing her own.

Their powers mixed, not quite combining but feeding off each other. They threw a blast towards Raksh, which the demon deflected with a whip of the chains.

Freya's panting increased, as did Brennan's – for different reasons. She glanced at her partner, noticing the slight sheen of sweat on his forehead. She tapped into their link. *You okay?*

I'll live.

Freya nodded and called on air, fire – and lightning again. The clouds had grown heavy, and low enough that they almost touched the tip of the remaining part of the castle. She cast a glance at Brennan, and he nodded.

"Let's do it, like before."

Raksh's eyes widened and smoke covered him. By the time Freya forced air to dissipate the fog, only an empty place was left.

"He's gone." Brennan's mutter had Freya close her eyes in despair.

A shuffle had her open them, only to notice Brennan on the ground, drawing in deep breaths. "Bren! What's going on?"

She knelt over him, and a quick scan of his aura confirmed his heartbeat was slow – too slow. "You used too much." She frowned, a thought occurring. "How the hell did you expect to unite our powers, then?"

"I didn't," Brennan laughed. "I was bluffing."

Before Freya could scold him, a cough behind rose her to her feet.

"Seamus!"

But when she got to the old professor, he was no longer alone. A white tiger stood by his side, watching over him.

"Tyr?"

The animal lifted its head, but rather than green eyes, she met grey – much like her own. Then, to Freya's utter surprise, another feline stepped out from the rubble, joining the first one.

She knew Brennan was seeing the same when his curse echoed in her ear. "What the bloody *hell*?"

Chapter 7

F reya gaped at the vision before her, unable to comprehend what her eyes were registering. She turned to Seamus, who was trying to stand, holding onto the grey-eyed tiger. His feet gave way, and Brennan stepped forward to help.

He placed Seamus' arm around his broad shoulders and straightened, wrapping his other arm around the man's waist for balance. "I got you, professor."

Freya snapped out of her daze and headed towards them. Every few seconds, her gaze drifted back to the two tigers, now side by side. When she reached Seamus, she searched his clouded eyes. "Seamus?"

He blinked, and with painful tries focused on her. "Freya..." He lifted his hand to touch her cheek, and gulped. "Meet... your parents." As if the words had been too much, he went limp against Brennan, who swore under his breath. Somehow, he managed to hold the elder Sage's weight.

Freya whirled around to the beasts, her jaw wide open. "That's impossible!"

The bigger of the tigers stepped forward, with eyes as green as emeralds. Much like with Tyr, Freya heard his voice in her head.

Nothing is impossible when it involves the gods, daughter.

Freya looked to Brennan. By his frown, he'd heard it too. She shook her head and took another step backwards from the tiger. "You... What guarantees you're not some pawn of Raksh?"

A growl escaped the animal, and he moved closer. *I am not!*

The second tiger joined him, and she spoke in a softer voice. *We are who we say we are, Freya. But if you doubt us, get your Wiseman friend to read us. He can confirm.*

The Sage's expression closed at the suggestion. "I think not. My home was just attacked, and my main duty is to care for the man who raised me."

She gestured for Brennan to follow her. "Come on."

With a contrite glance to the tigers, he stepped behind her, bending under Seamus' weight. Freya was way ahead, increasing her pace as if to put as much distance as possible between her and the tigers.

Brennan sensed the waves of confusion, anger, and sorrow she tried to keep hidden. He bit his tongue, knowing she needed to deal with it in her own way. "Frey, wait up!"

She stopped in her tracks, wiping at her face. When she turned to him, her eyes glistened, but her voice was firm. "What is it?"

Brennan grimaced, "A little help? Your mentor's heavy when he's all dead weight."

Freya's expression cleared, and she joined him, ducking under Seamus' other arm. The Wiseman didn't need her help, but it was the best he could come up with, to coerce her nearby.

They shuffled around the debris until they reached the untouched wing of the castle. A glance over his shoulder confirmed the tigers were trailing far behind, but heading their way.

"So, um..."

"Don't," Freya cut him off, her voice breaching no argument. "I don't want to talk about it."

Brennan continued walking in silence, supporting most of Seamus' weight. Their feet took them to the untouched part of the castle, and the library within it. It was the same one they'd spent countless hours in, and relief flooded him that all the books were untouched.

They deposited Seamus on it, and Freya placed a rolled-up sweater under his head. She knelt by the professor's side, holding one of his hands in hers. A shudder ran through her, even as she tried to scan his body to see how far gone the injuries were.

At the obvious distress in her aura, Brennan joined her on the floor. He removed Seamus' hand from her grip and pulled Freya against his chest. She struggled at first, muttering under her breath, but eventually surrendered against him.

Then the sobs came. Heart-wrenching, body-shaking, they rattled through Freya's slim body. Her tears soaked his shirt, and no amount of comforting words could ease her sorrow.

Shadows caught his eye, and Brennan turned to the door of the library. Both tigers stood there, gazing down at them. He tried to extend his mind, trying to tell them to stay away, but one crossed the threshold.

Brennan recognized the bulkier tiger and blazing emerald gaze. *That's Freya's dad.*

And that's my daughter you're holding.

And she's my girlfriend. Brennan's jaw clenched, and he lifted his chin in defiance. Unaware of what was happening, Freya continued sobbing in his chest.

The smaller tiger took a cautious step forward, nudging the other one backward. *Enough, Mark. This isn't how we pictured our reunion, but what else can you expect? She's lived her whole life without us.*

I would have expected my daughter to know... Mark trailed off, staring insistently at Freya. After a long moment, he turned away and stalked off.

The female inched closer. *My name is Evie. This must be confusing, but I swear we are who we say we are.*

What proof do you have? Brennan frowned, recalling Freya's suspicions.

Evie glanced between him and Seamus. *I know you care about Freya, but you must also care for her mentor. If she doesn't trust us, he could die. There is no amount of healing you can do for him... Not as we can.*

Brennan glanced between Seamus and the tiger. *What do you mean, as you can?*

The gods themselves sent us here, Brennan. This time, with no restrictions, unlike Tyr. I can use my vital energy to heal his wounds, make them less fatal.

Will it hurt him?

No, I swear it.

Brennan's arms tightened around his devastated girl-friend. He knew it was only the shock of Seamus' injury that was keeping her from catching the conversation between him and her would-be parents. *Freya will sense it.*

Evie's grey eyes were solid on his. *I suppose it's up to you she doesn't.*

His eyes widened at the implication. She was asking him to keep Freya's senses occupied. But could he? And more importantly, would she see it as a betrayal?

&&&

Brennan's warm arms wrapped round her. His strength allowed her to let go, to be vulnerable. And for once, Freya didn't fight it.

To have Seamus ripped away from her, then find out her parents were alive... It was the cruelest twist of fate. She'd been looking into their deaths, wanting to avenge them for years. And now, she'd just found out they were alive.

And yet, were they? Tyr had been a spiritual being... And was the creature gone now? What did it all mean?

Amid her sorrow, something nagged at the back of her mind. An intrusion, but not in her own thoughts. Rather...

Freya looked up from Brennan's chest, to see his gaze locked on someone else. She glanced over her shoulder, and pulled away from his arms.

"What the *hell* are you doing inside?" With a shaking hand, she pointed to the door. "Get out!"

If I don't help Seamus, he will die, Freya.

"As if I'm going to believe you. Get. *Out.*"

Brennan stood behind her and placed a hand on her shoulder. "Frey, listen to her."

"Her? It's a freaking animal!"

His eyes blazed. With a nod to the tiger, he pulled Freya against him and kissed her. She slammed her fists against his chest, but he only held her tighter. Freya's senses were too fraught to fight, so she surrendered to his lips... Just as someone wrenched him from her arms.

By the time she'd blinked and taken in their surroundings, the larger tiger was atop Brennan, growling in his face. The Wiseman had his hands dug into his mane, and she caught the energy of an attack rolling off him.

"Stop it!"

Freya lunged at them and pushed the tiger away. "Get *off* him!"

By the time the animal listened, Brennan was back on his feet, scowling. "I was trying to help."

"Like hell you were!" Freya yelled, her eyes narrowed. Before she could continue the conversation, another energy caught her attention.

She turned to the sofa where the smaller tiger was stepping away from Seamus. Some color was back in his cheeks, and his chest was rising and falling with a steadier rhythm.

"What did you do to him?"

Instead of the tiger, it was Brennan who answered. "You're welcome."

With one last glare at the male tiger, he took off, slamming the door behind him. Freya took a step forward to follow him, but hesitated to leave Seamus alone with the tigers.

No. If I'm being truthful, it's not Seamus I'm afraid to leave alone with them.

She looked back, and they were side by side, nuzzling each other. Over their animal bodies, the images she knew superimposed themselves – a woman with long, raven hair and her fairer companion.

His arms had held her as a child, tossed her in the air, played with her. And the woman, she'd sung to her, lullabies and soft melodies...

Tears threatened and Freya gasped, feeling like her chest was being ripped apart. The tigers – her parents, because she couldn't deny it any longer – turned to her in tandem. Unable to deal with their all-knowing gazes or her emotions, Freya took off.

&&&

It was sunset by the time Brennan wandered into the forest and found Freya sitting on the grass in her meadow. She looked up at his arrival, frowning.

"I'm sorry," she said when he knelt next to her. "This whole thing's messed me up, but I know you only wanted Seamus' well-being."

Brennan grasped her hand in his and nodded. "I do. And your mom –"

"She's not my mom."

The Wiseman refrained from rolling his eyes. "If you'd let me read them, I could confirm it. But, trust me, they're related to you."

His tone caught Freya's attention. "Meaning, what?"

"Your dad nearly ripped my throat out for kissing you." He arched an eyebrow. "Need I remind you?"

Freya winced and glanced away. Brennan didn't give her time to ponder the matter further. He tapped her nose with his index finger. "You need to talk to them, Frey. We don't have time for this, not with the Countess and Raksh. Plus, if they're half as powerful as Tyr, it'd be nice to have some damn help for once."

The Sage sighed, picking at the grass. "You really think so?"

"I do."

Another few moments passed, and Brennan tried to rein in his impatience. He could understand Freya's hesitation, but didn't agree with it. If the opportunity had presented itself to speak to his grandfather again, he would have jumped on it, not wasted time being angry.

As though she'd read his thoughts, Freya said, "I just... There's so much anger. All my life, I dreamt of being reunited with them. And now that I am... Why did they lie? Why pretend to be Tyr? I have so many questions!"

Brennan sighed, his thumb caressing her cheek. "And *they* can answer them. But isolating yourself won't do you any good."

Freya kept her gaze solid on the ground, but Brennan stood and gently tugged her to her feet. She didn't stop him when he retraced his steps to the castle.

All around them were ruins, and the powder was still settling. It was a good thing the castle was set on the coastline, with nary a soul in sight.

They came to a stop in front of the massive library. The door was still half-open, and Freya sensed the presences inside. Brennan released her hand and kissed her forehead. "This is all you now."

She searched his eyes, then nodded once and walked in. The tigers had been watching over Seamus, but they turned to her.

The room seemed to narrow on their presence, and Freya felt air was missing. Wringing her hands, she managed to say a single word. "Hi."

&&&

Brennan waited by the door, if only to make sure things went smoothly. When he heard sobs, he peered within. Freya had collapsed on the floor, her face buried in one of the tiger's furs. The other was nuzzling her back.

Finally. He knew he'd been right to push her towards her parents. It was the right thing to do, if only to ensure she'd give them a chance and wouldn't have any regrets. But much as he was happy for Freya, a feeling of utter loneliness spread in him, and he walked away.

He'd been sitting on a demolished boulder when Sam floated up the hill, Anya close behind. His panicked expression eased when he saw Brennan.

"What the hell happened?"

Brennan tossed the handful of rubble he'd been toying with. "Raksh happened." He caught Sam up to speed, after which the young boy shared his own findings.

By the time he filled him in, Brennan gestured for the ghosts to follow him. Much as he wanted to give Freya time to get reacquainted with her parents, the situation left no room for debate.

He burst into the library. "Sorry to interrupt family time, but this can't wait. Sam, tell them."

Once the younger ghost had related their findings on the Countess and the chains of fire, Freya was back on her feet. She glanced at Seamus. "Will he be okay?"

Sam floated to her, touching her hand. "I and Anya can keep watch over him. If anything happens, one of us will come get you. But you need as much help as you can get on this, Frey-Frey."

A faint smile tugged her lips at the nickname, and she bent to kiss his cheek, hugging him one-handed. "You're a good kid, Sam."

She turned to Brennan. "What do you say?"

Her partner's tone was firm. "We can't let this woman keep tormenting innocents. We have to stop her."

Freya inclined her head in agreement, then walked to Seamus' bed. She grasped his hand, squeezing it. Tears came to her eyes, and she fought to see through her now-blurry vision.

Seamus coughed, then opened his eyes and stared at her. "Don't cry, Freya... This isn't worth it."

She dropped to her knees, dropping her forehead to his chest and hugging him as softly as she could, considering his injuries. "Don't say that! You've been mother and father to me all my life, Seamus... I don't want to lose you."

He inhaled sharply, fighting back against his own emotions. Over Freya's head, he saw the two tigers watching them, emotions swimming in their own infinite gazes. With his free hand, he patted Freya on her back.

"My darling, I am not going anywhere, I promise. I may be weak and unable to come with you, but I will be here when you come back."

Freya pulled back and wiped at her face. "Swear to me?"

Her voice, so like a child's, tugged at his heart, and he made a promise he didn't know if he could keep. "I swear it, Freya." *May the gods bring truth to my words.* "Now you have to go... And please be careful."

Brennan moved closer, wrapping an arm around her shoulders. "I'll protect her with my life, Seamus."

"I know you will." The elder Sage glanced behind him and lowered his voice. "You may want to watch your public displays of affection around her father, mind you. Mark is nowhere as laid back as I am."

Though Brennan tensed, his arm remained around Freya until they walked out of the room.

The tigers moved around the bed. *Once he shows us the spot, Sam will return to you and act as a messenger between us. If anything happens, Seamus, send him to us. Please.*

O'Keeffe was already dozing off. "I will," he whispered.

&&&

Osiris nodded at the jackal guards, who stood straighter in his presence. Two accompanied him as he descended deeper in the cavernous prison, where a cage stood in the middle.

Its bars confined his brother, Set. Made of steel mined from the Underworld itself, they were reinforced with spells from Isis, designed to last a lifetime – and then some.

The prisoner's hard gaze landed on Osiris, then the guards. He snickered, not bothering to stand up from his cot. "You fear being in my presence, brother?"

Osiris scowled. "I am not here to play games. Call off your rabid dog, Set. He is interfering with things he does not understand."

Set laughed. "I know not what you speak of."

Osiris approached the cage, gripping the bars. "Yes, you do. *Raksh*."

The name hovered mid-air, and Set's eyes glinted. "He does his master's bidding. Can you fault him?"

Osiris let go of the bars, his expression darkening with warning. "You will not win this. Whichever play you aim for, I will be there to stop you, brother."

He took off, ignoring Set's maniacal laughter. Isis had been right – it was a mistake to visit him.

&&&

Backpack on her shoulder, Freya glanced behind at the castle one more time. Half of it still stood in ruins, but the other half harbored Seamus. She didn't feel right leaving her mentor behind injured, with only two ghosts to keep him company.

We will be here until you land at your destination, Evie reminded her. She and Mark were standing in front of the castle, to see them off.

Freya bit her bottom lip to hold back a smartass remark. Her relationship with her parents was already off to a rocky start, and she didn't want to make it worse. I should remember how much I've wished for this, rather than hold on to this anger.

"He'll be fine," Brennan tried to reassure her, squeezing her hand. He'd caught her worry of Seamus, and his presence alone was enough to calm her.

And Sam will let us know if any complications arise, Mark reminded her.

With one last glance at the library, Freya turned to walk away. Brennan saluted the tigers, then followed in her tracks. The plan was to fly out to Slovakia, then meet up with the tigers at Čachtice Castle for a full-on assault on the Countess' domain.

Let's hope it's not one of those situations of best laid plans failing, Freya thought. She couldn't help the unease in her stomach, which only knotted deeper in her entrails with each step she took away from Scotland – and Seamus.

Chapter 8

F reya was nodding off on his shoulder, but Brennan was too wired to sleep. They'd arrived at the Heathrow Airport two hours earlier, and had been waiting for their connection to Bratislava, Slovakia. The Countess' castle was in a region known as the Čachtice village.

Brennan recalled the dream he'd had. *As if it's not bad enough that hawk is hunting us, now this woman...* He glanced down at Freya's sleeping face. He wanted to tell her, but then she'd want to fix it. And she had enough on her head as it was, with her parents.

Though the teenagers travelled alone, Mark and Evie planned to meet them outside Bratislava, from where they'd make their way to Čachtice. The tigers couldn't appear in the village since they didn't know what –if any – barriers the Countess had set. So they had to do the remaining journey on foot.

As if the mere thought of them called them out, a voice resounded in his head. *Where are you?*

Brennan scowled and debated not answering. The thought occurred to him that if he didn't, Mark would try contacting Freya, and he wanted her to get some rest.

Landed at Heathrow and waiting for our connection flight.

And Freya?

She's sleeping.

The exchange was terse at best, and Brennan tried not to take it personally. Mark had missed a lot of his daughter's life, it was only natural he'd have extra doses of protectiveness. *Still...*

Freya turned into his chest, mumbling something, and he tightened his grip on her. If an angry dad was all he had to put up with, Brennan planned to suck it up.

The Wiseman's eyes fell on the panel announcing flights, and he swore. Their flight had the tell-tale *Delayed* sign.

What is it?

Our flight got delayed.

By how long?

He pinched the bridge of his nose, trying push away his annoyance. *I'm about to find out. Would you mind?*

No answer came. Brennan moved Freya so she was resting her head on their carryon bag. Satisfied he hadn't woken her up, he moved to the information center. After a painful conversation, he found out there had been a political riot in Bratislava, which meant no incoming or outgoing flights for at least two days.

Two days! We don't bloody well have two days!

I agree, Evie said. *Are there flights anywhere else?*

Brennan scanned the panels, then returned to the information desk. *There's one leaving for Vienna in forty-five minutes. We can hop on it and walk the rest of the way.*

Silence came from both tigers.

You realize it's close to thirty hours walking, meaning at least three days if you don't want to be left without feet?

Brennan bristled at Mark's condescending tone, but kept his level. *I do.* He pulled out his phone and plugged coordinates into the maps application. *You can meet us outside Gajary. It's a village in western Slovakia, and the closest one to Bratislava. Map shows lots of green nearby, so we can use the cover of the mountains to get by unnoticed until we reach Čachtice.*

Evie sighed, *We can meet you there, but when?*

Brennan glanced at the time. *We should land around midnight in Vienna and get a full night of sleep. If we leave early morning, it's about a twelve-hour hike to Gajary. We can shorten the distance with buses or trains, whatever we'll find.*

Okay, let's say by tomorrow evening. We will be outside the village. Contact us when you are close by.

Deal. Brennan waited for some sign from Mark, but the man had fallen quiet. *Probably annoyed I took over planning,* he mused.

With a shrug, he walked over to Freya and shook her awake.

&&&

Freya followed in Brennan's footsteps off the plane, then cleared customs half-asleep. She recalled her boyfriend mentioning he'd gotten a room at a hotel for the night, and couldn't wait to dig into a bed.

As if he'd been reading her mood, Brennan took care of everything. He hailed them a cab, made small talk with the driver, and checked them in. The minute they were in the room, he excused himself to go shower, leaving Freya alone.

She wanted nothing more than to call Seamus and hear his voice. But they'd only had a landline at the castle, and that evaporated along with everything else in the ashes.

There was another way, but it involved contacting one of her parents. Freya wasn't sure how she felt about it. She moved around the room, taking in the oak desk, plush carpet, and twin beds. She liked that Brennan had gotten them separate beds, though she wasn't sure she could sleep alone.

All she could see was Seamus' expression when the sword had stabbed him, and his pale, ashy face after the healing. After a short debate with herself, she slid to ground near the window and closed her eyes, leaning her head against the wall.

Mom?

Evie's voice answered. *Freya! Is something wrong?*

No, I... Brennan filled me in. She cleared her throat. *How's Seamus?*

He's better. He woke up today and Sam made him eat something. She paused. *He will get better, darling. Believe me, he's a stubborn man.*

I.... okay.

The silence lengthened, and Evie said, *How was the flight?*

Good, um...tiring, I guess. But I have to go. Need to get some sleep.

Of course. Freya sensed her disappointment across the distance. *Let us know when you've reached Gajary.*

Yup, will do.

Freya broke the connection and opened her eyes. Brennan was hovering over her, watching her with a peculiar expression. When Freya met his gaze, it cleared, and he gave a half-smile.

"Parents?"

"Mm. I tried to check on Seamus."

Brennan crept lower, wearing only a pair of night sweatpants and no shirt. His muscled chest drew her attention, and Freya sensed a blush creep over her cheeks.

She realized Brennan was still talking to her and forced her eyes back to his face. "Sorry, what?"

His worried expression eased into a smug grin. "Seeing something you like?"

Freya reached out a hand and shoved him. Because he'd been crouching, he lost his balance and toppled backwards. His chuckle echoed in the room, and a smile crept on Freya's face, too.

"Stop being arrogant. What were you saying?"

Brennan lifted his head and propped himself on his elbows. "How's Seamus?"

"Mom says he's better, and he's eating. I... Thanks, for distracting me so she could heal him. Even if it got you on my dad's wrong side."

Brennan shrugged and straightened up. "Something tells me I would have been on his bad side, anyway."

Freya frowned. "What makes you say that?"

Another shrug, then he looked away. "Think about it. He's been out of your life for so long, it's only natural he'd try to do everything at once. Especially when it comes to protecting you."

Freya said nothing, shuffling her feet on the carpet instead. "It's weird, Bren, having them back. I've been so long without parents that having them worry and want to protect me is almost alien. Stifling. Does that make me a bad daughter?"

Brennan's eyes softened. "No, Frey. You're only human."

He extended his hand and helped her to her feet, then bent to kiss her lips. "And it'll take time to build a relationship with them. It doesn't happen overnight."

"But I don't..." She bit her lip, before saying, "What if it doesn't happen at all? I feel so weird and guilty, but..."

Brennan lifted her chin and looked her in the eyes. "Try, Frey. If I had a chance – as small as it was – to see my grandfather again, to talk to him... Hell, to have him boss me around? I'd take it in a flash. Don't let your fear of losing them again stop you from enjoying this."

Freya hugged him, burying her head in his chest.

"Now, your turn to shower. I need to put some balm over your back scratches after."

Freya was in and out of the shower in a few minutes. She returned to the room in shorts and a tank top, drying her hair with a towel. Once she perched herself on the bed, Brennan pushed her strap aside and pulled the material down, then slid his hand underneath to rub some gel onto the wound.

At the cool touch, Freya gasped and tried to pull away, but Brennan held her shoulder in place. "Relax, only a few more seconds."

She cringed, but tried to relax into his touch. "I wish I could just use my spiritual energy to heal it."

"Maybe," Brennan whispered, "but there's a chance if you try, it could cause something. If this is really a tracker, I'd imagine Set will be keeping a close ear to the ground. See if we try to mess with it, and all."

Freya's heavy sigh shook her entire frame. After he finished with the last lathering, Brennan replaced the tank top.

She turned to face him, biting her lip. "I know you got twin beds, but do you mind if I sleep with you tonight?"

Brennan searched her expression, then nodded slowly. He reached over to the carryon bag and threw her a sweater, grinning. "But put on a sweater. I'm still a teenaged boy, remember?"

Freya did as he asked, though she couldn't help rolling her eyes. Snuggled in bed next to him, she soon fell asleep.

&&&

Freya jumped off the back of the truck first, followed by Brennan. They waved at the nice farmer who'd given them a ride from the last town to Gajary, taking pity on their lost expressions.

The journey hadn't been easy. Between the language and culture difference, and the large expanse of land, Brennan was already weary. *And to think I'm about to hang out with my girlfriend's parents for the better part of the next three days...*

He slid a side-glance to Freya, watching as she huffed and pulled her hair back in a ponytail. She clamped the baseball hat lower on her forehead and readjusted her backpack. After a few more moments he faced him, sensing his eyes on her.

"What?"

"Nothing," Brennan grinned. "You ready for this?"

"You mean spending quality time with my parents, while heading to a crazy witch's castle of tortures?" Freya snorted. "Sure."

They walked in silence for a few moments, taking a path that would lead them towards the forest rather than the city.

"What about you?"

Brennan frowned at the question. "I'll survive."

Freya stepped in front of him and hugged his middle, then lifted on her tiptoes to kiss him. "You'll be fine. *We'll* be fine."

Brennan grinned against her lips and pulled her closer, deepening the kiss. Freya leaned against him and wrapped her arms around his neck, hanging on to him while the simple peck turned into a lingering embrace.

A low growl had them jump apart guiltily. Brennan looked to find Freya's parents – in tiger form – only a few feet away.

You were supposed to tell us when you were close.

Mark's reproachful tone had Brennan groan internally. *So much for making a good second impression.*

Evie threw him an amused glance, and Brennan guessed she'd caught his thought. Mark, meanwhile, stepped towards Freya. *It's a long journey, and you'll need plenty of stops. Let's get going.*

Freya opened her mouth to argue, but one glance at her father's annoyed countenance, and she dropped it. With an apologetic look over her shoulder at Brennan, she took his hand in hers and pulled him on the path.

&&&

They spent the first hour of their hike in silence – the awkward kind. A million things went through Freya's mind, a thousand questions she wanted answered. But getting them past the lump in her throat, was another problem.

Brennan had started by her side, but he'd moved ahead for a bit. Mark was on his heels, not that she could feel them communicate. Her mother, on the other hand, had been walking by her side for the better part of the walk.

Why don't you speak what's on your mind, Freya?

The Sage peered at the tiger in surprise. The grey eyes so similar to hers stared back, and she sighed. "I don't think you'd want to hear it."

The tiger stepped closer to Freya, nuzzling her hand. *Try me.*

Freya chewed on her bottom lip. "Fine, let's talk about your death. It was Raksh who was involved, right?"

Evie nodded. *Yes, the demon had been hunting us for a long time. He'd found out I was the guardian of the dragon manuscript, and its secrets.*

Brennan glanced over his shoulder, slowing his gait, and Freya smiled her thanks to her mom for including him in the answer. To her boyfriend, she said, *I guess now we know which part of Tyr was playing matchmaker between us in Spain.*

He gave no outwardly sign of reaction, but Freya sensed his suppressed laugh in their bond. She turned her attention back to her mother. "And Thomas?"

Evie looked at Brennan's medallion. *Yes, he was also a victim of Raksh.*

"But why was he killed so much later than you guys?" He frowned, recalling the time he'd found his dead body. "Freya said you were attacked when she was four."

And so we were, Evie confirmed. *From what I observed as Tyr, Raksh is tied to his domain. He cannot be on Earth for long periods of time. And time does not work everywhere as it does here.*

"So you're saying Raksh took longer because he didn't realize the time?" Brennan scowled. "That sounds like bull to me."

Evie's gaze sharpened on him. *It is also quite probably it took him longer to find Thomas, than us. By the time we realized what treasure we protected, it was too late to hide. Your grandfather was better at keeping secrets.*

That, he was, Brennan thought, but kept it to himself. Instead, he said, "How are you alive, then? And why isn't my grandfather?"

Brennan hadn't meant the question to sound accusing, but Mark joined their tighter group and glared at him.

The gods brought us all back – our spirits, at least. We were meant to go to the Underworld, not roam the Earth, because of our powers. But Isis and Osiris had other thoughts. Because we wanted to help, and protect you, we agreed.

"Are you saying my grandfather didn't?"

Thomas was no fool, unlike us. Mark's tone was bitter. *We didn't know that in agreeing to help, we'd become their puppets.*

Honey, it wasn't –

Mark threw Evie a look, and she sighed. *Regardless, it is thanks to them we have been able to return, and spend a longer time on this realm.*

"Yeah, how come?" Freya asked. "As Tyr, you told me you needed to replenish your energy. What's changed?"

Her parents shared a look, and Mark rolled his eyes. *We were limited, Freya. It's not impossible to understand, is it? Do you think we wanted to keep our identity away from you?*

Freya tensed, her eyes narrowing on her father. "And if I do?"

Her tone stunned Mark into silence, giving Evie a chance to intervene. *We did need more power, as Tyr. The entity was under the gods' thumb. When Raksh attacked Tyr and they fought, the injuries suffered were too much. Isis and Osiris had no choice but to separate our souls.*

Evie glanced at her husband, admitting something she hadn't until that moment. *To be perfectly honest, I think they only meant to save one of us. The fact we both survived definitely put a wrench in their plans.*

Mark's gaze turned speculative. *You may be right, darling.*

"I'd say she definitely is," Brennan said. When Mark glared at him, the Wiseman only shrugged and kept his attention on Evie. "So, what changed, then? Did you get upgraded superpowers or something?"

Not quite, Evie chuffed, the sound a soft snort coming from her rather bulky tiger shape. *Part of having joint souls meant we needed twice the energy to move about. Now that we're separate, well...* She tilted her head to the side, perusing the two teenagers. *It's easier, is all.*

Brennan rubbed his chin, pondering her words. There was a question on the tip of his tongue, but he didn't want to appear too eager. Freya, as always, read his mind and beat him to it.

"Why?" Freya frowned. "Why do you say Thomas was no fool?"

Because he refused to help, and disappeared. He realized the game better than we did and tried to warn Seamus. Mark sighed. *It's not like we could ever be as direct as he was.*

"And... Is he alive, then?" Brennan asked.

In the same way we are, yes, Evie said. *He is a Dreamwalker. While he may not cross realms, he can show up in dreams.*

Freya caught Brennan's hurt through their bond. His grandfather hadn't tried to contact him in a while. The question – the fear – that he wasn't good enough, worthy of the slightest effort, was nagging at him.

She stepped closer to him and intertwined their fingers, squeezing his hand. Comfort passed between them, enough to calm down Brennan – for the time being.

Mark was quick to jump in, saying, *Hiking while holding hands is dangerous.*

Freya scowled at her father. "Too bad."

Evie tried to diffuse the situation. *We asked the gods to pardon Thomas, should we help this far. That is how they granted us permission, and the spiritual strength, to return here.*

And be with you. Help you in this mission – both *of you.* Not that Mark appeared pleased at the prospect of working with Brennan.

Freya looked between her parents and her boyfriend. *Is that enough for you?*

For now, Brennan shot back.

"Then let's keep moving, shall we?" Freya's hand in his, Brennan took the lead once more and marched onwards.

Chapter 9

Freya woke up first. For a few seconds, she stayed immobile, scanning the surroundings with her senses out of habit. Once she was awake and realized they were in the forest, her body relaxed.

She rolled over to Brennan, who'd been sleeping nearby. To her surprise, he wasn't around – and neither was one of the tigers.

He left to refill your water.

Freya looked to the side, meeting her father's green stare. "Did you bother him again?"

Last night, when they'd camped, Mark had made it a point to force Brennan to sleep away from her. She'd found it annoying and had voiced as much – not that it had mattered.

No. Mark rose from the ground and stretched his feline body. *Your mother talked me out of it.*

"Good."

Freya packed up the blanket she'd slept on and grabbed a new shirt from her backpack. She avoided his gaze and changed shirts, then cleaned up camp.

It was only once she finished that she allowed herself to look at Mark – and noticed the waves of fury rolling off him. "What's gotten up your butt?"

The tiger's muzzle was only a foot away, and his breathing came out in short, huffing pants. *Who did that to you?*

"Did wh—" Freya hit her forehead, realizing he must have seen the scratches on her back. "No one. It was from the last fight with the ghosts."

Mark growled. *I know that's a lie.*

"And *I* don't owe *you* any explanations."

When she tried to step away, Mark blocked her path. *Freya, please.* The green gaze softened. *I know this is a change, but your mom and I are both trying. The least you could do is reciprocate.*

With the waterworks close at bay, Freya pursed her lips. She looked away and blinked until they disappeared. "Fine. I got them in a dream." When he sat on his hind and appeared to listen, she explained how the hawk had scratched her.

May I see?

Freya sighed and turned her back on him, dropping to her knees. Mark's muzzle got close to her shoulder, and he took a few deep breaths.

When he stepped away, he shook his head. *That's no Dreamwalker. It smells divine.*

"Divine? Like a god?"

Mark nodded. *You said it was a hawk?*

"Yeah, with dark eyes."

It cannot be Horus, he's been on another realm for ages, ever since humans stopped worshipping him. Set must be using his nephew's spirit animal, which means he can escape his prison to some extent.

Freya's eyes narrowed. "And if he can do that...."

"Yeah. We're screwed." Brennan made his presence known by pushing off the tree he'd been leaning against, and headed over. He bent and kissed Freya's lips, then picked up both backpacks. "Ready for day two?"

&&&

Brennan slowed down his gait, dropping to the back as Freya inched closer to her parents. He knew she was still conflicted about their presence, but at least she wasn't outright shunning them.

The idea should have made him happy. It should have encouraged him, even, to form his own relationship with Evie and Mark. But it was hard for him to reconcile the tiger he had grown used to – the presence in his mind – with these two radically different beings.

Brennan rubbed the back of his neck, shuffling along the path. They'd been walking in silence for close to four hours, and his feet were feeling it.

Even worse was the nagging in his chest, the jealousy that Freya had discovered parts of her missing family, while he was still alone. He looked away from her smiling face, unwilling to see more of it. Yet as if to spite him, his gaze returned to her.

To stop the conflicting thoughts, Brennan muttered something about having to take a leak and took off into the bushes. He would find their trace later, but a few minutes of peace would do his mind good.

After taking care of business, he stepped further away, until he reached a small stream. He dropped on his knees, dipped his hands in to wash them, before splashing cool water on his face.

Closing his eyes, Brennan tried to wrestle his wayward emotions. *What use is being a Wiseman if I'm all over the place? You'd think at least I could learn control.*

"Get a grip." His muttered curse resounded in the silence. While it didn't help, speaking aloud released some of his pent up emotion. After releasing one last heavy breath, Brennan opened his eyes.

His reflection in the stream was no longer alone, rather accompanied by a tiger. He glanced at the eyes, trying to figure out which of the parents he was dealing with. The soft grey hue put him at ease, and he lowered back on his haunches.

"Evie, is it?"

Freya's mom inclined her head, but her gaze never strayed from his. *What troubles you, Brennan?*

Unwilling to aggravate his girlfriend's parents, he muttered an excuse under his breath. When he moved to stand up, Evie stepped closer to him, forcing him to remain down.

You may try to fool yourself, but I was in your head for a while, if you'll recall.

"I do." Brennan winced, as another thought struck him. "You *and* your husband."

Evie snorted, and he could have sworn her eyes twinkled. *Is that what this is about? You are uncomfortable because of our previous connection?*

Brennan wanted to jump on the excuse, but before he could, Evie spoke again. *No... It isn't that. But it's related to us being here, right?*

At a loss, he dropped his head on his forearm and sighed, before nodding. He was silent until Evie took one last step and touched her muzzle to his hand. *Will you tell me?*

Brennan looked up, brows drawn in consternation. "I don't mean to feel this way, but now that Freya has you two, it only enhances all I have lost... and am left without."

And sharing her must not be easy after months of being together.

Brennan grimaced, but inclined his head in agreement. "That, too."

I cannot promise you that this will easily fall into place. Mark is complicated, and with your own stubborn character, there are bound to be obstacles. But yours and Freya's relationship has grown so much, in so little time, it gives me hope for the future.

Evie paused for a moment, then nudged Brennan's hand once more. *It takes time, Brennan - adjusting. But Freya is still your partner. Nothing about us being here will change that. And as for what you lost...*

A shuffling interrupted her words, and she whirled around, muscles tense and ready to launch. When Freya stepped through, followed by her father, Evie relaxed.

Brennan stood up, forcing his expression to remain neutral, even as he tried to regain control of his emotions. Mark's green eyes landed on him, peering past his defenses and he had the uncanny sensation the man could guess what had transpired.

Rather than mention it outright, Mark only said, *We thought we'd lost you.*

Brennan needed fresh water, and I didn't want to leave him alone.

Mark's gaze shifted from the Wiseman to his soul mate, then he nodded. *In that case, let us be on our way.*

When Brennan passed by Freya, she lifted a hand to his arm, tugging on his sleeve. "Are you okay?"

He looked down at his girlfriend, the faint smile playing on her lips and relaxed, almost softened countenance, and shook his head. *No way I'm going to ruin this for her.* Unsaid words clogged his throat, even as he kissed her ever so softly.

"I'm good, love. Shall we?"

Hand in hand, they followed her parents.

&&&

That evening, they made camp in another secluded area of the forest – those were easy to come by. Between mountain tops dusted with snow, old trees that stood the test of time and the roughened terrain, even the tigers needed a break.

While Brennan set about making camp, Freya joined her parents. "I've been thinking about this morning. If it's true what you say, then Set's been playing us for some time. And with Raksh in the game with the Countess, we'll be dealing with a lot once we reach Čachtice."

That's why we're here, Freya, to help. Evie nudged her daughter's hand.

"But if something happens, I and Brennan need to be ready. You two were friends with Thomas, you've spent time with the Wiseman. Isn't there a way you can help us train?"

Brennan joined her, smirking. "Aren't you getting enough exercise, love?"

Freya grinned at him. "Sure. But you know I'm right."

He rubbed his chin and his speculative gaze fell on Mark. "Depends what your dad thinks. Last thing I want is to get my ass kicked – again."

I don't see the need for training, Mark said. *We're here. It's not like before.* He stared his daughter in the eyes, willing her to believe him. *I swear it, Freya, we'll have your back.*

Freya's expression softened, and she reached out to rub behind his ear. "And yet, things never seem to work out the way we plan," she said gently. "I want to have a backup plan...dad." She waited a beat, before saying, "Please."

You always were an independent child, Evie chuckled. Her eyes were shining, the moment not lost on her. It was the first time Freya had called Mark *dad*, marking yet another milestone in their relationship.

Mark didn't seem convinced, and he moved off-camp. With a sigh, Evie went after him. Freya took advantage of her parents' inattention and grabbed Brennan's hand, leading him a few feet down and behind a tree.

"What are you doing?" Laughter coated his voice, but he didn't stop her.

When they were out of sight, Freya pushed Brennan against the tree and rose on her tiptoes. Her lips met his in a hungry kiss, and she wrapped her arms around his neck. There was no hesitation in the Wiseman. His arms slid to her waist, pulling her closer and deepening the kiss.

After a moment locked in the embrace, Freya pulled back. "I missed that."

"Mm." He rested his forehead against hers and sighed. "Me too, love. But it's bad enough your dad hates my guts. I'd rather not give him more ammunition, hmm?"

Freya searched his expression, probing with her senses at the same time. Brennan resisted at first, before letting her in. She caught the sadness he'd kept so well under wraps, and her heart lurched.

"There has to be a way of contacting Thomas. We'll find it, you'll see." She rested her hand against his cheek, running her fingers over his light stubble. "I wish I could do more."

Brennan dropped his mouth to hers once more, this kiss more heart wrenching than the last. When he pulled away, Freya felt like she was missing something.

"You're doing enough."

But still, he took her hand and led her back into the camp. They took a seat on a fallen tree, and he pulled her into his side.

A few moments later, the tigers joined them.

You win, Mark said. *We will help as much as we can, but this does not mean you pursue the mission without us. Understood?*

Both teenagers nodded under his severe gaze.

Good. Now, before we get to the practice, there's a theory we need to dig into. How much do you know about Elizabeth Báthory?

Freya shared a look with Brennan, and he nodded. She summarized everything they'd discovered in their research, ending with, "There's also the matter of the necklace she has."

"And the chains of fire Raksh promised her."

Damn these gods and their toys. Mark's massive paw swiped at the ground, sending a good chunk of pebbles and grass fly. At Evie's glare, he settled and sat on his hide. *There's another thing you won't find in any book.*

And it has to do with Seamus, darling.

Freya looked at her mother, frowning. "What?"

Elizabeth is a cunning enemy. No matter what you deal with in Čachtice, remember that. She will find your weakest point and exploit it. And she likes to make a meal out of young men's unsuspecting hearts.

Mark's heavy gaze landed on Brennan, who bristled under it. "Are you joking right now?"

I am not.

Freya's expression darkened. "I thought you said you'd give Brennan a break."

This has nothing to do with my feelings for the boy. It is the reality of what you're facing! He looked at his wife. *Feel free to jump in anytime.*

Evie rolled her eyes and stepped closer to Brennan. *I won't, because I disagree. And we're not talking about Brennan here, but Seamus. How about you stick to the facts?*

After a short staring contest, Mark nodded. *Fine. Elizabeth bewitched Seamus. Enough so that the last time we were here, he fell into her clutches and fought against us. Thomas helped us figure out a way to undo the spell – she'd used dark magic.*

"How?" Brennan asked.

By combining his powers with Evie's. The two sides broke the emotional aspect and returned Seamus to us.

Freya glanced at Brennan. "That should be fine. We've mastered the combining, right?"

He nodded, but his expression was still serious. "And if my grandfather hadn't been there?"

Mark pawed the ground in response, before meeting Brennan's wary expression. *Seamus would've been gone.*

Freya bit her lip, trying to ignore the nagging sensation in the pit of her stomach. "Okay, so we'll practice combining our powers. No biggie."

For the Countess, no. The demon, he is another story. Those chains of fire drain the spiritual energy of anyone powerful enough to be on its radar.

Sage, Wiseman, psychic, witch. Nothing escapes it, Evie added.

Freya thought back to the attack on Seamus, and his incapacitated state for days on end. "We can't let them touch us, if we're going to follow the map. So, what do you suggest?"

You need to work on your barriers, Evie said. *Offensive strategies alone cannot win you this fight, much as your father enjoys those. I can help you practice with the barriers tonight, and you can test them on each other.*

Freya nodded and jumped to her feet, holding a hand out for Brennan. They walked on the other side of the camp and took a stance side by side, facing the tigers.

"We're ready."

As soon as she gave the okay, Mark stepped forward. He opened his jaws and roared. A puff of light energy escaped him, heading for the teenagers.

Freya lifted her palms and concentrated on getting air to bend to her will. Brennan dug deep and focused on his need to protect Freya. After two failed attempts, he joined his barrier to hers.

Mark's attack bounced off, and he nodded. *Very good.*

But there isn't substance, Evie said. *You are acting as two separate entities when you should move as one.*

Mark threw her a look. *They can work on that later.*

Evie ignored him and said, *Try harder. Freya, be the outside the barrier. Brennan, fill the inside. It will drain your energy less.*

She stepped away, then nodded to Mark. *Again.*

The tiger lowered his head and sent another attack towards the teenagers. This time, Freya did as her mother suggested. She bid air to encompass Brennan's little spurt of energy and widened it to swallow them up.

The attack bounced off again, and she jumped in Brennan's arms. "Hell, yes! We got this!"

He laughed in her neck, before setting her back on the ground. "How about something a little more physically exhausting?"

Mark's growl pulled his attention, and he rolled his eyes. "I meant *sparring.* Your daughter and I do this daily."

Go on, Evie nodded and pushed her husband away into a corner. They watched as the teenagers danced around each other.

Freya jumped into attack mode first. She tried to hit Brennan, who blocked the punch and ducked under her. He landed a flat-palmed hit to her hip, causing her to wince and dance out of the way.

They toyed with each other, then Freya aimed a kick at Brennan's head. He caught her foot, and she dropped to the ground, rolling over her shoulder.

He's taller than you, try a lower kick, Mark suggested.

Freya rose from the fall, throwing a scowl over her shoulder. "Thanks, *daddy*. But I've been handling it well enough on my own, so how about some quiet?"

Mark chuffed, shaking his head in amusement, but no further instructions came. Freya faced Brennan once more, cracking her knuckles. "Ready?"

This, he was used to. The banter, the energy passing between them – enough to raise hell itself. Thoughts of jealousy and isolation left Brennan in favor of the adrenaline surging through him.

He grinned. "Always, love."

Chapter 10

Freya tossed and turned in her sleep, but Brennan lay away next to her. Mark's gaze was heavy on him, no matter how much he tried to ignore it. He blocked his mind, unwilling to let the man find evidence of his transgression.

Last night, he'd dreamt of the Countess again. It was the second time, and just like he'd been warned, she was trying to seduce him. She talked to him of power and what he could achieve by her side.

None of that interested Brennan, but he wanted to try and get in her head. If any information could be gained through the special contact, he had to attempt to retrieve it, at least.

The only problem was he was getting more and more annoyed that he couldn't keep Elizabeth out of his dreams. *Grandpa, I wish I had your help right now.*

Movement drew his head up, and he watched Mark head over to Evie. Since the training session when she'd pushed for him and Freya to combine their powers, Mark had kept a distance from his wife.

Now, he headed to her, bowing his head. Brennan couldn't tap into their private communication, but Evie shifted to the side, allowing him by her side next. *I wish my problems went away as easily.*

Brennan lowered his head and stared at Freya, willing sleep to take over. He reached out for her hand and grasped it in his. Eventually, he fell asleep.

&&&

The desert was hot in the day. Above, the sun burned like a million ovens, and Brennan wiped away at his forehead. In the distance, he could see a hill.

Get past it.

The words weren't spoken, more like a nagging at the back of his mind. He moved, little by little, but his body was heavy. The sun's rays shone brighter, and he tripped over his feet, rolling to the bottom of the hill.

"Brennan!"

Freya showed up by his side and helped him up. "You too?"

He nodded, trying to case their surroundings. "No hawk tonight?"

"Guess not." She pointed in the distance. "Are you getting the same feeling I am, that we're meant to go there?"

"Yeah..."

They moved as one through the sand. Freya lifted a hand, willing a breeze to cool them off. It was faint, but it answered still.

Freya grinned at her boyfriend, and they continued onwards, refreshed. Time seemed to pass by slow, and the hill never got closer. They looked over their shoulders, trying to gauge the distance they'd crossed. When they faced the sun once more, the hill was there.

The teenagers shared a confused look and headed closer. As they neared it, they noticed it wasn't a hill, but part of a rock mountain. Carved in the cliff were two gigantic statues with the head of a canine animal.

At first glance, they appeared almost jackals. But a closer look showed a slender canine shape, closer to a greyhound. Each statue had a stiff tail, forked at the end, and their ears were erect. Mirror long noses poked the air with arrogance. One statue was red with golden areas where the tunic and jewelry would be. The other was black, similarly clad with gold.

Shivers ran through the teenagers, and they shared another glance. "That's no jackal, is it? It's —"

"—the Set animal," Brennan nodded. "Totemic animal of the god himself, also called a sha in ancient times." He clenched his fists. "You think he's in there?"

"Only one way to find out."

Freya lifted her hand to calm the wind, but it didn't listen. Rather, it picked up further, enveloping them in a cloud of dust.

"Brennan!" Freya put her arm over her eyes to protect them, but she couldn't see the Wiseman anywhere.

"Freya!" He called out to her from nearby, unable to see past the blasted sand. "Make it stop!"

"I'm trying!"

Despite her best efforts, the wind wouldn't let go. Through it, she noticed someone watching them. A shape was in the entrance, but Freya had to squint through the sand tornado. He was tall, with dark hair – and then the sand obliterated her vision.

Freya!

It wasn't Brennan's voice in her mind, but her mother's.

Freya, stop it!

&&&

Brennan woke up first. The first he noticed was the dip in temperature, and his freezing body. Then he looked around, and his eyes fell on both tigers leaning over Freya.

He took a moment to understand why. A strong wind had picked up around them, and was twisting the trees, breaking branches. The sky was too dark to see anything, obscuring both stars and moon.

"What..."

One tiger glanced at him – Mark. *What the hell happened?*

Brennan crawled to Freya, trying to shake her away. "Is she doing this?"

Yes! Evie sounded panicked. *You were both sleeping when the wind picked up. We took a minute to realize it was coming from Freya, and by that point it was too late.*

If she doesn't stop soon, this storm will reach the nearby village. Snap her out of it.

"Easy to say," Brennan muttered, recalling their previous issues with the dreams. He glared at the tigers. "I have an idea, but you won't like it."

Just do it!

Brennan held Mark's gaze for another second, waiting for him to agree to Evie's approval. When the tiger inclined his head, he crawled over Freya.

After a slight hesitation, he bent his mouth to her lips. Behind him, the growls of the tigers got lost in the howl of the wind. Freya answered in her sleep, her lips moving under his.

Brennan waited until she gave him full access to her mouth, opening under his, before tightening his grip on her hand. He extended the barrier of his mind and reached within hers. Picturing the protective bubble they'd created together, he expanded it around his girlfriend.

Work with me, Frey. I need you to snap out of it.

Freya was still kissing him, but she was trying to pull her hand out of his grip. On a subconscious level, she must have caught his intrusion. He pushed further, trying to scan for what was driving her wild, making her powers get out of control.

Then he sensed it – the alien, unknown string of an outside influence. With all his mental might, Brennan pushed against it – until it snapped.

Freya went limp under him, and he froze, pulling back. His wide eyes scanned her body. "Shit! Freya?"

The wind had died off, but she was too still. Brennan shook her once, twice –

"Ow," Freya muttered, blinking awake. "I'm not a rag doll, Bren, cut it out!"

He dropped his head on her chest, sighing in relief. "Holy shit."

Indeed.

Brennan froze and pulled off Freya, noticing the tigers' gazes on him. He gulped. "How much trouble am I in, on a scale of one to ten?"

Evie shook her head, but Mark beat her to it. *I may not agree with your methods, but you did a good job.*

Stellar, Evie added, showing off her canines in a feline smile.

Freya looked from one to the other and frowned. "Stellar job, at what exactly?"

&&&

In the palace of the gods, Isis jumped awake in bed, her heartbeat flying out of her chest. She touched Osiris' shoulder, shaking him awake.

"What is it, beloved?" His sleepy mumble almost caused her to be silent – almost.

"Your brother."

Osiris was up in an instant, searching her expression. "What did Set do again?"

Isis thought back to what she'd seen in her dream. "He is trying to gain control of the teenagers. Both of them, one of them – it matters not to him."

Osiris' fist clenched the bed sheet. "What else can I do, save kill him myself?"

Isis looked at him with pity in her eyes. "You know that is not possible."

Osiris slumped back on the bed, throwing an arm over his eyes. His mind whirred, trying to find a solution to an impossible problem.

"Damn."

&&&

The Sage stared at her parents and boyfriend, waiting for the moment they'd say it was all a joke. But their expressions were identical in seriousness, and she sensed it was a vain hope.

"I don't understand. How would I be doing in real life, what I did in a dream?"

Her parents shared a look. *Same as the scratch on your back. Set's involvement in this – for I have no doubt it's that coward who did this – is altering the barrier between dimensions.*

Not to mention he has divine powers. An encounter with him is harder to escape than, say, a vengeful demon. Evie sighed. *Be careful in your dreams. Block your mind before you fall asleep, and if you find yourself there again, will yourself awake.*

"I tried," Freya whispered. "I really did. But it was impossible, and the sandstorm kept going." She turned to Brennan. "How did you make it out?"

He shrugged, "I honestly have no idea. One minute I was there, tasting sand, the next I was waking up here in a tornado."

Freya bit her lip. "Is the village okay?"

Yes, Mark said. *Brennan woke you in time.*

Freya recalled the intrusion in her mind and scowled. "Yeah, he definitely did."

Uncaring of the parents, Brennan pulled her hand in his and leaned close. His brown-golden eyes shone, willing her to believe him. "I had no choice, Frey. Otherwise, you'd still be with him."

The anger left her as easily as it came, and Freya squeezed his hand back. She leaned her head on his shoulder, drawing comfort from his presence and calm demeanor.

Inside, she was panicking. If Set could get to her so easily, how could they ever hope to fight him?

We will help, Freya. I swear to you.

She looked at her mother and nodded, wanting to believe her. But something told her it wouldn't be as easy as they all thought.

Another thought occurred. "Why do we keep seeing him in the desert? And that place... Was it his temple?"

"It might have been," Brennan said. "But I felt something else before we ran into him. Almost like something meant for us to go in one spot, but ended up somewhere different."

What are you talking about? Mark asked.

Freya explained him the sensation she'd had, the command towards the hill. "We never made it. Set side-tracked us."

Evie turned to her husband. *Do you think it's...*

He nodded, his expression grim. His green eyes were full of something when they fell on his daughter once more. *It's not a sensation, but the map. It leads you to the relics.*

And Set wishes them for himself.

Brennan's hand tightened on Freya's. The agitation within him caused a slight tremble down his fingers, and she zeroed in on it. *If we have the relics, they could help him reach his grandfather.*

He glanced at her, and she knew he'd followed her thoughts. She squeezed back, but tried to keep her expression from giving her away.

"We'll be careful," Brennan promised. "But we also need sleep, if we're to survive the last day of hiking."

And you can get your rest.

&&&

Brennan was dreaming. The moment he realized it, he pulled his barriers up and tried to stay alert. But the mountains he was in were not in the desert, rather his hometown. And the cabin...

His heart thudded in his chest. "Granddad?"

Noises came from within, and he ran towards the entrance. When he barged in, the cabin was empty. Brennan walked in slower, taking in the two cots in a room, the small kitchen, his grandfather's desk.

Tears hit his eyes, and he blinked them away. "Why am I dreaming of this?"

"Because I needed to see you."

Brennan froze, not trusting his ears. For so long, he'd dreamt of seeing his mentor, his friend, his only family again, and he wanted desperately to believe the voice was real. But when he turned around, his grandfather *was* there. Dressed in an old shirt and jeans, he pulled a straw hat off his head, releasing the grey hair that fell to his shoulders.

The Wiseman stared at the man he'd seen dead for a beat – then ran into his arms, tackling him into the wall. "Granddad!"

He tightened his grip on him, afraid he'd disappear again. A loud guffaw escaped Thomas, and he pushed his nephew away.

Tears shone in his eyes when they met Brennan's. "I've missed you too, nephew. But we haven't much time."

"Why haven't you... If you're a Dreamwalker..." Brennan was having a hard time stringing a sentence together.

Thomas smiled. "You've learned much in my absence, I see. Yes, I can dreamwalk, but it wasn't until recently the gods got off my back." He glanced around and sighed. "Speaking of gods, it's time I give you a lesson in history."

Brennan sat on one chair while Thomas grabbed the other. "Long ago, before humans thought for themselves, they worshipped the gods of Ancient Egypt – and other pantheons. These deities still exist, but they are far removed from Earth now." He paused. "Except for Isis, Osiris and Set. Their feud started eons ago, from brotherly jealousy."

"I know the story," Brennan said. "Set cut Osiris up in pieces, and Isis was the one to put him back together and bring him back to life with her magic. Osiris became Lord of the Underworld, and Isis put their son in hiding. When he was older, Horus challenged Set and won – with that victory came the throne of Egypt." He frowned. "I don't want to waste time with you on their squabbles."

Thomas patted his shoulder and smiled. "I know. And you would be quite right, Brennan, except for one details. That fight never happened. Horus never fought Set, because Osiris imprisoned his brother in the Underworld long before he could hurt his son. Set's been in there since, cultivating relationships with demons."

"Like Raksh."

Thomas' glinted. "Yes, the coward who killed me. He wanted the medallion." His knowing gaze dropped to Brennan's empty neck.

"I'm sorry, he—"

Thomas lifted a hand. "It does not matter. You absorbed the map, and that is most important. The relics, they will not bring me back. When you get them, destroy them."

"Why?" Brennan frowned. "We can keep them safe."

"No. There is a battle for good and evil whose balance tipped a hundred years ago."

"When the ghosts entered here."

"Yes. And demons and angels alike will come for those relics. It is best you destroy them – especially if you want to vanquish Set." He paused, and his expression darkened. "I know you believe those relics can help bring me back, but they will not."

Brennan's stomach lurched in response to Thomas' firm tone. "Why?"

Thomas' expression softened for a split instant, and he patted Brennan's shoulder. "I am long gone, Brennan, whether you wish to accept it or not. And it was time for me, you know? But you..." The grip on his shoulder tightened. "My boy, you can be so much more than I ever could. You can have a family, a life outside of this." He glanced around, smiling sadly. "A better one than me."

Brennan followed his gaze, taking in the meager possessions and the quaint décor. It had been little, but it had been theirs. He wiped at his face, removing the tears that weakened him. "Why can't we kill Set?"

Thomas met his gaze once more, and nodded. Pride shone in his eyes, and he opened his mouth as if he would say more. A thunderstorm outside drew his attention, and he paled. "I'm running out of time. It seems the gods are not keen on me spilling their secrets, after all." He took Brennan's hand in his. "Do not trust Isis and Osiris. Do what feels right, *always*."

"Wait, granddad –"

Thomas hugged him once, whispering in his ear, "I believe in you, Brennan. Always have, always will."

In the second it took Brennan to blink back tears, Thomas had vanished.

Chapter 11

Freya shifted the rucksack on her shoulder, trying to roll it. She'd been training with Brennan in the morning, and her muscles were sore.

"Let me," he said from behind, and picked it up. Without effort, the Wiseman shrugged the extra bag on his free shoulder, and grinned at her. "And don't start."

Freya rolled her eyes but said nothing. Instead, her gaze shifted back to her parents. For once, they were walking ahead, leaving the two teenagers with some alone time.

"How are you doing?" Brennan's soft question drew her attention to him. "With them, I mean. Any better?"

She nodded, and a slow smile spread on her lips. "Yeah, you were right. I shouldn't be giving them a hard time when all I've wanted my entire life is to have them back."

Brennan grinned and squeezed her hand. "There's something I have to tell you. I had a dream last night."

"Oh?"

"Yeah, it was my granddad."

Freya stopped in her tracks, staring at him. "Thomas? But I thought..."

Brennan shook his head. "He's not dead, but a Dreamwalker. Like your parents." He glanced at the tigers, before lowering his voice. "Granddad said we shouldn't trust the gods, because they're only after their own interests."

"That's not surprising," Freya said and walked again. She kept her voice to a whisper, not wanting her parents to overhear. "Remember all the research we did? Gods are fickle."

Brennan threw her an amused look. "Now you sound like my grandfather."

Freya shrugged. "What else did he say?"

"That we have to destroy the relics. If we try to keep them, we'll be targets to both demons and angels."

A sigh escaped his girlfriend, but Brennan squeezed her shoulder in reassurance. "And we will, I promise. He said the relics can't bring him back, and I believe him."

Freya's gaze landed on the tigers once more. "Which means, it can't bring them back either."

"No."

She swallowed past the lump in her throat. *The idea was nice, while it lasted. But at least I'll have this little time with them, if nothing else.* She met Brennan's golden-brown eyes. "I'm with you, whatever it takes. You know that."

Before Brennan could say anything, Mark switched directions and headed to them. *What are you whispering about?*

Evie came to their rescue. *Leave them be, Mark. They've earned a little alone time, no?*

The male tiger snorted, checking their surroundings. *I think here's a good enough spot to set up camp. Time for round two of your training.*

Freya groaned. "Do we have to? We had a morning session, dad."

Mark rolled his eyes. *Yes, you do. Enough with the complaining. If I recall, it was you who insisted on our help.*

She sighed and let go of Brennan's hand. After he'd set down both rucksacks, they moved to the center of the meadow. This time, the tigers seemed to have a different training in mind.

You can relax, Evie said. *It would be best if you sit, and face each other. Try to touch hands – it should help for the first time.*

First time? Freya thought, glancing to the Wiseman opposite her.

Brennan's expression mirrored her confusion for a beat. Then he smirked, and she knew the exact moment his mind dropped in the gutter. Read the laughter in his eyes, she shook her head. *Don't even think that around my dad!*

Too late, Brennan laughed mentally.

Luckily for them, Mark seemed too busy pawing the ground, designing some kind of circle around them. When he finished, he said, *All right. So we know heading to fight the Countess won't be a walk in the park, but she's the least of your worries.*

Raksh is the most powerful opponent, Evie picked up. *And if our theory is correct and this has all been planned, you cannot meet him again without being able to unite your powers. Yes, combining is fine, but* uniting *is what will get you the win.*

Freya gaped at her parents. "But, we haven't... I mean..." She pleaded to Brennan for help.

"What Freya means, I think, is that we haven't really practiced that part. At all, to be honest."

No better time to try than when you're not under fire.

They sighed at Mark's wise words and dropped to the ground, facing each other. Freya rested her hands on her knees, palms up. Brennan gripped them in his and winked. It relaxed the Sage, who'd tensed without knowing why.

"So, how exactly does this work?" Freya asked.

We'll give you a head start. You need to surround yourselves with a barrier, using the circle I drew.

Then, Evie said, *we'll attack as we did this morning. But we'll attack from different sides, in ways you cannot predict. Eventually, the barrier will break.*

And when it does, you two need to be ready to hit us back with a strong, joint *attack.*

"What if we hurt you?" Brennan asked.

Mark snorted. *You won't, believe me.*

"Okay," Freya said softly, and focused her gaze on Brennan. "Let's do this."

They closed their eyes, tuning in to their bond. Freya felt Brennan's gentle nudge, and rather than rebuke him, she allowed him closer. She pleaded with air to surround them with a barrier while Brennan used his vital energy to strengthen it.

Very good, Mark said.

Freya sensed their energies mingling, but not jointly. Before she could press further, she sensed something bounce off the shield.

One glance around confirmed both her parents attacking with bursts of spiritual energy. Freya squeezed Brennan's hands in hers. *Bren, we need to get ready.*

Only, when she turned to him, Brennan was staring – and not at her.

&&&

Brennan was still in the meadow, but not quite. Rather than the soft shadow of the trees, trunks with ugly roots surrounded him, their ominous vibes throwing him off.

"Pretty boy, pretty boy, what have you brought me today?"

The Wiseman spun around, only to see the woman from his dreams. "I...what?"

Her blue eyes shone in delight, fixated on something in his hands. When Brennan looked down, his jaw dropped in horror – he was holding a heart.

"What the hell is this?" He tried to let go, but something glued it to his hands. Blood dribbled to the ground, coating it in burgundy.

The Countess smiled and stepped closer to him. Brennan tried to move away, but his gaze was drawn to the necklace around her throat.

"You've been a good boy," she whispered in his ear. She walked around him, her nails caressing his back. "A heart for me, and so fresh. Tell me, was it *hers*?"

Brennan started, still unable to move.

"Was it your beloved's?"

&&&

"Brennan!" Freya tried to shake him awake, and the surrounding attacks grew worse. Her parents couldn't catch something was off because of the barrier, but the air itself was stifling, filled with something...wrong.

At a loss on what else to do, she dug her nails into Brennan's hands and closed her eyes. With all her might, she tugged on their bond, trying to reach him. Only, when she did, he wasn't alone. Another presence was with him – a woman.

Freya pushed her confusion away and pulled Brennan back to her. She sensed it when he was present once more and said, *We have to unite our powers, now!*

The dam of the attacks burst the bubble and rained showers around them. Freya threw the elements as a barrier, but it was futile. Brennan tried to back her up with a burst of energy, but it was out of synch.

Stop, Mark!

The attacks paused and Evie was by Freya's side in an instant. *What happened?*

Mark, meanwhile, focused his attention on the Wiseman. He sensed his shock, his guilt, and a full whirlwind of emotions running at top speed.

Freya opened her eyes and stared at Brennan. Hurt and pain mingled in her grey stare, which darkened with each second. Then her expression closed off and she pulled her hands from Brennan's. Before he could say anything, she got up and stalked off into the woods.

Mark meant to follow her, but Brennan's whispered words stopped him in his tracks. "You were right."

&&&

Brennan knew the time to hide was long gone. He met the tigers' gazes and told them everything – the dream, and the last daydream. When he got to the part about the heart, he sensed their agitation increasing.

Elizabeth should not be able to contact him so, not with us around! Evie paced, grumbling under her breath.

Brennan looked instead at Mark, who was uncharacteristically quiet. "What, you're not going to say I told you so? Warn me off your daughter?"

No, I gather you're doing enough of that on your own. The fact remains, while you feel this guilt and block yourself from Freya, uniting your powers is impossible.

"I know," Brennan sighed and dropped his head in his hands.

This also puts you at risk with Raksh, Mark continued. *And because of you, Freya is also in a precarious position.*

Brennan remained silent, knowing he was stuck between a rock and a hard place. *I won't leave Freya to fight this alone,* he resolved.

Mark's next words surprised him. *But, to be fair, it's not your fault you're this weak.*

Rather than retort something sarcastic, Brennan asked, "What do you mean?"

I don't think Elizabeth is playing fair any longer.

Evie stopped pacing, her ears twitching at Mark's words. *Are you saying...*

She is close to becoming a Cursed One, yes. Her ability to enter Brennan's dreams, to influence him, is not that of a regular ghost.

"You forget the necklace she wears," Brennan reminded him.

That necklace doesn't have the power to ignore godly-enhanced barriers, Mark said. *And even if Raksh was helping her, it should still not be enough. Unless she is becoming a Cursed One.*

"Like Cortés?" Brennan recalled the conquistador, and how he'd been focused on becoming a demon, on having the power of evil.

Some ghosts that blasphemed of their living knew it only took more sins in their death to turn over to evil, and gain the true power of darkness. They'd become tangible, able to wield such forces for their own benefit. In the end, they would no longer be invisible – not unless they so chose.

Yes, Mark said. *Exactly like him.*

Brennan ran a hand over his face, then sighed. "Was she on my grandfather's list, too?"

His list? Evie stepped closer.

"Yeah, Seamus told us in Spain that's how he knew about the Cursed Ones. That my granddad had a list of them."

Mark rolled his eyes. *Quite possibly, yes. Thomas always was good at keeping records. After seeing what happened to Seamus, it would not surprise me if he'd written down Elizabeth's name as well.*

Evie lifted her head and sniffed the air, turning around. *Enough about Elizabeth, Brennan. Go to Freya. She is hurt right now, and needs an explanation only you can provide.*

Brennan sighed and got to his feet. It took only a quick scan to sense where she was. Each step in her direction was heavy, as was his heart.

After a few minutes of walking, he ended up by a stream. Freya was perched on a rock, wiping at her cheeks. His heart clenched at the thought he'd hurt her, without meaning to.

"Freya..."

Her back tensed, but she didn't turn his way. Brennan crossed the remaining distance and hesitated. He stepped around the stone and knelt in front of his girlfriend.

Her grey eyes were rimmed with red, and her nose was more crimson than usual. She avoided his look, wiping at the dried tears on her cheeks.

"I'm sorry," he said, putting all his regret in those two words.

Freya was silent for a bit, before asking, "Who is she?"

He tried to reach for her hand, but she moved it out of his reach. "It's not like that," he tried. "I'm not being unfaithful to you."

"Really?" Freya's eyes blazed, meeting his. "So how do you explain what I felt? Because I'll tell you, it sure as hell didn't feel innocent!"

Brennan dug his hands in his thighs, clenching them. Everything was spiraling out of control, and the fear of losing Freya – the one who'd been there by his side these last months – weighed on him. His chest constricted, his vision narrowing down to her accusing eyes.

Thump-thump-thump. The sound of his heart was loud in his ears, and air was scarce in his lungs. He inhaled desperately, then dropped his head on the rock next to her thigh.

"Frey, I'm *so* sorry. You can't... She came to me in my dreams." The words poured out, and with each syllable that passed his lips, he felt lighter. His breathing quieted, and he left nothing out – not the dreams, not his feelings, not Elizabeth's promises. He even told her Mark's theory, that the Countess was becoming a Cursed One.

After long moments of his voice alone echoing in the forest, he finished with, "I didn't want you to worry. Between Set, the attack on Seamus and your parents coming back, you had enough on your mind. I realize how stupid that was... Forgive me, Freya. *Please.*"

Silence surrounded him for long moments. Only the river made any noise as water passed over stones and trickled down into the forest.

A few moments later, he felt a hesitant touch on his head. Brennan looked up, and Freya dug her fingers in his hair. Her grip was strong, and for a moment he wondered if she was getting ready to bash his head into the rock. But rather than punish him, she bent over and rested her forehead against his.

"You can't lie to me, Bren. Never again."

He reached for her hand, and this time she allowed it. "I swear it."

Freya's grey gaze, so dark when they'd first started talking, lightened a shade. "Dealing with a Cursed One is nothing new for us, Bren. But losing trust in one another... That, we can't afford to do."

Brennan closed his eyes in relief, and nodded.

"How touching."

Both teens froze at the voice. Brennan jumped to his feet, angling his body in front of Freya to protect her. *What the...* His eyes couldn't see anything in the shadows at first.

Freya gripped his shoulder. *There.*

He followed the direction of her gaze and noticed a pair of red eyes staring back at them. *Raksh?*

Laughter echoed through the forest, and Brennan moved backwards. He kept himself in between Freya and the wraith.

It's not him, Freya said. *There's more than one.*

Brennan cast out his senses and caught another presence...and another. He gulped. *Try calling for your parents.*

I already did. I think the demons are blocking us.

Freya....

She squeezed his hand in silent reassurance. *We got this, Bren. Just like we've been training.*

A fourth presence stepped out of the shadows, and any idea of escaping vanished from their minds.

Shit.

Chapter 12

They couldn't back away any further. With no knowledge of the layout, Freya and Brennan had ended up on the outskirts of the forest. They were at the edge of a cliff, and water lay below.

She glanced at the Wiseman. *We're screwed.*

Brennan looked back to the forest, and the four demons advancing towards them. They had skin white as ghosts, eyes the color of blood and clawed talons. *Maybe not. Let's try the barrier your parents taught us.*

Freya reached within for her energy, knowing as well as he did that it was their only hope. She dug into air and water behind them, and a force field escaped her aura, then wrapped itself around them. Brennan's energy filled the bubble from within, enhancing it.

The demons moved closer. "You cannot essscape us, foolsss," said the farthest one on the right.

"You have sssomething we need," another added.

They're not Raksh, but they sure as hell were sent by him! Waves of fury rolled off Freya, mingling with the barrier around them and turning it static.

Brennan's jaw dropped, and he turned to her. *You're doing this?*

The Sage only shrugged, narrowing her eyes on the wraiths. *Guess so. Let's try pushing it towards them.*

Focusing on their energies, the two imagined the barrier having a life of its own and advancing towards the demons. Grass crackled underneath it, but it moved... inch by slow inch.

The wraiths hissed, showing yellowed teeth and lengthened fangs. Then one of them shot his hand forward. A black, viscous mass escaped his fingers, and rolled towards the teenagers. By chance, the barrier shattered it before it could get to them.

Something tells me we shouldn't let any of their shit touch us.

Freya gulped. *You think?* The nefarious vibes she sensed off them made her skin crawl. Speculatively, she glanced over her shoulder.

Don't even think about it, Brennan warned.

She met his gaze. *Why not? It wouldn't be the first time! And if we could survive the drop, I'd be able to use water to shield us more.*

Freya, jumping off a cliff is a bit more dangerous than hopping off your hotel balcony into a pool.

But we did it, once before.

Brennan's gaze fell on the demons. Their heads tilted at an odd angle, looking almost dislodged. Beady eyes stared at the barrier, trying to see how to undo it.

Then he looked back at the cliff. *I don't like this.*

Freya grinned, knowing he'd agreed. *On three, okay?*

She waited until Brennan nodded, and counted aloud. "One... two.... *three*!"

As one, they turned their backs to the demons and made a run for the cliff. They jumped off, bodies cutting through the air like arrows. Shrieks of annoyance escaped from behind, then faded away.

Freya focused on the water below. She pulled on air, sensing Brennan's energy as a backup. By the time they were low enough to make contact, they practically floated to the large river underneath.

They dropped in, and Freya was first to break the water. She looked around, and Brennan resurfaced a few feet away. He swam to her, pulling her in his arms and kissing her.

"That was mad," he whispered against her lips.

Freya grinned and glanced upwards. No sign of the demons. "Maybe, but it worked."

Brennan froze, sensing something she didn't. He looked everywhere, deaf to Freya's words, until he saw it – the viscous mass was rolling down the hill, and heading to them.

"Get out of the water!" he shouted and pushed Freya.

"What, why?"

"The freaking curse or whatever it is, it's heading this way. Go!"

Freya swam away, Brennan behind her. They reached shore and stepped onto the ground's safety. The minute they were on land, the mass filled the water. From a clear blue, it turned an ugly black, bubbling under their very eyes.

Brennan stepped closer to Freya, pulling her into his side and kissing her forehead.

"Good catch," she whispered, pressing a hand to his chest. She shivered at the chill in the air. With their wet clothes, they were pretty uncovered against the elements.

They also had no time to relish their escape. Brennan froze, his narrowed gaze scanning their surroundings. "They're here again."

"Thought you could essscape usss.... Foolsss. We are darknessss, we are everywhere..."

Their hisses surrounded the two teenagers, causing them to shiver in the cold night. Before they could create another barrier, the wraiths struck. The first demon flew in the air, tackling Brennan away from Freya.

The second burst from the water and grabbed her ankle. She shrieked and tried to pull away, but his iron grip only caused her to fall to the ground. Inch by inch, he pulled her closer to the water – and whatever lay beyond it.

"Freya!"

She tried to grasp at the ground, but came off with a fistful of it. In the darkness, her eyes sought Brennan's. He had a demon on top of him, and the creature's claws wrapped around his throat, cutting off his air supply.

Through their bond, Freya felt the double assault. Her panic mixed with Brennan's loss of oxygen, and it was enough to get her to hyperventilate. There was no rationale, no reason, only fear – and her spiritual energy answered in kind.

Wind picked up, and the tainted water rolled in waves. The demon stopped pulling, glancing around himself. The sky above darkened with clouds, obscuring the remaining light, and thunder echoed. Freya dug deeper under the earth, aware of the danger.

I can't....lose control. Not again.

The last time she'd done so, in Spain, it had nearly caused the hotel to be blown apart. She'd promised Seamus to watch herself, and never let it get out of control again.

Another voice entered her mind, a plea. *Do... it.... Frey.*

She met Brennan's golden-brown eyes across the distance, saw a second demon now had his arms pinned while the first was strangling him. Fury replaced the fear within her, and Freya screamed – a raw, primal cry.

Everything happened at once.

Fire raced across the distance, from the cliff and into the water. It became a blaze and within seconds consumed the demon that had captured her ankle. Freya pulled her foot out of the way in time, avoiding a burn. The demon's mouth was open in a mute scream of terror, even as it became barbequed.

Free now, the Sage rose and thrust her hand at the earth. It answered by rolling under Brennan and forcing the demons off him. Trees' branches lengthened, wrapping themselves around one demon and imprisoning him.

The next demon was in the air holding his throat, and it took Freya a second to realize why. Brennan was on his knees, panting for air, but he had one palm lifted. She saw it tremble, but it wasn't from fear. Rage unlike anything she'd ever felt from him filled him, coating his entire being in a silvery light not unlike her own.

Freya glanced at her body, noticing the glow she'd missed at first. She heard a crack, and looked up to see the demon crumple to the ground like a broken doll, its joints at weird angles.

Brennan stood next, and the golden flecks in his brown eyes shone fiercer, glinting almost unnaturally. "Freaking prick," he cursed, and walked to Freya. "Are you okay?"

He cupped her cheek, and she leaned into his touch, grateful they'd survived. "Yeah," she nodded. "But Bren, what *was* that?"

He shrugged, and the surrounding glow diminished. "No clue. Where are the other two?"

Freya pointed to the imprisoned demon. "I haven't seen the fourth one." She looked up at the cliff where the fire still raged, and unto the water. She gently entreated the element to vanish, and it disappeared, leaving behind burnt grass.

"How did fire come into this?" Brennan asked, frowning.

"I think from the shield we left up there. Remember the static?" When Brennan's expression cleared, Freya finally hugged him. "You realize what this means, right? We faced off four demons – and lived."

"For now."

The voice had them break apart. The fourth demon had appeared, and he was grinning like a maniac. Shivers ran down Freya's spine, and Brennan pulled her against his side. He wavered, and she sensed his energy draining.

The demon smirked as if catching their weakness. Before they could do anything, murky water wrapped around their ankles and imprisoned their movements. Freya struggled to get away, but nothing worked. When she tried to influence the element, it was useless.

"Time to get what I came here for." With a wave of his hand, he released the other demon. Then he advanced towards them with a blank face and lifted one hand with talons to Freya's face first.

Get the hell away from my daughter, demon!

Freya could have dropped to the ground in relief. A roar echoed from behind, and though she was immobilized by the ankles, she managed to turn slightly. Evie was on the cliff they'd jumped off of, standing tall against the horizon.

The second released demon moved forth. "Ssshall I?"

Before either could do anything, a low growl echoed around them and Mark stepped from the shadows. *I believe my wife asked you to leave our daughter alone.*

There was a brief silence, like before a storm, followed by a flurry of activity. The demon closest to Mark attacked him and, in a flurry of activity, Evie jumped onto the ground, tackling the second one.

Next to her, Freya caught Brennan's stumble. The water around his ankles kept him immobilized as well, but now that they weren't fighting, the energy loss was getting to him.

Freya tried to hold Brennan up and tugged on his hand. "Help me, Bren. Let's escape this."

He met her gaze, appearing to have a hard time focusing. After a long moment, he nodded and rested his forehead against hers. "Okay."

The Sage closed her eyes, searching for their bond. With Brennan as exhausted as he was, she knew the clock was ticking. She caught their energies, and imagined them mingling, uniting... No barriers...

A shudder ran through them. It centralized on their joined hands, and tremors ran up and down their arms. It felt like the energy was internalizing, then snapping back like an elastic band.

Freya was aware – *too* aware – of Brennan, of his every breath, the touch of his fingers on hers, the smell of his cologne, and the other, *earthlier* scent on him. She leaned towards him, as if pulled by a magnet.

The Wiseman was staggering, having a hard time standing up – then no more. Freya's energy balanced him out, and he was able to straighten up, steady on both feet. He didn't have to look to know she was there, facing him, supporting him – being *in* him.

Their auras shone for a brief second, obliterating all else – then the chains around their ankles disappeared.

Freya's eyes snapped open and met Brennan's shocked gaze. "Did we just..."

He looked down at his feet, and a slow grin spread on his lips. "We bloody did!"

Celebration would have to wait. The struggles of the tigers' fight rang all around them. Without needing to consult, Freya headed towards Mark and Brennan went to Evie. They extended their hands, energy boiling underneath the surface.

Freya shot her blast of air first, blowing the demon off her father. He got back in a crouch and hissed like an animal, but she wasn't impressed.

Get out of here! Mark ordered, his green eyes filled with worry.

No, Freya said. *We got two of them, dad. We can get the last two.*

Surprise flashed in his eyes, but the demon attacked before he could voice anything. He rolled to the ground with Mark, and Freya didn't have a proper shot. She jumped on the wraith's back, wrapping her arms around his neck and ignoring his rancid stink.

Freya, no!

The demon slammed her into a tree, and Freya's back hit the trunk full-force. She groaned and had to let go of the beast, slipping to the ground instead.

Mark lunged in the air, wrestling the demon.

&&&

On the other side of the riverbank, Brennan blasted his spiritual energy at the demon. It only served to further infuriate him, and he jumped on Evie.

Shit! Brennan ran towards them, clenching his fists.

Before he could reach them, the wraith had managed to get his claws around Evie's massive throat, and a rivulet of blood was already escaping. Her eyes met Brennan's, and he read in them the fear of losing, of no longer being able to protect that which she held most dear. *Keep Freya safe, please.*

I will. But there's no way I'm letting you die.

With no thought for his safety, he grabbed the demon's shoulder and shoved him off Evie. He followed it with a punch to the jaw and watched as he flew backwards.

Evie rolled to her paws, shaking her head. *Thank you.* She glanced at the demon, who seemed out of a commission for the moment. *Brennan, what happened? Why didn't you call out for help?*

"We did! The demons blocked us. One minute, I was apologizing to Freya, and the next they had us surrounded." His glare landed on the cliff. "We had to jump off."

Evie followed his gaze, and said, *That explains it. Once you hit the water, it broke whatever curse the demons set up. That's when we knew something was wrong.*

Brennan shifted on his feet, nervously looking around. "I need to find Freya. I don't feel good knowing –" Something slammed into him from the side, and he fell to the ground.

His head hit a rock and everything spun. By the time he'd blinked, Evie was back to rolling around with the wraith. With a swipe of her paw, she ripped his throat out, and watched him shake until he was dead.

The tiger walked to Brennan. *Let's find them.*

&&&

Freya got back to her feet in time to see her father knock the demon out. Mark stood over the creature, his paw raised, nails glinting – yet he hesitated.

"What is it?" Freya asked, stepping closer.

The demons, I smell... His blazing gaze scoured the area, unable to pinpoint the source of his uneasiness. The scent of blood hit his nostrils. He glanced back down, finding the demon awake – and grinning.

"You....lossse...."

Freya didn't understand the shiver until she saw it. "Dad, look!" She pointed to the demon's wrist, and the blood now flowing into the ground. A sense of sickness took over her, enough to make her nauseous.

No! Mark tried to shake the demon, to no avail. At a loss, he ripped its throat out, then pushed his inert body into the water.

Mark?

Freya tore her gaze from the murky waters, and met Brennan's. He and Evie were running towards them, and without a second thought she jumped in his arms, wrapping her arms around his neck.

Brennan wrapped both arms against her waist, holding Freya tight to his chest. Her breathing, her aura surrounded him, and he relaxed – knowing she was alive, unharmed, was enough.

Evie and Mark nuzzled each other in mute greeting. It was not their first fight with demons, but it was the best they'd survived in a while.

Vengeance is finally ours, darling, Mark said.

Lost in their reunion, neither pair noticed the darkness. Water rose behind them, swirling until it formed a black mirror in the air, floating parallel to the river.

Mark was the first to catch sight of it. *Watch out!* he tried to warn – too late.

A breeze sifted amongst them, but rather than push them away, it pulled them closer to the flat mirror. While the tigers were able to dig their paws into the ground and anchor themselves, the teenagers lost their balance and were thrown inside.

Before either parent could do anything, Freya and Brennan had disappeared through it.

Mark was already taking a step forward when Evie cried out, *Mark, don't!*

Her plea didn't deter him. *I'm not letting my daughter face any demons alone.* He jumped in, shortly followed by Evie. But when they came out on the other end, more forest met them – but no teenagers.

Shit!

&&&

Seamus opened his eyes when he felt a presence in the room. Sam's whispering got to him first, before his gaze fell on the massive tigers.

Green eyes turned to him, and he gasped in shock. "Evie? Mark? What are you doing back here? Where are Freya and Brennan?"

The tigers shared a look, then Evie stepped closer to the bed. *Demons attacked us, on our way to Slovakia. Freya and Brennan were remarkable in fighting them, but it was a trap. Once they died, a portal formed. We followed them through but it kicked us back here.*

A growl escaped Mark. *And we're stuck here. We tried to return, but we can't move anywhere.*

Seamus inhaled sharply and looked to Sam. "What about you?"

The ghost shook his head. "I can't leave either, professor. Anya has the same problem."

"This has Set written all over it."

My thoughts exactly.

Seamus tried to stand, but fell back against the pillows with a groan. Sam hovered nearby, biting his lip. "What can we do to help?"

"Go get Anya... We may at least gather more information for Freya and Brennan."

Evie shared a look with her husband. *In the meantime, we have to consult with the gods.*

&&&

In the Underworld, locked in his cage, Set stretched from his sitting position. Cat-like, he paced across the small cell, and grabbed onto the bars. His dark eyes shifted from the guards to the cavernous ceiling, though he couldn't see beyond it.

It will not be long now, brother. The time of my vengeance nears with each passing day.

He returned to his cot, laughing under his breath.

Chapter 13

The energy vacuum spit Freya and Brennan out in a similar forest to the one they'd left. They rolled on the ground, dizzy from the switch and their surroundings.

Brennan was the first to stand, though on wobbly feet. Between the fight, depletion of energy and the unwelcome travel through space, his vital forces were at an all-time low.

He looked around, holding his head with one hand. They were in a forest, true, but little changes made it different. The trees were thicker, older. The air was chillier, and he shivered in his pullover – still wet from the water dip.

No matter where his gaze fell, one thing was clear – they had no rucksacks, no clothes. *Shit.*

His gaze landed on a shape not too far off. "Freya!" Brennan ran to her, kneeling by her side and turning her on her back. He pressed his ear to her chest, and the sound of her heartbeat calmed him down.

She's just out of it. Thank the gods.

On second thought, the Wiseman wasn't sure if the sentiment should be voiced or not. *Where the hell did we end up?*

With none of their supplies, and no idea where they were, Brennan was getting anxious. One more scan of the area settled it. *We cannot stay here. If those demons come back, we're done for.* Despite his weakness, he picked Freya up in his arms and moved.

An hour went by. Then two. And Brennan still didn't stop. His vision was blurry, but he focused on putting one foot in front of the other. He'd used a lot of vital energy in their fight, even more so when they'd united their powers.

Our powers... He glanced at the hands holding Freya now, then at his girlfriend's peaceful face. *I'll get us out of this mess, I swear it.*

He didn't know how, but he'd do his damnedest.

Night fell harder, and everything around him became darkness. Brennan couldn't see past the next few feet, and his breath came out in foggy wisps. His hands around Freya were getting colder by the second, numbing his muscles.

Yet he knew stopping was not an option. He had to find shelter, and force one last burst of energy to warm them up. Brennan took another deep breath and moved. "I got this."

His whisper echoed eerily around him, as if the forest itself was listening. For a second, Brennan thought he'd seen a glowing shape. But when he turned, no one was there.

He took another step – and lost his footing. No scream escaped him, because in the next second he was tumbling to the ground, taking Freya with him.

&&&

"Anything?" Seamus sat up straighter in the armchair, setting the book he'd been researching through away.

Sam looked up from the massive tome he was carrying around and shook his head in answer. "Nothing, professor. We tried again and still cannot leave."

A glowing shadow behind him poked her tiny head, and Seamus sighed. Anya followed Sam around like a lost puppy. It was neither of their faults that something stuck their spiritual forms in the Scotland, but he was growing more worried by the second for Freya and Brennan.

"There has to be *something* we can do," Seamus muttered under his breath. He wished pacing was a possibility, but in his current weakened state it would be useless to try. It had been a chore to drag himself out of bed and to the chair. The last thing he wanted was to waste energy better used on researching a solution.

"Maybe only the gods can help," Sam whispered. He was worried for the Sage, but nothing they'd tried had helped so far.

Seamus' expression darkened. "But will they?" His gaze shifted to the window, wondering how Evie and Mark were faring.

&&&

Are you sure it's this way? Mark asked.

Evie refrained from rolling her eyes. *Would you trust me?*

I do. But wouldn't Stonehenge be a better conduct of energy?

No, not today. This cave will work much better. As she finished speaking, the tigers emerged from the dense forest around Seamus' castle onto a small path.

Evie threw a victorious look to her husband and continued onwards. When they'd both inhabited the same consciousness as Artemis, Freya's white cat, they'd explored the castle grounds, always watchful for any dangers.

One such a day, they'd run across the cave – which, apparently, her dear husband had forgotten all about. It had been impossible for Evie not to recall the power she'd sensed inside.

Impatient to get it over with, she quickened her trot and within moments had reached the cavern. Mark joined her side, panting. Though the entrance wasn't big enough to allow humans in, the cave was the right size for them.

The tigers stepped in, and Evie sensed the ancient power imbuing the grounds. *Feel that?*

Mark grunted behind her. *Aye, hard not to. And you're convinced this will work?*

Yes. The cave has enough spiritual power to negate whatever spell Set put on the place. It won't be enough for us to escape, but it should be enough to connect to the gods, and help them bring us back to their realm.

Mark sighed. *All right, we have nothing to lose.*

Moments later, they emerged into an underground pool area. Clear, crystalline water filled up the entire basin. Evie jumped in without a second thought – and Mark followed.

Let's try it now.

Mark nodded. *Isis! Osiris!*

His shout was unanswered, so Evie tried. *Gods, we need you!*

Mark growled loud enough to echo in the cave. *I should have known they'd discard us as soon as things turned ugly!*

Mark, stop it! Evie's eyes flashed. *We need to get to Freya. I don't care if Thomas was right or not, they have to help!*

The tigers shared a look, neither speaking. Mark was ready to say something when the pool surrounding them lighted up. Evie's gaze shifted around, and excitement had her tail flicking in the water.

They heard us!

The vacuum that started pulled them under, and they vanished.

&&&

"Finally!"

The tigers landed on the marbled floor of the palace. With one wave of her hand, Isis returned them to human form, which left them spluttering and coughing water all over.

The gods moved closer and waited for them to regain their strength. Evie was first to stand, pushing away locks of her long, raven hair from her face. Her gaze was wary. "You heard us."

"You...." Mark stood, his fists clenching and clearing his throat. "Could've done it easier, no? Did we have to nearly drown?"

Osiris' expression darkened. "I apologies for being un-concerned with your hybrid-immortal lives, when the relics are about to land in my brother's hands!"

Mark narrowed his eyes on the god and took a step clos-er. Evie's hand on his begged him silently to reconsider. But it was too late. "My daughter is out there, taken from us by demons under Set's command. Be careful you don't cross me, Osiris. God or not, I can easily take Freya out of the equation and make sure she's far away from either of your reaches."

Anger rolled off Osiris. His usually warm onyx eyes were cold, and he clenched his jaw. Isis' hand was on his, in a mirrored gesture to Evie's.

"Think about Freya," Evie whispered in his ear. "Please."

Mark tensed under her hold, then all fight flew out of him. He bowed his head and relaxed his hands. "My apologies. We worry for our daughter and..." Tears choked him, and he was unable to speak past the lump in his throat.

"What happened?" Isis asked, redirecting their attention to something more important than fighting.

"We'd been trying to teach Freya and Brennan how to share their powers. Mid-way through an exercise, Brennan got distracted, and it upset Freya."

Evie didn't tell the gods the entire story on purpose. What good would it do if they knew about the Countess and her influence on Brennan? For all they knew, Osiris could decide the Wiseman was no longer fit for protecting the relics and replace him.

Mark's side-glance to her and squeeze of her hand let her know she'd chosen right, so she continued. "Freya took off, and Brennan followed her. They were out of our sight for less than half an hour, and we lost contact. By the time we found them, they'd already battled and eliminated two demons. But with the remaining two...."

Mark shook his head. "It was my fault. I wasn't paying attention to their leader, and he cut himself. His blood mingled with the earth, some kind of demon magic. Before we knew it, a portal opened and Freya and Brennan were sucked through it."

Evie blinked back tears. "We tried to follow through, but ended up in Scotland instead of wherever they are. And we couldn't leave!"

Osiris' gaze shifted from Evie to Mark. Realization crossed his features, but he said nothing and instead paced. Isis followed him with her eyes before settling her intent gaze on them. "The good news in all this is that Freya and Brennan defeated two of the demons. For youths like them, to live and tell the tale is an accomplishment."

"That worries me," Osiris said and turned to his wife. "It is almost *too* easy. What if someone meant them to succeed?"

"Are you saying it was all a trap, not just us being stuck?" Mark frowned at the god. "It would explain why Raksh was not among the demons."

"Yes," Osiris agreed. "But what worries me is where Freya and Brennan ended."

"Can you locate them?" Evie whispered, holding onto Mark's hand for reassurance. He wrapped his arm around her shoulders, pulling her into his side.

"I believe so," Isis said. "And if we find it, we should be able to send you back to them."

"Please... Tell us what we have to do."

Isis looked into Evie's pleading eyes and nodded. Then she stepped to the fireplace where they'd watched the teens more than once before.

&&&

Freya groaned and tried to move. Her entire body was frozen, and she couldn't move her fingers or toes. She tried to open her eyes, only to feel them heavy with – ice?

Her eyes snapped open, and she moaned in pain as the rest of her senses returned full-force. The bite in her feet, in her entire body. The cold was overpowering, numbing her. Teeth chattering, she tried to stand, but only ended up rolling downhill.

She stopped and risked lifting her head up. In the distance, she saw a shape. *Brennan.*

"Bren..." The whisper got past her split lips, but Freya couldn't speak any louder. *I have to do something, otherwise we'll die before we ever reach our destination.*

She couldn't explain the change in temperature, so drastic from their previous location. Unless they'd travelled north, nothing else made sense.

Despite the urge to sleep, Freya forced her fingers to move, digging into the crusty earth. She went past the frozen top – noticing the absence of snow – and dug deep into it. She pulled at her emotions, her senses, her spiritual energy, forcing everything to the surface.

A current ran through her, and this time her eyes snapped fully opened. From her fingertips, the current ran through the ground and to the tree behind her, and it caught fire. Its flames didn't spread, but they were enough to thaw Freya out within the next moments. As soon as she was able to, she lifted her other hand and pleaded with air to help.

Brennan's shape stirred in the distance. Another few moments, and the element helped bring the Wiseman closer to her. Freya pulled his head in her lap, and directed air to force the smoke from the tree to ground-level. It wasn't the best option to inhale it, but it was the safest in case any other demons were out looking for them.

In her lap, Brennan moved, coughing. His eyes opened, and their golden-brown hue settled on her face. He smiled. "Some road trip, huh?"

Freya chuckled, drawing in the heat from the fire. "I'd say. How are you feeling?"

Painfully, it seemed, Brennan got up in a half-sitting position. He took in the burning tree, and the smoke being redirected to the ground – but away from them. An eyebrow rose in surprise. "Your idea of warming us up?"

Freya shrugged, then turned to face the tree, lifting her hands to draw in the heat. "We need shelter. I don't know where we are or why the heck it's so cold, but we won't survive without supplies for much longer."

Brennan nodded, then reached for her shoulders and pulled her into his arms. He inhaled the scent of her hair and sighed. "I'm just happy we're alive."

Freya looked up at him, a smile tugging at the corner of her lips. "Me too."

She was about to rest her head against his shoulder, but hesitated. Her eyes caught Brennan's golden-brown gaze, and she stopped breathing for a split second. Then she closed the remaining distance between them and pressed her lips against his.

Life's too short to hesitate, Freya told herself. *He's mine, and he's safe. It's all that matters.*

As if hearing her thoughts, Brennan responded in kind. One arm snaked around her waist to pull her closer, while the other rubbed her cheek gently. The embrace lasted longer than it should have, when they were both so tired, but it was a much-needed connection on both sides.

Moments later, Brennan pulled away and kissed her nose. "We'll make it."

Freya buried herself in his arms, trying to draw reassurance from his grip. *I hope so.*

&&&

"Well?" Mark asked, running out of patience.

Isis turned away from the fireplace and wiped at her forehead. "They are near Čachtice Castle, only an hour's walk, maybe two at the most."

"How is that possible? Because of the training, we were at least a day away!"

Osiris shrugged at Evie's question. "It must be where the demons wanted Freya and Brennan."

"You mean, where *Set* wanted them," Mark corrected.

Neither deity said anything, and he turned to Evie. "If Elizabeth is truly turning into a Cursed One, Freya and Brennan won't have much of a chance. Not against her mind tricks and the demon."

Tears shone in his wife's eyes. "We have to help them."

"The barrier Set prepared...." Isis trailed off, shaking her head. "It is strong. He could not have done so from his prison, meaning Raksh must have helped."

Realization dawned on Mark. "The attack on Seamus."

Osiris nodded. "Everything is linked."

"Can you send us back, yes or no?" Mark asked.

"Yes," Isis said, "but only one of you. More than that will attract unwanted attention, no matter where you go. Your energies are full of our scents, which makes you targets for the demons." The goddess looked from one parent to the other. "You need to decide who goes and who stays, and fast. The window of opportunity is closing."

Mark turned to Evie and took both her hands in his. His gaze searched hers, reading her permission. "I'll bring her back safe and sound, I promise."

She nodded. "And Brennan. Swear you won't give up on him, Mark."

He kissed her in response, then turned to the gods. "I'm ready."

&&&

A growl woke Freya up, and she found herself in a pair of warm arms. As she moved, they tightened around her, forcing her to relax back against his hard chest.

"Brennan, something's here."

Only the lightest of snores came from him, and Freya sighed. "You're seriously going to sleep through an attack?"

A ferocious snarl had the effect she was waiting for. Brennan released her, jumping to his feet and putting his body between her and the perceived danger.

You're both lucky I'm no enemy.

Brennan stared for a beat, then rubbed his eyes to push the last remnants of sleep away. "Mark?"

"Dad?" Freya stepped forward, looking around. "Where's mom?"

Back in Scotland, if I was to guess. We had to ask the gods for help, and because of the strength of the barrier, they could only send one of us through. Any more, and we would have attracted attention. He checked their surroundings, adding as an afterthought, *Or so I was told.*

"Great, more godly mind tricks." Brennan scowled in response. "So what was the rough wake-up for?"

You had your paws all over my daughter, Wiseman. You do the math.

A faint blush covered Brennan's cheeks, but he pushed forward a step. "It's not like I was doing anything or had bad intentions."

Really? Because I don't recall you ever talking to me about your intentions concerning my daughter.

"*Dad*!" Freya's hiss had no effect on Mark, whose cold green gaze was steady on Brennan's.

The Wiseman shook his head, lifting his palms up. "I meant nothing by it, Mark. It's cold as hell, we were trying to stick together and keep warm. As for intentions..." He grabbed Freya's hand in his and kissed it. "They are but the best."

Freya glared at her father. "Is that enough for you?"

Mark made a non-committal sound, then said, *We have to go. The castle is nearby, but it's not safe to be out in the open.*

"Castle?" Freya frowned. "Is that where we are?"

Yes, and we can reach it before nightfall and set camp there.

Without further words, he moved. Brennan and Freya followed behind him, hand in hand.

So much for peace of mind, Brennan snorted.

&&&

The castle, if someone could name it such, loomed in the distance. With the sun setting over the horizon, Čachtice loomed like an angry beast. The mountain's silence didn't help the overall feel of stepping unto forbidden ground.

With each step they took closer, the air became sharper – chillier. Mark had explained the Countess' dabbling in evil was the cause, and had urged them to stay warm as much as they could.

Nonetheless, the minute her eyes landed on the ruins, shivers ran up Freya's spine.

"It's like some unspoken signal is telling us to run away, far away, from the evil that lurks in this place." Brennan's whispered words did nothing to quiet her discomfort.

Even Mark, outspoken until then, kept silent.

What did we get ourselves into?

Chapter 14

"This is useless!" Seamus threw the book to the ground, grunting in disgust.

Sam glanced up from the floor where he'd been reading with Anya in whispers. The two shared a look, then he straightened and floated to Seamus. "Should I go by the library again and fetch another book?"

"No," Seamus shook his head. His hands gripped the sides of the armchair, and he pushed himself up. He grimaced at the pain in his stomach, then inhaled sharply. "I want to go there myself. Help me up."

Sam moved under his arm, and Anya went to Seamus' other side. Though he'd been healed of critical injuries, his body still had to recover. Between the two, Seamus could use them as crutches and they made their way down the hall.

When they got to the top of the stairs, Sam hesitated. "Are you sure this is a good idea, professor? If you fall..."

"It will be fine," Seamus hissed through gritted teeth. A faint sheen of sweat coated his forehead, but he nodded. "Go on."

Inch by painful inch, they headed down the stairs. Sam racked his brain, trying to think of something that would take Seamus' mind off the pain he was in. But nothing came to mind.

It was Anya who came to the rescue, in her accented voice. "It is good they do not harm the library."

Seamus glanced down at her in surprise, then nodded. "Yes, we were very lucky. I could rebuild the rest of the castle, but that library took years to compile."

"*A tudás hatalom*," Anya whispered.

Sam tried to catch her eye and ask what she'd said, but Seamus nodded as if he'd understood. "Knowledge *is* power, yes. That is a beautiful saying. Anya, were you a scholar of your living?"

Laughter bubbled up from her, light like a fairy. "*Apa*...My father, he was a merchant. I was with him in Čachtice for a summer festival, when he went missing. And I died."

"Was it Elizabeth?"

Anya nodded, and Seamus squeezed her shoulder in understanding. "I am sorry for your loss, my dear. What you did, finding us, it was very brave. Please accept my gratitude."

She turned her large brown eyes towards him. They were filled with pain and anguish, but still she said, "You are welcome. I hope Freya and Brennan defeat her. Evil like the Countess cannot continue."

"Aye, indeed," Seamus said. Before he could add anything else, they reached the bottom of the stairs – and they were not alone.

A white tiger with black stripes stood waiting for them. When the familiar grey eyes settled on him, Seamus felt his heart stop. "Evie, what happened?"

&&&

Freya tossed and turned on the ground for close to an hour before giving up. Rather than wake Brennan with her constant movement, she shifted away from him and the toasty fire.

Her feet carried her near Mark, whose gaze was glued to the castle in the distance.

Why are you not sleeping?

Freya glanced behind her. "Brennan needs it more than I do." She took a seat on the tree's roots, leaning her back against it. "Anything to report?"

It's quiet out there.... Much too quiet.

The Sage followed his gaze, letting it land on the castle. Or, rather, its ruins. In the moonlight, they shone like large giants against the backdrop. On a hill less than an hour's walk from them, it still seemed too close. Distinguished by its horseshoe tower, it had been in decay for ages.

It's not as scary as it looks.

"I'm not scared," Freya scoffed. "After the Vikings and conquistadors, you really think a Countess makes me shiver?"

Mark threw a look her way. *She should.*

"Well, she doesn't," Freya whispered. She glanced behind at Brennan again, her mind going back to what she'd felt – the intrusion in their bond.

It's not his fault.

Freya's eyes narrowed on her father. "What?"

Elizabeth's influence on him. Brennan did nothing to ask for it, nor can he truly fight it. Thus, he's not to blame.

"I wouldn't have thought you'd defend him, you know."

I'm not. Mark paused, then sighed. *Maybe I am. But only because Seamus has already suffered through it once. And you know how strong-headed he is.*

Freya nodded, then bit her lip. "How is he?"

Fine when I was there – for as little time as I was.

"Yeah, you didn't fill us in on that. What happened? How were we split?"

The demon engineered the plan so we would not end in the same spot as you. It sent your mother and me back to Scotland. And unable to leave.

Freya frowned. "How so?"

Seamus thought Set had prepared a barrier around the castle, something that was activated the minute someone destroyed the castle.

In her exhausted mindset, it took a minute for Freya to realize the implications. "Are you saying the attack from Raksh, that whole thing, was just a smoking gun?"

I'm afraid so.

Freya clenched her fists, reining in her temper. "That bastard!"

Mark shifted closer to her, resting his massive head on her thigh. *There is no point getting angry. Raksh will get his due – sooner, rather than later. And I intend to be the one to deliver it.*

Another pause followed, and both father and daughter found their gazes drawn to Čachtice Castle once more.

I, for one, am glad we get a second chance at eradicating this evil. Elizabeth was always mad, but to think she has slipped into the Cursed One's life. He sighed, and trailed off.

Freya shivered at the cold, and his words. Brennan had told her about the possibility, but hearing it there, in such proximity of the castle, was another experience. She hesitated, then said, "I won't let her get to Brennan." When Mark only responded with silence, she poked him. "Did you hear me?"

I did.

"So why aren't you saying anything?" When his silence alone responded, Freya pushed his head off her thigh and forced him to look at her. "You don't think Brennan will be able to resist, is that it?"

Mark looked away.

"Why not?" Freya pushed, refusing to give up. "Are you so intent on disliking him that you won't give him your vote of confidence?"

Mark jerked his head her way. *It has nothing to do with that. Yes, I think you're too young to be in a relationship as heavy as what you two have. But I understand it. However, I have seen more than you, Freya, and the influence Elizabeth has on Brennan has not waned. No matter how much I want to believe he will fight it, I cannot.*

"Well I *do*! He's not Seamus, he has someone else to care for!"

So did Seamus.

Freya frowned. "What are you talking about? He never married."

That's because Seamus has always loved only one woman – your mother.

"My...*what*?" Freya gaped at her father, even as she tried to grasp the magnitude of what he was telling her. "How are you guys even friends, then?"

Mark laughed under his breath, and it sounded like the low rumble of an earthquake. *You are young, Freya. Some things, time does heal... And Seamus was too good a friend to leave us.*

"But... He's never been happy, then."

What makes you think so? Mark's green eyes glittered. *He got to raise you, while we were not around. And he had something else to live for besides being a Sage. I think he's as happy as he can be, Freya.*

She was silent for a bit, then said, "Be that as it may, I feel it in our bond, stronger than ever. We can unite our powers, dad! What, do you think that I'll let that witch get into his head?" She looked towards the castle. "The so-called Countess has another thing coming her way, if she thinks Brennan is hers for the taking."

Throughout the rant, Mark remained quiet, and his silence alone spoke volumes. With another scoff, Freya stood and walked away.

Where are you going?

"Away from you," she muttered under her breath.

Her steps took her back by Brennan's side. She curled up into him by the fire, breathing in his scent and relishing his strong embrace. *I won't let anything take you away, Bren. I swear it.*

&&&

Seamus blinked at Evie, then blinked some more. Finally, he ran a hand over his face, and said, "So only Mark could follow through?"

Yes. I can only hope he re-joined Freya and Brennan by now...

He sighed, leaning back against his chair and feeling more fatigued than ever. Evie picked up on it and neared him, nuzzling his hand. *What is it, old friend?*

"I fear for them. Elizabeth's influence was strong on me, and I was fully trained. How can Brennan hope to fight it off?"

He has Freya. They have each other. And Seamus, they were able to unite their powers. It might have been a small feat, but it was huge. Evie paused, taking in the library. They were alone, Sam and Anya having left them. *You did good, you know? With Freya.*

Seamus met her eyes then, and his shone with unshed tears.

The way you raised her, taught her... Even how you delivered the news of her legacy. We both want you to know how grateful we are, Seamus. That night, it was the hardest thing we had to do. Giving her away, knowing we would die, yet wanting her to live.

Seamus leaned forward, placing both hands on Evie's head. "I know," he whispered, his voice hoarse. "Believe me, I know."

They stood like that, staring eye to eye, for long moments. Then Evie pulled away, and Seamus cleared his throat. "Now what?" he asked.

Now, we wait. There is nothing else we can do.

&&&

The Countess stepped from the fog again, this time dressed even more provocatively. Brennan kept his eyes steady on her face, unwilling to be drawn into her web.

"What is it you wish of me?"

She smiled, showing perfect pearls of teeth, and luscious lips. "Your soul, my boy. I could do much with one such as you."

"Too bad I'm taken."

Elizabeth smirked. "Is that so?" Step by step, she walked in a circle around him. By the time she touched his shoulder, Brennan couldn't move – let alone breathe on his own.

She leaned over his shoulder and whispered in his ear, "Do you still belong to her? Or are you ready to recognize your new master?"

&&&

Morning came by much too soon. Brennan was shaking her awake, and Freya got back on her feet. Grumbling, she swallowed the meager food he'd found them – some dried up and half-frozen berries – and set to walking.

She ignored Mark's look and instead headed by Brennan's side. As they hiked towards the village nearby, Freya made it a point to stick close to him.

"Did I miss something?"

She looked up at Brennan's question, noticing the curiosity in his eyes. When he glanced from her to Mark pointedly, Freya shrugged. "Nope, nothing."

He wasn't fooled. "Are you guys fighting?"

"Just drop it, Bren."

Something in her tone must have gotten to him because he let it go. But only moments later, he stopped in his tracks. He scanned their surroundings, twisting this way and that, as if trying to sniff out something.

"What are you doing?" Freya frowned.

Mark, too, had stopped and was watching them. Under their bemused gazes, Brennan got off track and walked towards what looked like an abandoned inn.

After a second's hesitation, Freya followed him in. She pushed the creaky, half-destroyed door open, and stepped inside. It took a second for her eyes to adjust, but the glowing forms were recognizable even in the dim morning light.

Freya stared at the gaggle of girls, avoiding the urge to scratch her head in consternation. They were all of various ages between ten and eighteen, some beautiful, some less, but all scrawny and dressed in rags.

Brennan was next to a girl taller than most, and waved her over.

Dad, stay outside, Freya said. *It's best you sit this one out.* She could only imagine their reactions if they saw a white tiger.

Without waiting for an answer from Mark, she headed to the Wiseman. "What is all this?"

"Victims."

Only, the answer didn't come from Brennan, but from the young ghost by his side. Freya turned to the young girl, her expression fierce. It was enough, apparently, to cause her to step back in fright.

Brennan lifted his hand and whispered, "It's okay, she won't hurt you, Elena."

"Elena?" Freya glanced between them.

"Yeah, she's Anya's friend. I felt their scared energies from the outside." His gaze was heavy on Freya as he added mentally, *It was impossible to miss it. I've never felt such terror in my life.* Out loud, he added, "And I came in here asking if anyone knew Anya."

"Anya... she okay?"

Freya's expression softened. "She is, Elena. She's safe in my home." Her gaze then travelled over the scared ghosts. "I don't understand. If you can all leave the castle why not leave here? What does she have over you?"

Ominous silence answered, then small voices said, "Our families."

"Our souls."

Although the words were spoken in Hungarian, Freya had no trouble recognizing them. Anya had said something similar, after all.

&&&

"Ssshe isss here..."

Elizabeth's turned from the bathtub she'd been admiring her reflection in. Though her body could no longer feel virgin's blood on her, she relished watching it nonetheless. The memories it brought were some of her fondest.

And soon, I might enjoy it once more.

She nodded to the human peasant cowering in a corner. The woman dropped the bloody knife and scurried out the door, bandaging her wrists as best she could. These days, the Countess found she could make most mortals do anything she wished. And all it took...was a simple suggestion.

"Who is?" Elizabeth asked the shadows.

"The Sssage..."

A cold laugh escaped her. "If she is here, then so is her friend. I have been dying to meet him in person."

&&&

Freya shared a look with Brennan over the head of one ghost. They'd divided to conquer and tried to speak with as many girls as possible, hoping to get more information on the Countess before they fought her.

It hadn't proved fruitful due to the language barrier, but Freya had gained enough insight to deem herself ready. She was about to head to Brennan when a blood-curling scream escaped from a corner.

Freya spun on her heels, noticing a young girl, no older than ten, with pale blonde hair and blue eyes. Her mouth was opened in a never-ending screech, loud enough Freya had to cover her ears.

The screams of the young girl raised the hair on her skin, but Freya forced herself to appear strong. "What got into her?"

When only silence answered her, Freya looked to Elena. But her large eyes were set on Brennan, filled with wariness and fear. "She said... that he is touched by the Countess."

No... Freya turned to Brennan, willing him to deny it, but his expression spoke volumes.

The help of the girls depended on her next reaction. Once the realization sank in, Freya shook her head and met Elena's gaze. "He is not. Our powers make us immune to it."

Elena appeared unconvinced, so Freya kicked it up a notch. She lifted a hand, creating fire and a mini-tornado within her palm. "See?"

The screams stopped, and the girls gathered closer. "We are immune, I swear it," Freya said.

The lie tasted like ashes on her tongue, especially when pair after pair of vulnerable eyes turned on her.

&&&

"You swore to me it was done," Freya said the minute they were out of the inn. They'd told the girls to stay inside for the time being, while they headed on to the castle.

Brennan jogged up to her side, reaching for her hand. "She showed up in my dreams, Frey!"

She pulled out of his grasp, whirling on him. "Again. She showed up in your dreams, *again*. Isn't that what you mean?"

The Wiseman noticed Mark's eyes on them. "What did you want me to say? That some dead woman wants me to be her lover?"

"For one, yes! But I would have settled for honesty!" Betrayal had taken the glow out of her cheeks, and she shook her head. "I trusted you, Brennan."

He stepped closer to her, grabbing hold of her shoulders even as she tried to fight him off. He met her gaze, forcing all the walls down in his own expression. "Nothing happened, Freya. I was trying to get inside her head, but instead she got into mine. Other than that, nothing, and I mean *nothing,* happened. I swear to you."

Freya searched his eyes, feeling the truth in his words, but unwilling to believe it. Mark's appearance saved her from answering.

We have to leave, now. Trouble is coming.

Chapter 15

Freya scowled at her father. "We're not going anywhere, except there." She pointed to the castle, less than five minutes' walk.

Freya, that's a bad idea.

She didn't listen, fuelled by the need to show the Countess that she couldn't mess with her. The Sage marched ahead, and Brennan had no choice but to follow. Mark closed up the ranks.

They walked in silence until Freya stopped. In the shadows of the beat-up houses, she'd sensed something. *An evil...* She looked around, past Brennan and her father, to no avail.

We should leave, Mark repeated. *Here, in the open, we're easy targets.*

"No," Freya said. "We're going to the castle and I'm going to show that witch she shouldn't be messing with us."

"And how shall you do that, dear?"

The voice was sweet, overtly ill. Freya's eyes flew to Brennan, noticing his shocked expression. She thought she heard Mark's groan in her head, but dismissed it and turned around.

A few feet away, at the end of the road, stood a woman. She had on a dress the color of blood, which enhanced her ruby-red lips. Her blue eyes shone even in the distance, enhanced by the darkness of her hair. The glowing aura around her almost made her look angelic – were it not for the murdering intent in her expression.

Freya made a move towards her, but Brennan grabbed hold of her arm. "Freya, hang on a second. I smell a trap."

He is right. Listen to us!

Her blazing grey eyes rose to Brennan's, and she pursed her lips. "I'm taking her down. You two can either fall in line, or get out of my way."

Freya wrenched her arm from Brennan's grip and stepped forward. The Countess didn't move, waiting for her to get closer. She merely lifted her chin, a haughty expression on her face.

The Sage stopped a few feet away and sneered at the woman. "Are you so bored with your immortal life you have to seduce young men?"

Elizabeth laughed – a rich, throaty laugh. Her eyes shifted to Brennan, whom Freya could feel behind her. "I did not hear any complaints."

Freya's jaw clenched, and her vital energy rose to the surface. It was one thing to hear it from Brennan's lips, but the Countess' arrogant demeanor rubbed her the wrong way. She pulled onto air, then jerked her hand towards Elizabeth – the ghost didn't move.

"What the..." Brennan's shocked whisper behind her unsettled her more than the Countess' apparent immunity.

We fought demons, Bren. We can take this witch on.

He didn't answer, but she sensed his resolution at her back. Freya couldn't see Mark, but she refused to get distracted. Instead, she trusted in the promise he'd made her earlier – that he'd protect her, no matter the cost.

She angled her body, preparing another onslaught. *On my count.*

Before she could launch it, something flew in the air behind the Countess – a white mass of something. *Dad, no!*

Elizabeth turned around in slow-motion and smiled. It was cold, devoid of any emotion. Then she flicked her fingers and chains of fire materialized in her hands.

No!

&&&

Evie was pacing in the library, unable to sit still, when she dropped to the ground. Tremors shook her body, and roars of pain escaped her – strong enough to shake the walls.

Seamus snapped to from his sleep. He tried to head to her, but fell on his knees. Cursing his weakness, he crawled to the tiger, trying to see what was wrong. Without his powers, he was clueless.

Sam and Anya floated in, their young faces mirrors of shock. "What happened to her?"

"I don't have the slightest clue!" Seamus ran another hand down her fur, but Evie trashed around too much. Then, she went limp.

&&&

In the palace of the gods, Isis jumped up from bed. In a frenzy, she ran to the fireplace, falling to her knees. Her hair was a curtain around her face. She leveled a determined gaze into the flames, willing them to show her what had upset the balance.

Osiris' footsteps followed, and he joined her. "What is it, beloved?"

"The tigers. Something's hurting them, but I cannot see."

The god looked to the fire, noticing the smoke in the flames. It refused to listen to his wife, which was unheard of. With no care for his health, he dug his hand in the flames.

Its warmth tried to burn him, but he clenched his teeth against the bite. "Show us what we need," he ordered. He clenched his fist in the fire, picturing grabbing it. "*Show us.*"

The image cleared, and Isis inhaled sharply. "The Countess! She has the demon's chains of fire."

Shocked gazes clashed, and Osiris removed his burnt hand. Isis bent over it and healed it with some incantations, but her gaze kept shifting to the flames.

"We have to intervene, Osiris. If we let it go on that woman will do to them what the demon did to Seamus. We cannot allow it!"

Osiris hesitated, then nodded. "Very well, beloved."

Isis kissed his cheek, then got back to her feet and ran out of the room. She crossed the ballroom, the balcony, and straight to a small alcove. It contained various oils, but she was only interested in one.

&&&

"*NO!*" Freya's scream had no effect, as she saw her father writhing on the ground.

The Countess chuckled under her breath, then removed the chains – only to whip him again. Their fiery restraints wrapped around him, and he shook against their merciless hold.

Freya blasted another round at the Countess, to no effect. Brennan's strike made no impact either, and they couldn't get close enough to engage in a physical fight.

Then the air shifted, and the smell of roses appeared. Freya looked around, trying to see where it was coming from. Elizabeth did the same, narrowing her eyes.

Then a blast came – from the tiger's fur. It sent the Countess flying backwards, and the chains a ways away. Freya jumped on the chance and ran to her.

Get my dad!

Brennan nodded and headed to Mark. His breath was laborious, but he could lift his head. *Don't let those chains get on Freya. Whatever you do, Brennan. Protect her.*

He crawled away, knowing he was too weak to still be in the fight. Charcoal-like burns marred his fur, but his flesh remained intact. Brennan guessed the issue was more with his internal energy.

You would guess right, Mark said, and disappeared around the corner of a house.

Brennan turned to Freya then. She was fighting Elizabeth, dealing blow after blow. As a noblewoman, the Countess couldn't fight – but powerless, she was not. With each blow Freya dealt her, she stumbled backwards – and closer to the chains of fire.

Freya, watch out!

She didn't react, and he ran towards her. Mark's warning rang in his ears, as did Freya's words earlier. *I'm not letting this witch hurt her.*

&&&

Osiris raised his head from the match of senet he'd been playing with himself. "Well?"

"It is done," Isis nodded, wringing her hands. "I intervened as best I could, but she still caught my presence. Mark is safe, as is Evelyn. But they have a bigger problem on their hands."

"Elizabeth..." Osiris frowned. "Was Mark correct, then? Has she transitioned to a full wraith, a Cursed One?"

Isis nodded. "As good as. With the chains and that stupid medallion, she can enthrall most men." She shook her head. "That woman wields the fire's weapon as if she was born to it."

Osiris rubbed his forehead, sensing tension building up. "But she knows nothing about the relics."

"No... And let us hope she does not find out. With Brennan in her clutches, anything is possible."

"Then we should pray Freya knows how to save him."

Isis stared at her husband, narrowing her eyes. "Will we not help, other than what I just did?"

Osiris' gaze met hers, and she read the conflict he tried to hide. "We cannot enter Earth, beloved. If we do, the balance we have worked so hard to maintain shall shatter. And we cannot risk that." He moved another piece on the senet board. "Not even for those gifted younglings."

&&&

In Scotland, Evie inhaled and stood. Seamus was by her side, his worried expression clearing when he saw her move. "How do you feel?"

She groaned. *As if I got run over by a train.* A quick glance around revealed they were alone, without the ghosts. *Where are Sam and Anya?*

"Away," Seamus said. "Anya, when she saw you, thought it was the demon's weapon that did this to you. And I believe she was right. I sent them off to try dematerializing at different spots of the island, in the hopes they can find a break."

Evie nodded. *Good plan. And yes, that would explain it. But in order for me to feel it such, it must have been Mark who got attacked.*

"I only hope he is safe."

That they all are, Evie corrected. She looked around the library. *If Sam or Anya escape, we could send word to Freya on how to defeat Elizabeth.*

"And Brennan."

Evie shook her head. *For a moment, while I was unconscious, I saw through Mark's eyes. Brennan was standing next to Elizabeth, Seamus. She has him.*

Rather than despair, Seamus focused on survival. "Then it is even more imperative we find out how to destroy that necklace of hers."

I agree. Last time, neutralizing it worked, but there were more of us. Elizabeth needs to be put to bed, for good this time.

&&&

Freya only knew of the rage inside her. The woman in front of her had hurt Seamus, long ago, turned him against his friends. And she'd been trying to do the same to Brennan. *Not on my bloody watch.*

She clenched her fist and struck Elizabeth under the jaw again, sending her flying backwards. This time, she fell on the ground. But still she smiled, like she knew some secret Freya didn't.

"The gods may help you and that tiger of yours, but I am in no need of such pitiful aid."

Freya snorted. "I don't know what you're talking about. But how about we end this, once and for all?" She lifted her hand, searching for the energy she needed to blast Elizabeth to the great beyond.

Then Brennan tackled her out of the way, and they landed in the distance. Elizabeth laughed, and for a fearful second Freya thought she'd somehow controlled him. But no, the Wiseman was facing off against the Countess, breathing hard and holding back from hitting her.

He'd been pushing her out of the way to protect her, and take on the Countess himself. But there was one problem.

I know you have some code about hitting women, Freya shot. *But I swear it doesn't apply here.*

There was no response from Brennan. Then his body arched, and Freya noticed why when she got to her feet. Elizabeth had gotten hold of her chains of fire, and she was holding Brennan's wrists in them.

He struggled against their grip, and she sensed the energy trying to fry them both. Before she could move, Elizabeth did. She yanked on his wrists, pulling Brennan closer – and kissed him.

Freya saw red. She aimed another hit of air towards them, enough to blast Brennan backwards and away from her. Then she stalked to the Countess.

Elizabeth only stood and waited. She was the picture of calm personified, only a slight sneer curling her lips. The

Sage resolved to ignore it, instead pulling energy into her hands.

Freya, we need to go!

She caught movement out of the corner of her eyes, and sensed Mark was out of his hiding spot. Freya turned to tell him to leave, and instead gaped in shock at the spectacle before her.

The ghosts they'd met earlier were exiting the inn, one by one. The girls walked as zombies would, enthralled and brainwashed. Not one looked her way.

"What the hell?" Freya muttered.

Freya turned to her partner, expecting him to have her back. But rather than his warm eyes, she met the cold, calculating gaze of a monster. His palm shone with held up power, and she took a step back.

"Brennan..." It was him, but nothing about the young man in front of her was familiar. He was looked straight at Elizabeth, as if expecting an order.

The Countess stepped out of the shadows then, laughing. "He is mine now, my dear. All. *Mine.*"

"No!"

Freya moved to go to Brennan, but Mark stepped in her way, limping with his front paw. *Not now.*

"Let me go to him!"

I will not let you risk your life when there is a much better way. Come with me. Now.

When Freya still struggled against him, Mark growled. *You are my daughter, and as your father, I demand your obedience.*

A whimper of despair passed her lips, even as she let Mark push her backwards. She tried to catch Brennan's eye with every backward step, but his expression never changed. The last image she had was of the Countess stepping towards him, smiling.

&&&

Freya let Mark drag her away for a bit, feeling numb. Her heart was shattered, and a gaping emptiness filled her chest. Where before she'd had love, now she felt...nothing. She'd lost Brennan, all in the blink of an eye. The bond between them weakened, disappearing by the second –

She froze in her tracks. *It's weak, but still there! I still have a chance!*

Ignoring Mark's shouts behind her, Freya took off running back towards the Countess and Brennan. She could see their shapes in the distance, and the ghosts nearby. With all the force she could muster, Freya launched herself in the air – and tackled Brennan to the ground.

They rolled over once, twice, and she ended on top of him. Uncaring of their audience, she bent her head and kissed him. Hands by his face, she tried to push her mind against his, to touch him as he'd once touched her to break Set's hold on her mind.

But Brennan lay unresponsive beneath her – a statue. And then hands pulled her away, restraining her. It was two of the ghosts, under a similar enchantment.

Elizabeth stepped closer. "Did you really think you could break my spell?" Her voice was soft, but the way she played with the ruby necklace at her neck wasn't innocent.

The hairs rose at the back of Freya's neck. "You're pure evil. And I fight against evil. So, yeah." She grinned, but it was full of bravado she no longer had.

Freya fought against the urge to look at Brennan. Like a robot, he stood from the ground and dusted himself off, then straightened into an immobile stance. *I can't let her see how much this hurts, she'll only use it against me.*

Despite all the right reasons not to do it, she looked. Brennan's eyes gazed in the distance, his expression blank and unfocused. He was breathing, his chest rising in smooth rhythms, but he might as well have been a statue.

"Ah, so you *do* care." Elizabeth laughed, yet there was nothing funny about it.

"What did you do to him?" Freya blinked back her tears and tore her gaze from her boyfriend, focusing on the Countess. "What the *hell* did you do to him?"

"Enchanted him, of course." Elizabeth stepped closer to Brennan, forcing Freya to witness her actions. She struggled against her bonds, but the girls' hands on her were iron shackles.

"And such a lovely pet, he is. So kind to help me round up my rebellious girls." Elizabeth ran a hand down Brennan's cheek, petting him as she would an animal. "Indeed, he comes in handy."

Freya tried to keep her expression blank, but it was hard. She'd just realized why the ghosts were so amenable. Brennan was controlling them... like she'd once controlled the elements. She gulped, trying to swallow the lump in her throat.

His words rang clear in her head, from one of many sleepless nights in Seamus' library. *If I ever lose control, Tyr told me I'd be influencing everyone around me – emotionally. I could make them do anything.*

With a wicked look, Elizabeth kissed Brennan. Her lips moved against his, but to Freya's relief, he didn't react. Hands by his side, he was as immobile as a lifeless doll. *Maybe all's not lost.*

As if guessing her thoughts, the Countess turned back to her. "He will if I make him. Would you like to see that?"

Freya bit her lip to avoid screaming. A tantrum was no way to get out of the situation. But before she could figure out a proper exit strategy, Elizabeth waved to the girls.

"Remove her from my sight. I shall contact the demon, then dispose of them." Her glance lingered on Brennan. "Or perhaps he might let me keep you, darling."

Freya's scream was lost all the way to the castle, and then in the catacombs. The girls threw her in a cell below. She crawled away from the skeletons and rats, curling up in the darkest corner.

Far from light, hidden from view, Freya brought her knees up to her chest and dropped her head on them. And there, she let her sorrow out – screaming until she was hoarse, yet knowing no one could hear her.

Chapter 16

Seamus stifled a yawn and rubbed the back of his neck. Evie stretched from her spot near him, sighing. *We have been at this for hours. Perhaps a rest is in order.*

"No. If Sam and Anya come back with good news, we have to be ready." He rubbed his chin. "I worry for Mark, and the youngsters."

A soft puff of air from Evie had him glance up from the book in his lap. He realized she was chuckling. "What's funny?"

Nothing, I... Evie nuzzled his hand. *Thank you, Seamus, truly. This is my second time showing you gratitude, but it feels too little compared to all you have done. You have our eternal thanks for the care you took of Freya, for being there for her when we couldn't. Who knows what would have happened otherwise.*

His grey eyes crinkled at the corners when he smiled. "I only wish I could have spared her the hurt. She was so angry when I wouldn't tell her about you two..."

It was hard for her to grasp everything, and your reasons. Now that she does, she wants vengeance, despite us being here. Evie sighed. *Teenagers are a handful, are they not?*

Seamus laughed. It started as a chuckle, then morphed into a full-blown guffaw. By the time he'd settled, tears had run down his cheeks. He looked at Evie, falling prey to her lighter grey eyes, and the wisdom within.

"I missed you," he said. She answered with another nuzzling of his hand, and he rubbed behind her ears. Her purrs filled the air, then she stilled.

"What is it?" Seamus asked, worried something else had happened. But Evie wasn't staring into oblivion, rather at one of the books he'd discarded earlier.

Pull that up, Seamus.

He reached over and was about to flip the page when Evie nudged him. *No, there.*

Seamus listened to her and looked closer. He noticed a picture of a necklace. "That's Elizabeth's!"

Yes and read what is says under.

His gaze fell to the familiar writing. "Dragon runes..."

You know what that means!

Seamus nodded absently, already reading the rest of the text. When he'd finished, he looked up. For the first time since the attack on the castle, hope shone in his eyes. "Freya has to read these runes and absorb the power within. Their hidden force will complete the abilities she currently has. And when she uses them, her spiritual energy will destroy the necklace."

And free Brennan.

They shared an excited look, interrupted when Sam and Anya passed through the wall. Seamus noticed their eager energy. "Anything?"

Sam's grim face transformed with a smile. "Heck yes!"

"Language," Seamus muttered, but he didn't have it in him.

Sam knew it and ignored his comment. "We tried dematerializing at different spots on the island, but nowhere worked. After a few attempts, we tried it over shorter distances."

At their confused expressions, he explained, "Originally, we wanted to go straight to Freya. And that wasn't working. But when we tried to go the next town over, it worked!" The young ghost was bouncing up for joy, and even Anya smiled.

"This is great news," Seamus said to Evie. "It may take them longer, but they could get to Freya."

Evie nodded. *Tell him what we found.*

Once Seamus explained it to the ghost, he showed him the book page. "You cannot take this with you. As soon as you're away from me, you won't be able to hold on to it. So I need you both to memorize these runes."

Sam and Anya stared at the page. The younger girl said, "How does it work?"

"Since Freya does not have the book with her, she will have to rewrite them somewhere, and read them out loud. Preferably under a full moon, and near a place of power." He paused. "Is there such a place nearby Čachtice Castle?"

Anya frowned. "Like a church?"

Seamus shook his head. "Not quite. It has to be stronger than that. Somewhere used as a passage between the living and the dead realms."

While Anya thought, Seamus turned to Sam. "Freya's survival depends on these runes, Sam."

"I know," he nodded. "And I'll make sure she gets them."

A heavy silence fell on them, interrupted by Anya. "There is a pool under the castle. In the ancient times, priests used it as their ceremony ground. It is considered hallowed ground... or was, until the Countess."

Seamus nodded. "That would work. Make sure Freya gets there and speaks these runes."

Sam and Anya shared a look, then held hands. "See you soon, professor."

The instant after, they vanished. Seamus limped back to the couch, plopping down and sighing. "It is out of our hands, now."

They will not disappoint.

&&&

Freya woke up shivering. The damp cell they had thrown her in did nothing to warm her up, neither did her thin pullover and jeans. She rubbed her hands, blowing on them to instill heat.

A quick glance around showed a skeleton covered in rags. Grimacing at what she had to do, she crawled over and ripped some cloth. She returned to her corner and reached out to fire. The element soon ignited the cloth, and a small blaze warmed her up.

Within moments, Freya shivered less, and felt more awake. "I won't let this break me," she whispered to the flames. "There has to be a way to get through to Brennan."

"There is not," a voice whispered back.

Freya jumped and looked around. In a faraway corner, she noticed a girl. Like Anya, she wore rags, and seemed malnourished. Something about her struck Freya as familiar. "I've seen you before... What's your name?"

A hesitation followed. "Elena. You... You were at the inn. Do you really know Anya?"

"Yes!" Freya tried to hold down her excitement to avoid scaring the girl. She moved closer to the corner. "Anya came to get us, me and Brennan. She begged us to help you and the other girls out."

"But he got captured."

Freya opened her mouth to agree, then frowned as something odd struck her. "Hang on... How come you're not under his control, too?"

Elena hesitated, then moved closer to the bars of the prison cell. "I left the inn before he came, with some girls. We'd planned to disappear a long time ago. When we saw what happened, we stayed in hiding. I came here to see what happened."

Freya looked around, not noticing the ghosts she spoke of. "Where are they?"

"Safe," Elena responded curtly and folded her arms over her chest. "And why do you need to know, anyway? Your *partner* got captured."

Freya had to clear her throat past the emotion. "Yes, but I know I can get through to him."

Elena's expression filled with suspicion. "How?"

"We have a bond, me and him."

A sneer formed on her face, so at odds with her otherwise gentle expression. "Elizabeth ruins everything. Everyone. She took my father from me, my brother..." She looked away, unwilling to continue.

"And your love?" Freya whispered.

Elena nodded, tears streaming down her cheeks. "She is evil incarnate."

"I swear to you, I can destroy her. We've fought an army of Vikings and conquistadors. I'm not scared of Elizabeth."

"But the chains..."

Freya's expression grew even more determined. "Help me get out of this blasted cell, and I'll take care of her. *I swear it.*"

"What about your partner? He works with the Countess now. His witchcraft could hurt my friends."

Freya hesitated, then figured she might as well tell the girl everything she knew. "You know the necklace around Elizabeth's throat?" When she nodded, the Sage said, "If I destroy it, Brennan is free. Elizabeth loses her power." She paused, gauging the situation. "Please, Elena. Help me."

Elena stared at her for a long moment before finally nodding. She moved to the lock and used an old-fashioned key to let Freya out. The minute the door was open, the Sage extinguished the fire and stepped out.

She had no idea how to get rid of Elizabeth while Brennan was helping her, but she knew her starting point. "I need to see –"

A screech outside drew her attention. Elena cowered against the wall, but Freya thought she saw a flash of white and black fur. In the tiny window of the cell, a pair of green eyes glowed in the darkness.

Freya?

"Dad!" She looked to Elena and smiled. "It's okay, it's only my father."

The young ghost looked from the Sage to the tiger as if she'd lost her mind. Freya rolled her eyes, realizing how incongruous the statement sounded. "Long story, but I promise he's good news."

She stepped back in the cell, hoisting herself up on her tiptoes. Relief filled her tone when she asked, "What are you doing here?"

Rescuing you.

Freya bit her lip, holding back the emotions threatening to overwhelm. He hadn't lied – Mark had come back for her. The green gaze, glued to hers, softened and he whispered in her mind, *I told you I'd have your back.*

The Sage held back a snort and pointed at the opened cell door behind her, all the while trying to pretend she wasn't moved. "I'm doing fine with that part. But say, you wouldn't know how to free Brennan?"

Mark shook his head, but there was an odd glint of amusement in his eyes. *Not me, but I brought someone who does.*

He moved backwards, and a head of blonde hair and blue eyes replaced him. Freya gaped in shock at the newcomer.

"Sam!"

"Frey-Frey," he grinned, "good to see you. Staying out of trouble, eh?"

Freya laughed at that and reached through the bars until she could touch his hand. "What are you doing here? It's too dangerous with that witch around."

"We have something that can help, but I have to tell you face to face."

Freya glanced over her shoulder to Elena, who was nervously floating about and wringing her hands. "Is there a way to the outside that would keep us out of Elizabeth's sight?"

Elena nodded and pointed further in the catacombs. Freya looked back to her friends. "Can you follow my scent?"

Mark snorted. *I'm not a dog, Freya. But I can follow your aura, that's how I found you in the first place.*

"That'll do. Keep walking on the side of the castle. I should be out in a few minutes."

She let go of Sam's hand and took off on a jog, following the floating ghosts. Within minutes, they led her to another gate – this one in wood. Freya scowled at the obstruction and lifted her hand.

"Wait!" Elena moved closer with the same key and opened it.

Freya had to laugh. "Sorry. I'm used to barging my way in."

Elena only rolled her eyes, continuing down the path. Soon, Freya could smell fresh air, and she ended up outside. *Dad?*

The mental call was unneeded, she soon found out. Mark and Sam rounded the corner, and she pulled the younger boy into her arms, squeezing him. To her left, she saw Anya hug Elena, equally relieved.

She pulled back. "What did you need to tell me?"

Sam glanced around to make sure they were alone. "Seamus and your mom found a way to destroy the necklace. As soon as it's gone, Brennan should be freed."

"Are you sure?" Freya gripped his shoulders. *I can save Brennan!* Hope blossomed in her chest.

As sure as he can be, Mark said. *But there's a problem – the solution lies with dragon runes.*

Freya frowned. "Dad says it's dragon runes?"

"Yeah," Sam nodded, biting his lip. He, too, remembered what had happened last time she'd let dragon runes influence her mind. "Seamus had me and Anya memorize them. He said you have to rewrite them in a place of power, speak them aloud under a full moon, and the power will come to you."

Freya bit on her bottom lip and glanced upwards. The moon was past its apex, but no matter how far she extended her senses, she couldn't catch the vibe of a place of power.

She scowled at their surroundings. "This castle obscures everything with its black aura. Where can I do this?"

Anya stepped away from Elena. "There is a basin, under the castle. It could work."

Elena's eyes widened. "You mean the hallowed place?"

A quick exchange in Hungarian followed, after which Elena put some distance between them. "I am afraid to go."

"It's okay," Freya held her palms up. "You've helped me much already. Can you do something else?"

Elena hesitated. Her eyes darted around, and she hugged her middle. "What?"

"I need you to gather the rest of the girls, somewhere out of sight of the Countess. If I can talk to her, I could rally them to my cause."

Anya bit her lip. "They are terrified."

"I know, but I can offer them a chance to get their lives back – what's left, at least. Or I could offer them eternal peace. Please, Elena."

When she still appeared fearful, Anya floated closer. "She has imprisoned us, destroyed our families. I will not stand by and watch her kill more innocents. Help us."

Tears filled Elena's eyes, but she nodded. "You are right. The Countess deserves eternal death."

"And she will get it." Freya smiled at her, then turned to Anya. "Can you lead me to the underground pool?" Once she'd agreed, Freya pulled Sam in her arms again. "Watch over Elena, and keep an eye on the area."

"You got it, Frey-Frey." He smiled and disappeared back into the catacombs with Elena.

Mark stepped forward, his gaze intent on Anya. *Lead the way.*

Freya followed them back inside the castle, but this time they headed opposite Sam and Elena. She hesitated on the threshold, glancing outside once more. *I hope I'll get to breathe fresh air again.*

With one last deep inhale, Freya ducked inside.

Chapter 17

In their palace, Osiris waved his wife over. "Look, beloved."

She rushed to his side, peering over his shoulder into in the fire. At first, she had to blink – unsure of what she was seeing. There was Freya, in some kind of cavern lighted by torches.

Mark followed her, the light reflecting off his fur. They were both being led by a ghost to the middle, near a pool.

"Where are they?"

Osiris chuckled under his breath. "Underneath Čachtice Castle, my sweet. Is it not funny how everything comes full circle?"

Isis' wide eyes met his calmer gaze. "She's where Draykho entered the world through!"

"Mm, yes," Osiris smiled. "Which means she is about to receive more than she bargained for."

&&&

Freya trailed behind Anya, already sensing this was a place unlike any she'd been in before. *And I thought Dinas Emrys was something...*

189

All thoughts were wiped from her mind when she noticed the center of the cavern – and the pool in its midst. Clearer than the bluest sky, it shimmered of rainbow colors, reflecting the walls. At first, Freya didn't realize why, then it clued in.

Large chunks of amber and precious stones were embedded in the natural cavities, and they glittered. Her gaze was drawn to another aspect of the hallowed place that couldn't be ignored – a brass door, past the pool. Atop it were dragon runes, engraved in the material.

Just like the book Brennan showed me!

Freya recalled what they'd read, and took another look at her surroundings, this time with a clearer head. It wasn't just about saving Brennan. The entire quest had to do with saving innocent lives, like she'd always done.

Without hesitation, she knelt next to the pool of water and dipped her hands in it, then her face. Rather than the frigid liquid she'd been expecting, its warmth surprised her.

The crystalline water and torches on the side gave an odd hue to the place. Deep in her bones, Freya knew she wasn't in any cavern.

"Will this work?" Anya asked.

Freya glanced at the younger girl and smiled. "I believe so, yes." Recalling how unpredictable her powers could be, she added, "You should probably move back, just to be safe."

Her gaze fell on Mark. He was sniffing the pool and inspecting the area as if he sensed something she didn't. His silence put her at odds. "What is it?"

Nothing. Mark met her gaze and dropped his head. *I'll be off to the side.* He passed her and touched her shoulder with his muzzle. *You've got this, Freya. Be strong.*

After they cleared a wide radius around her, Freya set her hand to the ground and drew in it the runes Sam and Anya had shown her earlier. With each swirl of her finger in the dust, Freya became increasingly aware of the surrounding water, the air she was breathing, the earth she was touching, the fire blazing on the walls.

When she'd completed the last of the runes, she waited. Nothing happened, and she was about to turn to Anya and ask if she'd messed up – then everything happened at once.

Fire blazed from the torches and licked the wall, water splashed everywhere like they were amid a tsunami. Air blew fiercer like a tornado, twisting her hair around, and earth rumbled under her knees.

Freya dropped both hands to the ground, trying to calm her fast-beating heart. *Something's happening.* She knew it, but couldn't name it. Her being was tuned in to each element, each breath around her, each being nearby...

She was no longer Freya – a daughter, a pupil, a girl-friend. The Sage calling in her veins rose to the surface, responding to something beyond her understanding, and way past her imagination.

The elements all seemed to rush inside her, and it left Freya coughing, bent over. Her body trembled, but a hum of power rushed within her veins, enhanced.

Freya!

She lifted her head up from the ground, noticing Anya's worried expression, and her father near her. The Sage reached out to him, tugging on one ear.

"I'm okay," she said. Inch by inch, she stood, and took one wobbly step forward, then a stronger one, followed by another. Freya noticed her palms' reddish hue. "I'm better than okay," she whispered.

I should have known nothing could faze you.

Freya's narrowed on her father. "What?"

He jerked his head towards the pool. *You remember how Sages got their powers?*

She rolled her eyes. "Seamus only made me tell the story a million times. Through a dragon."

And remember what you and Brennan discovered?

Freya's mouth opened to speak, then she closed it. "I... The dragon from the Underworld, but..." She glanced at the pool, recalling the energy she'd felt. "Are you saying this is where he came from?"

More like this is where he came through. Everything in here is imbued with his power, which is why the elements responded such.

Freya clenched her hand in a fist. "I shouldn't have a hard time defeating the Countess, then." She turned to Anya, who'd been watching in silent shock. "When we find Sam and Elena, I need you to take them away, before things get out of control. I'll handle it from here."

Anya looked like she wanted to argue, but ended up nodding. "I promise."

Freya was already jogging towards the stairs. "Elizabeth must've sensed what happened."

Probably, which means we don't have much time until she starts her contingency plan.

Damn.

&&&

Freya's eyes surveyed the group of girls facing her, Elena at their head. It hadn't been hard to find them – they'll all come to her former cell. Her path had crossed theirs on the way to finding the Countess.

"I understand you're scared, and I'm not asking you to fight with me." She softened her tone. "The Countess has made each of you suffer through life and death, and she has kept you imprisoned by her side in this cursed immortal life you lead. Believe it or not, I can help."

Murmurs of disbelief rose among them, but Freya lifted her hand, summoning fire to her palm. She let the flame dance on her skin, showing them it wasn't hurting her. "You've seen what my partner can do. It's because of him Elizabeth got you all back here, against your will."

"He is evil," one girl spoke, and others nodded their agreement.

Freya turned to her father for help, and his green eyes were steady on her. *You can do this.*

"Brennan isn't evil," she affirmed to the ghosts. "Elizabeth tricked him as she tricked you, and many of your male friends. We've all lost something, but I'll be damned if I lose Brennan to her hands."

Freya took a deep breath, drawing strength from Sam and Mark's presences by her side. "I don't ask you to fight. There is but one thing I need your help with – the chains of power. Around me, you have a physical form. All I need is one of you to steal those chains and give them to me."

Only silence answered her, and Freya sighed.

Let me do it, Mark said. *These girls shouldn't be risking their souls.*

Freya glanced at him out of the corner of her eyes. *I've lost you once, no way I intend to do that again. And the chains have already left marks on you. With the ghosts, they won't.*

How can you be so sure?

Because I'll protect them, Freya said. To the young girls, she added, "This is not a woman you want to owe your soul to. If you help me steal her chains of power, I swear to dispose of her, and free you all."

The girls looked between themselves, then one nodded. And another.

But it was Elena who spoke. "We stand with you."

&&&

Freya stepped into the ballroom where Elizabeth was waltzing in Brennan's arms. He was stiff, blank expression, moving in a robotic way. The Countess, meanwhile, was laughing and twirling to her heart's content.

She came to a full stop and snapped her fingers. "Away." Brennan didn't bat an eyelash and moved to the opposite side of the dance floor.

Elizabeth turned to Freya and Mark by her side. Her lips curved in an evil smile, and she chuckled. "Have you come to fetch your boy?" The smile became a sneer. "You are more stupid than I thought."

Easy, Mark warned, sensing her gathering energy.

Freya unclenched her hand and met the Countess' gaze. "Let Brennan go."

"Or what?"

Rather than answer, Freya pulled on air with her lifted palm. She threw a burst towards the Countess, then ran towards her at the same time. She jumped in the air, foot extended, and enjoyed the collision with the woman's face.

Elizabeth dropped like a doll, and her nails scraped the floor. Mark moved closer, growling, and Freya took advantage of the distraction to go to Brennan.

He didn't meet her gaze, not even when she shook him. "Bren, please! Snap out of this!" She touched his cheek, tried to reach him behind the wall – but someone yanked her by the hair.

A quick look around showed her Mark in the distance, shaking his head and trying to get up. He must've gotten hit by... A flash of fire confirmed the chains were out, and Elizabeth meant business.

Her grip on Freya's ponytail was strong, and she dragged the Sage back – then hurled her to the ground. In the second following, the chains whipped the air, heading to Freya. She rolled away in time, avoiding their bite.

In a crouch, Freya spared another glance to Mark. *Are you okay?*

Peachy, her father said. *I didn't see the chains coming.*

Just as well. Freya's gaze landed on Brennan again, immobile in the distance. The moment of inattention nearly cost her life – Mark pushed her out of the way in time. The chains wrapped around his paw, and he was dragged into the wall.

Stay focused! He whined, trying to stand and failing. *That necklace is our priority!*

Freya shook her head to clear it and faced the Countess once more.

Her face was a mask of anger, and the Sage relished the emotion. She yanked on it, hoping to make her unravel. Aided by air, she jumped and kicked the Countess in the stomach. Though she tried to counter with the chains, Freya jumped and avoided their bite.

They engaged in a dance of hit and duck – Freya would strike, then evade before the chains could make contact. With each passing second, Elizabeth's breath grew more ragged.

When Freya tried to catch her, the chains slithered around her wrist. She fell to the ground, screaming in pain at the agony spreading through her. Energy left her in spares, and the ballroom spun around her.

"You are predictable," Elizabeth sneered. "The demon warned me. Which is why he gave me these."

Freya glared at her and focused on the chains. Her new-found powers rose to the surface, and her aura pulsed strong – strong enough to snap the chain holding her captive. Elizabeth's stunned expression was a gift in itself.

"Did he also warn you about that?" Freya's next strike had the Countess drop to the ground – and the chains flew out of her grip.

Her surprise didn't last long. "Take her!" Elizabeth yelled. Glowing shapes burst from the shadows, heading for Freya.

Elena's group countered them, stepping from behind Freya. The girls were not under Brennan's influence, and were able fight or duck the ones moving like zombies.

Freya noticed Elena pick up the chains off the ground, then disappear in the crowd. The Sage hit the Countess in an effort to distract her, before she could come to the same realization.

Ghosts swarmed on them, but Freya wasn't about to retreat. She rolled on the ground with the Countess – pulling hair, delivering slaps, anything to incapacitate her. Then a pair of strong arms lifted her off.

She tried to fight the ghost – but it wasn't one. Brennan's arms were holding her in an iron grip, his gaze unblinking and not recognizing her.

"Bren, no!" Freya's whisper fell on deaf ears, as he turned her around and held her to his chest. She took a moment to realize what he was doing. And once she did, despair threatened to overwhelm.

He's offering me up for killing.

Elizabeth stood from the ground, wiping at her mouth. She met Brennan's eyes over Freya's head and whispered, "Good boy. Now hold her." Her arctic gaze landed on the Sage. "Until I hear her scream."

She turned around, looking for the chains of fire. Elena was at the other end of the ballroom, near Mark. *Smart kid.*

"Give them back to me!" Elizabeth shouted.

Elena started, but didn't budge. Her gaze darted in fear to Freya, looking for an escape.

The distraction was all Freya needed. She slapped her palms against Brennan's thighs, clenching her nails through his jeans, gripping him. With all the will she could muster, she closed her eyes and cast her consciousness towards his.

Come to me, Brennan! Come back. Please.

The plea echoed in her mind, and his arms around her trembled. Then a loud screech caused Freya to lose her concentration. Her eyes opened, looking for the source.

In the middle of the ballroom, Elizabeth stood with her fists clenched. Her hair obscured her face, and when she lifted it, something filled her pale ghostly skin with veins. "You. Are. A. Pest. And I have had *enough*!"

Her second scream was louder than the first, and caused both sides of girls to fall back in consternation. *This is my chance!*

Freya moved one palm off Brennan and cast it towards the Countess. The force of the blast, filled with her spiritual energy, headed towards the specter with the intent of an arrow. Her necklace shattered in a thousand pieces, its ruby pieces littering the ground.

Elizabeth stopped screaming and stared down in shock. Her gaze lifted, blazing with fury, onto Freya. She thrust her palms and a flurry of insects flew from them. Dark, slimy, they carried trails of oil behind them. Freya tried to back away, but Brennan was still holding her captive.

I can't let her get to Brennan!

She slammed her palm against her boyfriend, and air blasted him backwards. Freya threw the element towards the creatures, but more insects followed in their wake.

Why isn't this working?

Her scared gaze met Mark's across the distance. *What the hell is going on, dad? Brennan should be back to me by now!*

He pawed one of Elizabeth's ghosts that came too close. *Weren't you listening when I told you? It took me, your mom and Thomas to snap Seamus out of it.*

But the necklace is destroyed!

Mark stopped his fighting and looked around. His emerald gaze fell on Elizabeth, and widened. *She's become a Cursed One,* he said. His tone was full of shock. *Freya, that's why it isn't working. She must have spelled Brennan with something else.* He took in their surroundings, looked for an escape. *We need to leave here, now! She'll turn this place into a tomb!*

Before Freya could move, however, Elizabeth flew to her like a banshee ready for war. Her outstretched hand was no longer smooth, but filled with claws as thick as a raven's. It aimed for Freya's face, but she ducked – not fast enough.

Elizabeth caught her by throat, and the force propelling her forward moved them into a wall. Freya hit it with her back and grunted in pain. But she couldn't even swallow, for fear of having her throat ripped out.

Freya struggled against the Countess' hold, feeling her air supply diminishing by the second. She focused on her rage, her betrayal, and in her hand lightning crackled. She slapped the Countess with it, and the woman flew back into a wall.

The Sage made sure to demand the elements keep her glued to it – until further notice. She glanced to her partner, then her father and Elena. *Go outside the castle, now! You can't be here when I try this.*

Mark took a step forward. *If you think I'm going to leave my daughter alone –*

Leave! Freya thrust a waft of air towards him. She ignored his growl and said, *Please. I beg you. You know I can't be worrying about your safety while I'm doing this!*

Mark moved back, shaking his head, pushing Elena with him – and the demon's weapon. *If you don't come out of this alive, your mother will kill me. Keep that in mind when you try something reckless.*

Freya gave a shaky smile, then moved towards the corner Brennan was in. He'd gotten up, and he was fighting against the rebelling girls. Freya made her way towards him, pushing past the attackers and straight into his arms.

She didn't care if it had taken two Sages and Wiseman to undo Elizabeth's hold on Seamus. This was *her* boyfriend, and she wasn't about to let him bite the dust just because a bloodthirsty Countess had become obsessed with him.

There has to be something I can do! Freya closed her eyes, tightening her hold on Brennan, even as he tried to push her away.

No matter how much he struggled, Freya held good. "It's me and you, Bren. Don't let this witch get between us."

One more time, she expanded her consciousness towards his. Something answered back – faint, but there. It was all Freya needed. She latched onto the sign of good faith, tugging on it until she practically sensed the veil lifting off Brennan's eyes.

He slackened against her, dropping to his knees. She almost feared meeting his gaze, but forced herself to glance down. The eyes that looked up at her were warm once more, and filling with tears. "What did I do?"

"No time to explain." Freya pressed her lips against his, lingering a second longer than necessary. "We need to do what we did earlier, Bren. Unite our powers. The Countess is a Cursed One, and I can't do this alone. I'm too weak."

Brennan's hand squeezed hers. A million emotions danced in his eyes, but all he said was, "I got you."

Freya looked at Brennan and smiled, squeezing back. "We can do this." *I hope.*

She could not guess how the recent fight would affect their bond, but she had to believe if she focused on it, they could do it. Brennan squeezed her hand, then faced the Countess.

Evil contorted her face, even as she struggled against the bonds. Freya lifted her free hand, and Brennan mirrored her. There was no hesitation when he aimed towards the Countess, drawing energy from his anger at what he'd been forced to do.

Freya ordered the elements to let go, replacing their hold with a burst of spiritual energy from herself. Much like she'd done with Cadmael, then Cortés, the power expanded from her aura and shot wards Elizabeth.

The Sage's strike hit its target first, followed by Brennan's soon after. Their powers mingled until her ghost shattered into nothing.

Once she disappeared, Brennan slouched against the wall, barely able to stand on his two feet. Freya walked to him, wobbling as well. "We did it."

"Mm, we sure did, love."

Freya's gaze fell on the girls, hovering in the background. "You are free now, as promised."

One by one, they came to hug them, then disappeared through the walls. Elena lingered, the chains of fire still in her hand. Freya reached out for them, and Elena seemed only too content to be rid of them. With one last nod of acknowledgement, she left.

The two teenagers stared at the weapon. "How do you think this works?" Freya asked. The chains felt smooth in her hand, and light as a feather. Still, their flame was as blazing and intimidating as ever.

Brennan's gaze shifted from the weapon to Freya, and he cupped her cheek. "Forget about the chains. Where's your father?"

Freya frowned, tilting her head to the side. "I kicked him out, was afraid of what would happen. Why?"

"Good. Then he can't stop me from doing this." Brennan dropped his free hand to her waist, pulling Freya closer to him. The hand on her cheek angled her head and his mouth fell against hers, taking and plundering to his heart's content.

When she responded in equal fervor, he groaned against the kiss, deepening it. Everything ceased around them – the ballroom, the castle, the battle they'd just found. The only thing existing was the sliver of their connection, alive and breathing once more.

Minutes later, they were left panting, and Brennan rested his forehead against Freya's. "Now, what's next?"

Her eyes searched his, relieved to see the warmth back in his golden-brown eyes. She spoke the truth they both knew, in their heart of hearts. "The relics."

Chapter 18

Freya and Brennan exited the castle, hand in hand. She still carried the chains in her free hand. They made it to the cover of the forest, when a twig snapped.

Brennan tugged the Sage behind him, lifting his hand pre-emptively.

Stand down, Wiseman. He relaxed at Mark's voice.

Freya went around him, kneeling next to the tiger that had emerged and hugging him. "I was scared you'd gotten seriously hurt this time!"

Mark pulled back and stared at his daughter, his eyes shining. *Not enough to put me down. And you were spectacular...* He looked at Brennan. *Both of you.*

"Freya?"

Two more shapes emerged from the forest – glowing in their immortality. Sam's face lighted up when it fell on her and Brennan, and he ran to the Wiseman. "You made it!"

Anya stayed behind, smiling at them.

Brennan chuckled and patted Sam's back. Though he seemed fine, Freya sensed something tugging at the edge of their bond. It was enough to make her wary. He'd been under the influence of the Countess... *Is it really all done? So easily?*

As if reading her thoughts, Brennan met her grey eyes and smiled. *I'm okay, Frey. I swear it.*

"So, where to next?" Sam interrupted their silent exchange.

Mark nudged the ghost. Anya was floating away, and Sam turned to her. "Anya, wait!"

She turned to him, her expression sad. "I have to go, Sam. Elena and the girls need me, and there is much to be done if we are to make this region safe, once more."

Sam bit his bottom lip. "But I can see you again?"

A smile as bright as the sun lighted her face. "You know where to find me." With one last hug and a wave to Freya and Brennan, she vanished.

Freya stepped closer to Sam, squeezing his shoulder. "Don't be sad, Sam. She got her freedom back, you know? That's worth celebrating."

He sniffled and turned to her, hugging her once more. "I guess whatever you got planned, I can't come with, huh?"

She shared a look with Brennan and her father. "No, Sam. It's way too dangerous."

He sighed and pulled back. "What should I tell Seamus and your mom?"

The truth, Mark said.

Freya nodded and repeated aloud, "The truth. That we're going after the relics, and won't be back until we neutralize Set."

Sam nodded, and with a last wave, dematerialized as well.

Freya turned to Brennan and held her hand out. "So, how do we do this?"

"Hang on a sec," he held up his palm. "I need..." He rubbed his temple, sighed, then said, "I remember a little of what happened. But I'm drained. Can we camp somewhere, for the night? Then take off in the morning."

Freya glanced at her dad, who nodded. *I don't see why not. The relics have been lost for ages, one more day won't change much.*

On his advice, they retreated off the main and secondary roads, and went into the depth of the forest once more. The air was less chilly than previously, which alone confirmed the Countess' presence had been affecting it. It was easy to find a bed of dry moss, and Freya lighted up a fire for them.

She lifted the chains towards her father. "How, exactly, am I supposed to carry these around? They don't fit in my pocket."

A rumble of laughter escaped the tiger. *No, they do not. Fire is one of your elements, is it not?*

Freya frowned. "You know it is. What about it?"

Use it. Ask it to make the chains portable. And when you need them, they can become.... less portable.

Freya stared at the chains in her hands. Behind her, she sensed Brennan's presence, his support, as surely as her next breath. *If we do this, we do it together. Screw hesitation.* She turned to him, holding out the hand with the chains, and silently asking for help.

Brennan's expression softened, reading between the lines. He placed one hand over hers, cupping the chains. "I'm here."

Their breaths synchronized, and time seemed to stand still. The flames covering the chains froze, waiting for a command. Freya passed a hand over them, and Brennan mirrored the gestured underneath.

In front of their eyes, the chains lost their fire-like aspect, and became as small as a key chain. Freya had no trouble fitting them in the pocket of her coat. "This better not light up overnight."

Both men laughed, then Brennan lay back down. "Won't you sleep, too?"

After a slight hesitation, Freya curled next to him. He wrapped his arms around her, pulling her tight against his body. To her surprise, Mark stepped further away, giving them some privacy.

Freya closed her eyes, ready for sleep.

A breath later, Brennan's voice inserted itself in her head. *Are you mad at me?*

The Sage kept her breathing deep, guessing he was keeping this conversation private from her father. *No, Bren. Sleep, you need it.*

He paused. *So you* are *mad.*

She sighed and wrapped her hand around his. *Hurt, is more like it. I thought this bond of ours was unbreakable, even by curses. But I guess I was wrong.*

Guilt and regret radiated off him in strong waves, and Freya turned in his arms, hugging him and burying her face in his chest. *Bren, let it go. Please. What's done is done.*

I... can't. Out loud, he whispered, "I'd do anything to take it all back."

"As would I," Freya said. "It was my fault you got captured. If I hadn't pushed us to go, maybe things would have turned out differently." Another pause. "We're both at fault,

Bren. But there's no use holding on to this. It will only rot us to the core."

He searched her eyes in the darkness, then lifted a hand and wiped a tear away. "Can you forgive me, though?"

"Of course I do," she smiled through her tears. "You're my partner."

His expression was still pained, desperately searching for a deeper truth. "And will you still trust me?"

She didn't hesitate. "With my life."

The answer seemed to suit him, and his body relaxed. Freya rolled over again and curled up in her previous position, closing her eyes.

A moment later, Brennan's whisper was by her ear. "How were we able to unite our powers so easily?"

A shuffle away drew their attention, and Mark came and sat next to them. His gaze lingered on Brennan's arm wrapped around Freya's waist, then he looked at the Wiseman. *Because while the Countess had you under her spell, you lost control. Like Freya did a while back, your powers took over and you could influence the emotions of the young girls.*

Brennan's sharp inhale indicated his surprise. "You're saying I upgraded my powers, too?"

Yes. And it's about time. Mark looked around. *Something is coming, and you will both need your newfound strengths.*

"Newfound?" Brennan peered at Freya in his arms. "Again, love?"

She shrugged. "Under Čachtice Castle, there was a pool and I..." The Sage paused, biting her lip. In the end, she told Brennan about the dragon energy.

The Wiseman sighed, recalling what they'd found out about the beast. "Why do I have a feeling we're only getting this upgrade because we'll be facing bigger foes?"

Freya didn't answer, and neither did Mark. Instead, the tiger returned to his spot by the tree. *You two should get some rest. We leave at first light.*

&&&

Seamus and Evie were walking the grounds when a glowing shape floated towards them from a distance.

"Sam!" The elder Sage stumbled over his feet in his haste to reach him. He grabbed the younger ghost by the shoulders. "What happened? Are they all right?"

He nodded and grinned. "Yep, fit as a fiddle! We defeated the Countess, Anya went back home, and Freya and Bren are heading to get the relics."

Seamus glanced at Evie, who'd joined them. Her wary gaze mirrored his feelings about the new development.

"The relics? So soon?"

If they are together, they should be fine, Seamus.

Sam nodded at Seamus' question. "There was no talking them out of it. They said to tell you to get better, and that they'll be home soon."

Seamus let his gaze wander over the remnants of the castle, and the water. "May luck be on their side..." His whisper carried on the breeze, but no amount of prayer or wishful thinking could unknot the sensation in his stomach.

&&&

The next morning, Freya woke up alone. She looked around and found Brennan in the distance, kneeling next to Mark. Something about their stance told her they were in deep conversation, and she didn't want to disturb them. No matter how curious she was.

Instead, the Sage got up and walked further. She could sense water nearby – a river. Its cool water was heaven on her face, washing the remnants of sleep away.

She lingered beside it, waving her hand in the water. At one point, she thought she felt eyes on her. But when she scanned the area, Freya caught nothing out of the ordinary.

Moments later, Brennan joined her and knelt next to her. "You should've told us you were leaving the campsite."

Freya shrugged. "You seemed deep in conversation, and I didn't want to interrupt."

Brennan glanced to Mark, who'd followed him there. "We were talking, is all."

His tone caused Freya to grin. "Dad, you'd better not be scaring him off."

Mark only snorted, then said, *We should get going, if you two are ready.*

After one last wash, Brennan helped Freya to her feet, and they headed down the mountain.

"Where exactly are we going?" she asked.

Mark glanced at them. *Now that there is nothing else lingering in your minds, the map will arise soon enough. It had spoken to you in your dreams not long ago. Before you know it, it will guide you to the resting place of the relics.*

Brennan's look was heavy on hers, and she guessed the question in his eyes. With a nod, she indicated he should voice it.

"What do you know about the protector of the relics?" Brennan asked.

Mark didn't even skip a beat. *They say a beast of the Underworld guards them.*

Freya gulped. "Like, say, a dragon?"

The tiger stopped, turning an inquisitive stare towards them. *What more have you learned?* Once they'd caught him up to speed, he growled. *Why should this surprise me? I knew of Draykho, and guessed he'd crossed the pool in Slovakia, under Čachtice Castle. But I never thought they'd make you fight your own maker.* He shook his head in disgust. *The gods really are fickle.*

Freya ignored that comment. "What I don't get is how we're supposed to beat an immortal being, when it's from him we get our powers?"

Mark sighed. *You aren't meant to fight him, because you would lose. The two of you would have to prove worthy of the relics that's all.*

That's all? Brennan asked. *It's like he's asking us to order a cheeseburger!*

Freya snorted. *We'll find a way. We always do.*

She reached for his hand and they continued in silence. Lost in their own thoughts, neither noticed the scenery changing. The surrounding trees grew sharper, until they weren't trees anymore, but statues. Freya slowed down, and Brennan mirrored her.

"Are you seeing this?" she asked.

"I thought I was imagining things."

At the end of the hallway they were in shone a golden door. And behind it, they felt rumble – a passage. Yet the minute Freya tried to head closer, the image shattered, and they were back in the forest.

Mark was watching them, his head tilted to the side. *The map?* He didn't seem surprised.

Freya nodded, feeling like she'd run a marathon. She glanced to Brennan, who was also out of breath. "I think it was telling us to go to Egypt, dad."

Of course it did. What better way to trap you? Mark grumbled, then turned tail and continued on his way. After a beat, Freya and Brennan followed suit.

As they walked down the mountain, Freya stumbled over a root and nearly fell. In the second between tripping and heading towards the ground, something flashed in front of her eyes.

Brennan caught her before she made contact, but when his hand touched hers, it only seemed to enhance the experience.

"I..."

Before Freya could say more, the image hit her full force with such brutality it wrenched her out of Brennan's grip, and she fell to her knees. By the time she came to, Mark was hovering nearby in worry, and Brennan was also on his knees, panting.

"What the bloody hell!?" He lifted worried eyes to Freya. "Are you all right?"

The Sage could only shake her head, at a loss on what happened.

It's the map, trying to stop you from continuing.

"Why would it do that?"

The map preserves the safety of its protectors. His eyes roamed the surroundings, trying to assess the peril.

"Are you saying we're in danger?" Brennan asked.

I'm afraid so. And from the scent of it, it's someone we all know.

As if on cue, Raksh stepped from the trees, his red eyes glowing in the dark.

I was hoping it would be you, Mark stated as he placed himself in front of the two teenagers. *We have some unfinished business, demon.*

"Perhapsss. But I'm here for the map in their headsss, not for your triflesss." Raksh followed the statement with a wave of his hand, which sent Mark into the nearest tree.

While the tiger rose back to his feet, the wraith advanced. Their bodies slammed like thunder, rumbling the ground. With a few well-placed hits, Raksh had Mark flying backwards. Bleeding gashes were on his body.

Freya moved forward, but Brennan grabbed her wrist. "Not like this, Frey. The chains. We have to use them."

She nodded and pulled them out, asking fire to reactivate them. The small key chain lengthened, and a blazing trail coated the enhanced chains. Raksh froze, staring at them with wide eyes. For the first time, Freya read panic in his gaze.

"Thought you had us, huh?" She smirked and whipped the chains to the ground. They sizzled in the air, loud and crackling.

Raksh took a step closer, his eyes glued to the chains. He lifted his hand as if asking for them back, but Freya snapped her wrist and they cut across him. He stepped back, hissing at them like a cat.

Then he lunged, tackling Freya and wrapping his talon-like hands around her throat.

"Freya!"

Brennan was building energy behind her, but she caught his eye. *The chains... Use them.*

He caught her meaning and rushed to them. With a flick of his wrist, they wrapped around Raksh's throat like a lasso, pulling the demon off the Sage. Freya got back to her feet, coughing. Out of the corner of her eye, she saw Mark stand too.

Stay down, dad.

Brennan moved halfway in front of Freya. With one hand, he kept the chains wrapped around the wraith. With the other, he held out his palm to her.

We have to do this right. Are you ready?

She glanced to her father, who was getting to his feet. Memories of years without her parents passed through her head with just as much intensity as the map had. *Yes.*

Their hands rose in unison, spiritual strength gathering. Focused on their task, neither heard Mark's cry of warning. The energy released and flew into Raksh. Rather than a counterattack, the demon stood and took it, disintegrating into nothingness.

Freya and Brennan shared a look, jaws slack. "Did he just..."

"... commit suicide?"

Mark's wail reached them too late. *Run! Both of you, run now! It's another trap!*

Before they could react, the ground shifted underneath their feet. Another portal formed, this one a green whirlpool. Freya and Brennan had no chance to get out – they were sucked in it within seconds.

Despite jumping the minute he saw it, Mark crashed on grass. The portal had closed before he could get through, and he was unable to follow them.

Damn you, demon!

Chapter 19

I n the Underworld, Set lifted his head, sniffing the air like a dog. His dark gaze turned to the jackals that had been watching over him for centuries. Since Raksh had killed his last guards, Osiris had doubled them.

Not that it matters...

Set flexed his hand, sensing the magic underneath his fingertips. With his demon's sacrifice, two gates had been blasted open. The one taking the two teenagers where he needed them... and the one keeping his powers under lock and key.

It had taken Set weeks to realize the potential of the teenagers. Though they held the maps within their bodies, they were also vessels to potent spiritual energy – the type that could break apart even the most powerful of enchantments.

Once he'd realized it, Set had given strict orders to Raksh. And, for all intents and purposes, the demon had carried them out perfectly.

Time to leave this prison.

He stood and walked to the cage bars. "Listen well," he spoke in Ancient Egyptian. "You have but a minute to leave here or join me. Otherwise, your lives are useless."

Two of the guards turned to him. Their muzzles snarled while the others remained indifferent. They carried spears, their tips anointed with poison.

"Your foolish choice."

Set stepped back from the cage and lifted his palms. Energy crackled this time, and with a single blast the doors spun open. Smoke created confusion, and he heard the guards' mutterings.

The god stepped behind one and pulled him in a headlock. He struggled against his iron grip, but Set removed his spear and pointed its poisoned tip at his throat. With one hard jab, the jackal dropped, unmoving.

I'd almost forgotten the sweet thrill of a fresh kill, he thought to himself and smirked. His dark gaze fell on his hands, filled with blood.

With the spear in his hand, Set moved. He lunged and ducked, swifter than a cat. The guards fell one by one, until a single jackal was left standing. Blind in the fog, he'd drifted to a corner, and was trying to blink into the darkness.

Set ruled the shadows, moving amongst them like he was born to it. Which, he was. He sneered at the poor guard and appeared out of thin air. He grabbed him by the throat, lifting him in the air.

"You, I shall let live," he hissed. "Give my brother a message. Tell him he should tremble because I will soon have his precious relics. And nothing he does will stop me."

He set the tip of the poison over the guard's bare chest. He collapsed to the ground, frothing at the mouth. The god smirked. "I said I would let you live... I didn't say forever."

With a cackle under his breath, Set turned his back on what had been his cage for eons, and walked out. Stairs led into a palace, then out in the desert. He inhaled the arid air, enjoying the sun's burn over his skin.

His hand crackled again, and he threw magic at air itself. A portal formed between worlds, and he grinned and stepped through.

&&&

A groan woke Freya up, followed by a string of curses. "Brennan?"

The muttering ceased, followed by shuffling close by. "I'm here. Are you all right?"

She blinked against the scorching sun, lifting a hand to shield her face against the glare. "I think so but... Where the hell are we?"

Brennan's silence had her turn around, noticing he was covered in sand from head to toe, and so was she. "You won't believe this, Frey..."

"After everything that just happened? Try me."

"We've gone back in time."

Freya shook her head, unwilling to believe it. "That's impossible. How do you even..." She stopped, fully taking in their surroundings. They were in the middle of what looked like a desert, with no buildings around for miles.

No buildings, that is, except...

"Is that... Are those..." Words died on her lips, choked as much by her astonishment as the dry desert air.

Brennan nodded to where she was pointing. "Yep. The pyramids of Giza. Or should I say, the unfinished version?"

In the distance, they could see large pyramids. The biggest one shone in the darkness, looking almost adrift in the red desert. Covered in limestone, it appeared brand-new – nothing like the weather-worn version Freya had seen in history books.

But what really astonished Freya was not its material or perfect architecture – rather the fact that there were only *two* pyramids. Dual monsters, witnesses to history, they rose against the backdrop of a starry night and cold moon. But there was no third pyramid, no matter where she looked.

Freya gaped, tearing her gaze from the impossible sight. "How is this even possible?"

"We both know how, Frey. And we knew we'd end up here... In Set's game."

As if on cue, a wind rose around them, strong enough to beat against their skin. They reached out for each other, in fear of this newest development try to tear them apart.

Yet the breeze quieted as soon as it had started, and it left Freya and Brennan facing a dark-skinned man with eyes of cold onyx. On his shoulder was a hawk, its gaze intent on them both.

The hawk... Freya glanced to Brennan, who nodded.

I know. We're screwed.

&&&

Osiris had been conversing with Isis when the attack happened. First, he felt the guards' confusion – then their pain. He dropped to the ground on his knees, deaf to anything else but their cries of terror.

Linked as he was to every spirit in the Underworld, the god couldn't have avoided seeing the massacre if he'd tried. Shocked by it, he was weak, held immobile by their last anguished moments.

He only snapped to when Set's message had been delivered. Isis was bent over him, trying to shake him to his senses. Slowly, Osiris stood, avoiding her eyes.

"I must go, beloved."

She was having none of it. Isis grabbed his wrist, stopping him from moving. "What happened?"

When Osiris met her gaze, the pain reflected within its depths. "Set escaped and killed the guards."

Isis read his mind before he could voice it. "I'm coming with you. And do not dare tell me otherwise. I will not allow you to face your murderous brother alone."

Osiris nodded, then turned to the fireplace and opened a portal. He stepped in, Isis behind him. They exited into the realm they'd imprisoned Set.

The stench of death was everywhere. Isis recognized the poison that had killed them – and the agony they'd endured. Tears filled her eyes, and she intertwined her fingers with Osiris' in a silent show of support.

Osiris stopped by each jackal, closing their eyes and whispering incantations designed to carry their spirits to a place of healing, and eternal continuance. When he reached the last one, he could still sense Set's conscience lingering.

He tried to press through it, and his eyes snapped open in shock. "He did *not*!"

"What is it?" Isis asked.

When Osiris only moved away, she touched the dead man's head and saw what he'd seen. Then she turned to her husband.

"He used *them*?"

Osiris nodded, avoiding her gaze. "Yes. He must have figured out their energies alone could break him out. When Raksh died, he pulled some of Freya and Brennan's energy into him, and acted as a conduit for Set."

"And released him," Isis scowled, waving her hand in the air. "What now? We cannot let them affront your brother alone, it will be their death!"

Osiris' tone was blank. "And what do you suggest we do?"

&&&

Brennan watched the man facing them, and the hawk that had been plaguing his nightmares for months. He recalled Freya's scratches due to the same bird and scowled at the god.

"Why did you bring us here?"

While his attention was focused on Set, a part of him also caught Freya's surprise, then her focused intention. She was trying to figure out a way past Set, and his job was to play distraction. *That, I can do.*

"To show you the truth." Set took a step closer to them, but Brennan lifted his palm, filled with spiritual energy.

"I think that's close enough, don't you?"

The god's eyes flicked between him and Freya, and he smiled. "I do not wish you harm, young ones."

Bullshit. Freya's tone in his mind was determined, and Brennan drew strength from the fact they were on the same page.

"Sure you don't," he rolled his eyes. "You wanted to chat, right? Show us how we've been wrong, following the wrong gods' orders and all?"

Set chuckled under his breath, and the red sand danced around him. "But you *are* wrong, young ones. And you *are* following a traitor's advice."

Anything? Brennan asked Freya. He could sense her spirit probing the god's aura, and he itched to join her.

Not yet. Keep him talking. And don't even thinking about hopping aboard this exhausting train.

Without blinking, Brennan said, "In your opinion."

Set's eyes narrowed, his sweet composure slipping. "What?"

"I said, *in your opinion.* Meaning, we're entitled to think differently. Since we're humans and have free choice, and all." His smile was as fake as the god's pretend-nice persona.

"Free choice..." Set tapped his chin as if considering the words, then nodded. "Very well, I will allow that. In the interest of gaining your support, of course."

"Support?" Brennan snorted. "You must be mental."

Set's gaze sharpened on Freya, and his hand lifted. In the next heartbeat, he levitated Freya in the air, and she was holding her throat as though she was choking.

"Stop!" Brennan stepped closer to her, but a quick scan proved his worst worry – Set was manipulating the elements, and not with spiritual energy. *This guy's using magic.*

He glared at the god. "Leave her alone!"

Set didn't even glance at him, and the hawk didn't budge. "Will you listen to me now?"

Brennan knew they had no choice. "Yes. We'll listen, all right? Just let Freya down."

Set kept her up for another few seconds, then dropped his hand. Freya fell to the sand, but Brennan was there to help her up.

"Now watch."

They shared a look, wondering how long it would be before the god lost interest in them and stopped toying with them.

A swirl of sand caught their attention, and the story shown to them entranced both Sage and Wiseman.

&&&

Set was sparring in the courtyard of a palace. When he paused enough to catch his breath, he turned to the shadows and smiled. There was no hardness in his expression, and warmth filled his eyes.

"Beloved, you should stop staring."

A laugh escaped the shadows, then a woman stepped forth. She had long, black hair with a beautiful oval-shaped face. Her full lips extended in a smile, and her grey-black eyes twinkled with laughter.

"When will you find a worthy opponent, husband?"

"Are you offering?" His grin was cheeky, and before she could escape him, Set pulled the woman in his arms. He buried his head in the crook of her neck and placed a kiss on her sun-kissed skin. "I have missed you, Nephy."

The goddess Nephthys pulled out of his embrace. "And I, you. But Isis needed help with a spell, and you know I cannot refuse my sister."

Set rolled his eyes. "And you would allow her to keep you away from your husband?"

Nephthys grinned wickedly. "Not for long, my love. Only enough to make you yearn for me."

Set chuckled against her skin, then dropped his mouth to hers. Their passionate embrace continued, on and on...

The scene shifted to another...

Set burst into a room, his eyes darting around in panic. "Have either of you seen Nephy?"

Isis lifted her head from Osiris' shoulder, smiling. "She went to search for ingredients to my spell."

"Again?" Set scowled. "It is dark outside, you should have sent someone with her."

"Breathe easy, brother," Osiris said. "Nephthys is a strong magician. She will be fine."

Once more, the scene changed....

A grief-stricken Set was fighting Osiris. "This is your fault!"

Tears streaked both their cheeks, and they could hear a woman's sobs.

"Nephy would have been alive were it not for you and your blasted spells!" Set tried to move past Osiris, to Isis. She was bent over a woman's body, crying her heart out.

"You will not touch Isis!"

Set's features contorted until he was unrecognizable. "A life for a life!"

Osiris reacted, punching his brother and pushing him away. His expression had darkened to cold fury. "You need to leave, brother. Now." He turned to Isis and pulled her away from her sister. "Let him take her, beloved."

Numb, Set moved to the body and picked Nephthys up in his arms. Step by painful step, he walked away, but stopped before the exit. "Mark my words," he hissed, "you will not know happiness again. Not while I live, brother."

&&&

Set dropped the illusion and faced the teenagers once more. Freya blinked, then glanced at Brennan. He seemed as shocked as she was.

There was nothing in the history books about this!

I know, he said. His gaze was glued to the god, frowning. *But why would he show us all this?*

The answer soon became clear.

"I show you this," Set said, "because it is high time to dethrone my brother as the god of the Underworld. You thought him all-knowing, all-merciful? He is but a selfish god, out for his own interests."

Set threw his head back, eyes glued to the sky. "For eons, Osiris used the relics to put himself in power. He allowed his wife to create the blasted things for him, with my beloved's blood. And he used that gift to ensnare the entire Underworld to his bidding."

Slowly, he leveled his gaze on the teenagers. "The relics he hid – the ones you protect – are key to dethroning him."

"And why the hell would we help you?" Freya narrowed her eyes on him. "You've done nothing but try to kill us all along! My parents are dead because of your demon."

"As is my grandfather," Brennan added.

Set glanced between them and grinned. "The relics can bring them back – for good. Forever. They will also allow me to control ghosts. I can remove the threats on your Earth, allow your normal lives."

His cold gaze shifted from Freya to Brennan, and he lowered his voice. "Would you not enjoy that? A normal life, away from the hell you have been facing? None of this was yours to fight... And I can make it so."

Freya tried to shake off his words, but something about the way he said it... Brennan's eyes were heavy on her and she turned. Was the golden-brown hue glazed? And why was the heat so scorching?

She inhaled, then shook her head. "No, you... It's not right, what you ask..."

"Why not?" Set asked, moving closer to them. His voice was alluring, entrancing. "Why is my world so much worse than what Osiris planned?"

Then he was in front of them, circling them. "He lied to you. They both did. Chose you as pawns, never revealing everything... You deserve better..."

"You..." Brennan started, then smacked his lips. His throat was parched.

Then everything went black.

Set stared at the youths by his feet, and a rumbling laughter escaped him. "You fools. I know you will not join me... Which is why I'll get the map out of you another way."

The hawk screeched and flew off his shoulder, and into the sky.

Chapter 20

Freya was no longer in the desert. She looked around, noticing the crash of a car in the distance. Seamus was gone, and she could hear cries for help inside the vehicle.

She stepped closer, led by pure instinct. Much like Seamus had done, she slammed her palms on the car and said, "Stop!" The blaze seemed to diminish for a moment. Before she even spoke, it burst higher, and it slammed Freya backwards by the force behind it.

The Sage recoiled back in shock. "Impossible..." She looked around, shaking her head. "This isn't... I can't be here..."

"Very much possible," a voice came from behind.

Freya spun towards it, recognizing its familiar pitch. She gasped when her eyes fell on Brennan. His golden-brown gaze was blank, and his palms were extended, vibrating with spiritual energy ready for unleashing.

"No, this isn't... You can't..." She staggered back. "You're the cause of this?"

Brennan passed by her and threw a blast of energy at the car. Flames erupted from within, and Freya heard her parents' cries. "No!"

She tackled Brennan, hitting him with her fists. "Why would you betray me? *Why!*"

"Because you're a fool," he sneered, allowing her hits. "I betrayed you with Elizabeth, and with your parents, and I will do it again. The only way to stop it is to kill me."

When Freya froze, he blasted something her way, and darkness followed. The silence of a tomb surrounded her, but it didn't last for long.

In the depths of the obscurity, a voice rose. "He betrayed you, Freya. You cannot trust him."

The Sage blinked, but couldn't see anything past her nose. "Who's there?"

"Brennan is a liar. A traitor. He *will* betray you again... The only way to survive it, is to fight him."

"I...." She shook her head, trying to clear it of cobwebs. "No, the Brennan I know wouldn't do any of this."

"Really?" The voice was in her ear now, whispering over, and over again. "Do you *truly* believe that, Sage?"

"I..." Freya tried to speak, but the words lodged in her throat. A sharp pain crossed her mind. Instead of a negative answer, she found herself nodding. "Brennan betrayed me, yes."

"Good girl... And what do you do to evil people who break your trust?"

Freya's eyes shone with determination. "I dispose of them."

&&&

The desert disappeared around him, and Brennan was in a cottage amid a forest. He recognized it – and the old man. He was sitting at a tiny table, writing on a piece of paper.

Long, grey hair was tied back in a ponytail, and he had warm hazel eyes.

Hunched over a paper, he didn't hear someone enter. Not at first. But a noise made him snap to, and he turned around. His eyes widened, and a glint of fear flashed, before his face became a blank mask.

"So, you came."

"Did you doubt it?"

Brennan froze at once, recognizing Freya's voice. He spun to her, watching her cold grey gaze land on his grandfather. "Where is it?" she asked.

"No," Brennan shook his head. "This isn't how it happened!"

But the scene kept playing in front of him, and he had no choice but to watch.

"Do not mess with me, old man. I need the medallion to lead me to the map. With it, I can bring my parents back."

Thomas' eyes flashed. "I do not know what you are referring to."

"Don't lie!" Freya shrieked, taking a controlled step forward. Her body were taut with fury, fists clenched. "You have the medallion, the key to it all. *I want it*!"

"I do not. Not anymore." There was an almost smug undertone to the words, despite his blank expression.

"Fool!" Freya growled. She lifted a palm, and a thin black mist escaped her index to travel in the Wiseman's nostrils.

Brennan gasped and tried to reach out, to help, but to no avail. She then stepped around Thomas as he choked to death and seemed to scan the area with her senses. Furious at not finding what she was looking for, she stormed out, leaving the poor man dying.

The vision faded, and he was surrounded by nothingness. The quiet didn't last for long, and soon a voice whispered to him.

"Freya is a liar, Brennan. You must cast her aside."

He shook his head, refusing to believe it. "She's my girlfriend. It was Raksh who killed Thomas, not her."

"Really?" The voice was in his ear now. "Do you really believe that?"

"I..." Brennan blinked, trying to clear his throat. "She..."

"She is *foul*! Admit it, Wiseman!"

Brennan rubbed the side of his head, trying to deny it. But instead, he said, "Yes, I... *Freya* killed my granddad."

"And what do you do to such evil creatures?"

The Wiseman's eyes burned in the darkness. "I kill them."

&&&

Freya blinked awake, looking around. "Where am I?" she whispered.

"Where you need to be." The cold voice came from a corner.

She stood, looking around, and her gaze landed on a boy. He was taller than her, with wavy brown hair and golden-brown eyes. They glinted back, and before she could ask questions, he struck her.

The Sage flew into the wall and groaned. By the time she got back to her feet, she was seeing red. She recognized his face – he was the one who'd killed her parents!

&&&

Brennan pulled on the fury within him and aimed it at the girl. He would not let her get away with killing his grandfather.

He'd recognized her face the moment he'd woken up and did not intend to leave the pit they were in unless she was no longer breathing.

Nothing else mattered, except her death – her soul, as payment for Thomas' demise.

&&&

Overhead, Set watched the teenagers battle. He was petting his hawk, biding his time. Once they were dead, or quasi-dead, the map would search for another host. And the hawk would be there – a perfect plan, considering he could cross dimensions without issue.

Now, if only they could hurry and kill each other...Then the map will be mine for the plucking.

&&&

Mark stumbled into the castle, praying to all the gods and beyond that he'd find them there. He managed to drag himself the rest of the way to the library, where Seamus was asleep on the couch, with Evie by his side.

Sam floated in the vicinity, his gaze lost outside the window. He was the first to notice the other tiger in the room.

"Mark!"

His joyous cry woke Seamus and Evie, who jumped to their feet – and paws. Seamus' hair was messy, and he rubbed the sleep out of his eyes as if not quite believing what he was seeing.

"You've returned," he whispered.

Where are they?

It was Evie's hopeful question that brought Mark to his knees. *I lost them, darling. We ran into Raksh, and after defeating him, another one of those blasted portals appeared.* He shook his head. *I couldn't follow this time.*

Evie stepped to him, rubbing her muzzle against his shoulder in a sign of affection. *You did everything you could, Mark. We can only hope it was enough – and that Freya and Brennan will survive this.*

Seamus gulped, looking older than his age. "Do you know where they could have gone?"

The last they said, was that they'd seen images of the relics' location in Egypt.

An ominous silence descended on everyone. Seamus dragged himself back to the couch, dropping on it as if he had no strength left. Sam returned back to looking out the window, tears streaming down his cheeks. And the tigers, they settled in front of the fireplace and prayed for mercy – for Freya, and her Wiseman friend.

&&&

They'd been sparring for what felt like hours. Too alike in strength, too similar in attack patterns, neither could win over the other. But their energies were growing weaker, and Freya was seeing double.

Only rage kept her going, and a strong will to survive.

Brennan's feet were as heavy as chains. He knew he was reaching the maximum of his strength – there was no way around it. But he didn't want to let the girl win. He'd do anything to bring about her death.

&&&

Another strike, and Freya used air to climb the wall, then land behind the guy. She kicked at him, and he hit the ground face-first. She caught him by the neck and they rolled around, until somehow she ended on top of him.

Hands on his throat, she used air to immobilize him. Then she looked into his eyes, wanting to see the life edge out of him – the person responsible for her parents' death.

He is not!

The voice was unknown in her mind, nothing like her parents or the gods. It was hoarse, old, but not unfamiliar. Freya didn't drop her hold on the guy, fearing it could be a trick on his end. After all, he'd killed her parents.

He did not, *Freya!* The tone was pleading, almost desperate this time.

Yes, he did, she thought, wondering why in hell she was speaking with someone in her mind.

A brief moment of silence followed, then, *And I thought you were smart – for a Sage.*

Before Freya could retort or tighten her grip on the guy's neck, images assailed her. Only instead of a killer, she saw warm, golden-colored eyes. He was laughing at her, stealing food, holding her and whispering sweet nothings. Then he was pushing her behind him, protecting her with his body. Brennan was....

"Brennan," she breathed, her eyes widening.

Before she could do anything, he buckled against her, breaking her hold and punching her in the gut. Freya landed in another hill of sand, spitting out blood and grime alike.

Brennan was heading towards her, fuelled as she was by a fire out of their control. She realized what had happened – what Set had done.

But how do I reverse it?

She could sense Set in the vicinity, watching them. When Brennan lifted his hands to strike, she rolled out of the way. But she couldn't make herself attack him.

Either way we look at it, Set will win. He'll either make us kill each other, or force us to exhaust our spiritual strength then kill us himself.

Her gaze fell on Brennan, now adjusting to strike again. Brennan, we have to fight against this! The haze of revenge threatened her brief respite as Set looked on. He'd sensed her cry, knew she'd woken from the illusion.

If I can, so can Brennan.

Fuelled by the thought, Freya jumped in the air, wrapping her legs around Brennan's neck and pulling him down with her. He was on top of her, and his hands reached for her throat.

She pushed them away, and lifted her head, pulling him closer by the neck. She pressed her lips against his, hoping it would work – same as it had with Elizabeth.

Rather than it working, Brennan pressed deeper in her throat, cutting out her air supply. Right when she thought she was done for, she heard his whisper in her ear.

"He's watching us, Frey. On the count of three, I need you to blast him with your last strength. I'll do the same."

Joy filled her, but she didn't move her head. She waited until Brennan straightened up atop her, pretending he was strangling her. She closed her eyes, putting all her trust in him – and gathered the energy in her hands.

At the last possible moment, Brennan rolled off her and shot his blast upwards, while Freya hit everywhere else. The surrounding illusion shattered, and they were back in the red desert. Set was scowling at them, the hawk on his shoulder.

Freya clenched her hand, gritting her teeth. Behind Set, Brennan's gaze locked with hers, and he nodded. Fury vibrated off him, fuelling his spiritual energy. Another wave escaped his aura, trapping the god within.

The Sage lifted her other hand, readying the last strike...

Then lightning poured from the sky, and something forced her and Brennan backwards, blasted into the dunes. When Freya had finished spitting sand from her mouth, she looked around – Set vanished.

In his place was Osiris.

"You've got to be *shitting* me!"

Chapter 21

Freya picked herself off the ground, trying to hold in her temper at the god's announcement. "Are you seriously saying we can't kill him?"

Osiris glanced between them, but said nothing. Isis had appeared by his side within seconds, equally quiet. It was impossible to mistake the gods, what with the crowns they wore and the gold regalia around their necks.

"That's why you're here and he's gone, isn't it?" Freya scowled. "You imprisoned him again."

By her side, Brennan leveled a glare on the gods. Yet Osiris and Isis maintained their composure.

Finally, Osiris deigned to answer. "If Set dies, it will upset the balance of the world as you know it."

Brennan scowled at that. "Seems hardly fair he gets to walk into another prison after all the hell he put us through."

Yet not that surprising, Freya pointed out as she recalled her father's words. *Gods will be gods.*

"There is much you do not understand. Suffice to say we did not expect him to escape – and now, he will no longer be able to."

Freya rolled her eyes. "Where have I heard that before?"

Brennan picked up the gods' resolution, and knew they were ready to leave. An idea struck him, and he held up his palm to grab their attention. "If you won't let us kill the ruddy bastard, will you at least allow us to destroy the relics?"

Anger vibrated in Brennan's tone, and Freya felt it radiating off his spiritual aura. *Breathe, Bren. What good would it do to make enemies of them?*

You heard what Set told us!

Yeah. And, at the end of the day, it's their squabbles. Let's leave it at that.

Osiris seemed to consider the possibility, unaware – or uncaring – of their internal dialogue. After a glance to his wife, he nodded. "Yes, we can allow that."

&&&

Freya glanced once more at their surroundings, then sighed. "Are you absolutely sure about this?"

Brennan only shrugged, then stepped into the cave.

After a rather non-eventful negotiation with the gods, Osiris had opened another portal. According to him, this particular door would lead them straight to the relics, because of the map embedded in them.

And it had.

They'd ended up in front of the cave of their dreams, the one Set had stopped them from entering before. Two large statues adorned each side, one red and one black, each decorated with jewelry.

After one last look around, Freya followed Brennan inside, surprised to see the hallway headed inwards into the earth, rather than continue straight towards the center. Glistening walls spoke of water and crystals, but the eerie silence was enough to lift the hairs on the back of her neck.

"This doesn't feel like Egypt anymore, Brennan."

Ahead of her, the Wiseman slowed down and waited until she caught up, then grabbed her hand in his. "I know, but we can do this. We've got to see it to the end, if only to make my granddad proud."

Freya bit her lip, debating for a brief second if it was the best time to reveal what had happened. Weary of secret, she ended up whispering, "He helped us, you know?"

Brennan threw her a glance over a shoulder, but didn't slow down his stride. "What do you mean?"

"When Set was controlling us, pitting us against each other. Thomas – I'm pretty sure it was him, anyway – spoke to me. He got through the mess in my head and made me realize the truth."

The Wiseman looked away then, exhaling heavily. His grip on her hand tightened as he said, "That's granddad, all right. Always to the rescue."

On and on they continued until they ended up in a deeper cavern with a glistening pool. They both sensed the presence, even before it made itself known.

The roar brought them both to a stop, and they stood staring at each other for a long moment.

I know you are here, Sage and Wiseman.

Freya jumped. The voice vibrated in the cavernous walls, and through their linked minds. She cast a glance to Brennan, who seemed as shaken as she was.

"Is that..."

Rather than answer, Brennan took a step forward, then another, dragging Freya by the hand. When they reached the end of the tunnel, they turned right and were greeted by an otherworldly sight.

A silver dragon stood perched on a column, its body wrapped around it. From afar, it could have been a statue... until his eyes opened to reveal startling blue irises.

Freya let go of Brennan's hand and took a step in his direction. "You're the dragon from the story... Estella's maker."

And so I am. A pause, and his eyes shifted from her to Brennan. *What brings you here, younglings?*

"We've come for the relics you safeguard."

Relics? I know nothing of such things. He closed his eyes, dismissing them.

The teenagers glanced at each other, and Brennan joined Freya's side. "With all due respect, we don't believe you."

The dragon's scaly tail lifted in what the Sage presumed was a shrug. *And why do I care what you think?*

"We've come a long way," Freya said. "We have to destroy them."

I do not think so.

Brennan stepped forward, gathering energy in his palm. In the next second, something blasted him against the wall, and fell to the ground.

You are fools if you think you can have what I have kept for eons.

"Stop, please! We mean you no harm! Osiris sent us!" Freya shouted.

Did he, now? The dragon didn't seem impressed. *And why do you seem to believe those are the magic words to avoid my wrath?*

Freya glanced over her shoulder at Brennan, silently begging for help. The Wiseman struggled to get up, but between fighting Freya and then Set, he was unable to.

From the ground, he looked up at the dragon. "Didn't you serve Osiris, in the Underworld? You promised him you'd safeguard the relics until such time as worthy champions came by to seek them." He gritted his teeth, pushing through without slurring his words, despite his weakness. "Why change your tune?"

The tail flicked again, and one wing fluttered. It moved air to such extent both teenagers were pushed further back. The blue eye staring in their direction was filled with amusement, but the large canines appeared ready to devour them.

Me, serve Osiris? Draykho snorted, and a puff of flames blew out of his nostrils. *You must have the wrong dragon, younglings. I suggest you leave, while you still have the chance.*

Freya narrowed her eyes on him. Rather than listen to its advice, she stepped closer to the dragon and placed her hands on her hips. "Are you *kidding me* right now?"

His eye, half-opened, blinked and stared at her again. *I should think if you wished something of me, you would be more polite, Sage.*

Freya scowled, biting back a curse. "My apologies, o mighty Draykho," she said, unable to keep the sarcasm out of her tone. "We may have been sent on a foolish quest, and you are entitled to think we are not worthy. But please stop wasting our time. We had to fight each other because a selfish god pitted us against one another, and now you make us run in circles." She shook her head. "Just..."

At a loss, Freya dropped to her knees, placing her palms face up as if begging. "Is this what you want to see? Us begging? Because I can tell you, I have no pride when it comes to the fate of the world."

"Nor do I." Brennan's voice surprised her, but then he crawled by her side and mirrored her position, palms pointed upwards. "Please..." Brennan sighed, barely able to keep his head upright. "What do we have to do?"

The dragon glanced between them. *Why do you wish to destroy these artefacts?*

"To make sure Set never gets them. He has come much too close, already," Freya whispered.

Wrong. You want to destroy them because you fear them.

In front of their bemused gazes, he unraveled his body off the column and stepped towards them. Freya and Brennan could only stare as his massive bulk, easily over forty feet, moved in their direction.

"We..." Freya cleared her throat, trying to get the words out. Her head was fuzzy once more, both from lack of sleep and overuse of her powers. "Set wants the relics, but so does Osiris, to some extent. We wish only to keep the world safe, Draykho. Help us..."

Rather than answer, the dragon stopped in front of them. His wings beat the air, extending to their full capacity – and still he had room to move in the cavern. Draykho then lifted a huge paw, hovering above their heads.

Freya tried to speak again, to summon up a barrier, but her strength was weak. She dropped next to Brennan on the ground. His hand found hers, and she gripped it like she would a life jacket.

Tears ran down her cheeks, but she didn't bother hiding them. "I'm so sorry, Bren," she whispered. "For dragging you into this."

He pulled her in his arms as best he could, rocking her. "It was both of us who followed this path. How would we have known it would end with our deaths?"

Freya continued crying in his arms. "If we die, we die united." Hands dug in his chest, she closed her eyes, attempting to find the inner peace she'd read so much about.

The dragon's claws, however, never tore through them. Instead, the air surrounding them crackled as if electrocuted.

Open your eyes, younglings.

When Freya did, she noticed the glowing aura around her and Brennan. "More powers?" she whispered.

No, something much more important – healing. After your adventures, it was much overdue. Both its blue eyes settled on them. *It was not Osiris alone I served, but Set, too. I have seen both gods lose themselves to power. And had you come here saying you wished to destroy the relics for one or the other, I never would have given them to you.*

Draykho snorted, luckily turning his muzzle away from them at the last moment to avoid flames touching them. *It was the reason I never told either god where I hid. Their fickle nature has no limits, nor does that of humans. Luckily, you did not ask me for favors on behalf of either deity. Your hearts are pure, and you wish only the best for the world.*

With a sigh strong enough to push them a few meters away, the dragon produced the relics. The orb and scepter appeared in his extended paw, looking no bigger than toys. The golden glow around them drew both teenagers' attention.

They are yours, to do with as you wish.

Brennan pulled himself to his feet first, then extended a hand to Freya. Once she got up, they slowly moved towards Draykho's outstretched paw. The Wiseman reached for the scepter, while the Sage picked up the orb.

To their surprise, both relics were light as feathers. Aside from the glow emanating from them, nothing could have indicated they were precious artefacts.

Under the dragon's watchful faze, Freya produced the chains of fire, her gaze glued to Brennan's. "Are you ready for this?"

He nodded and placed the scepter on the ground. "Together." Freya dropped the orb next to it, watching them glitter for a second.

She could sense their pull, their offerings – the fate of the Underworld, the souls of the dead, for their taking.

Then Brennan moved around her, wrapping his hand around hers. The chains were in both their grip, strong and flaming. Freya pulled on the energy within her, and Brennan's joined hers. Time seemed to freeze, and she was aware of his breathing against her ear, his heartbeat at her back, his strong grip on hers.

A glow formed around the chains, coating them with a silvery light. Freya glanced over her shoulder, meeting Draykho's blue gaze. He nodded, once.

Together, she and Brennan lifted the chains and flicked them – once, twice. Each hiss of the air touched a relic, shattering it into millions of glittering diamonds. They floated around the cavern like fireflies, finally falling into the pool – and vanishing forever.

They stared at the calm waters, before glancing at the dragon.

"It's over, then?" Freya asked.

"For good?"

Draykho inclined his massive head in agreement, then spread his wings. *Well over, I should say. You are free to return home now, and live the rest of your lives without this threat over your heads.*

Freya bit her lip, leaning against Brennan's chest. "And the ghosts?"

Nothing can undo what has been done, unfortunately. But at least no one can control them now.

Brennan nodded against her temple, and wrapped his arm around her shoulders. "Let's go home, shall we?"

Freya turned in his arms, lifting her gaze to his, and nodded.

If I may help...

In dire need of recovering their strength, both Freya and Brennan accepted eagerly. The last they saw of the dragon was its massive form returning to the pool, and disappearing within its calm depths.

Epilogue

Three weeks later...

"Brennan!"

Freya's shriek had the young man rush to the library, only to find her smiling and clapping as Seamus leaned on a stick.

"He's walking again!"

Brennan leaned back against the wall, folding his arms across his chest and returning her smile. "I see that. Good on you, old man."

Seamus snorted, waving the stick towards him. "Who are you calling old, boy?"

Freya moved to Brennan's side and kissed his cheeks, then he moved to her lips. "Where are your parents?" he asked.

"Somewhere in between worlds, I'd say."

After they'd returned to the safety of Seamus' castle, Evie and Mark had found out they were allowed to still visit. While they had to spend more time in the spiritual world to recharge, being able to see them occasionally was enough for Freya.

She nuzzled her boyfriend's neck, relishing the shivers that ran through him. "Why do you ask?"

"No reason," Brennan said, thinking of the conversation he wanted to have with her father. *If not now, then perhaps at some point. Might as well tell him my intentions for the future.*

"Hm?" Freya looked up at him, and he realized he would have to be careful, considering their tight bond.

"Nothing, love." He tightened his hold on her, hugging Freya close to his chest. Then his eyes drifted to Seamus. "Better now, then?"

The elder Sage smiled, having observed them all along. "You could say that. What's next on the agenda, besides waiting for Sam's latest updates?"

Brennan glanced down at Freya, raising an eyebrow in question. She shrugged, leaning her weight against him. "Who knows? Maybe once Sam returns from cavorting with Anya, he'll have news of some disaster or other."

"In the meantime, we can find other ways to keep ourselves occupied," Brennan whispered in her ear.

Seamus shook his head, waving a finger towards Brennan. "Do not let Mark hear you say those words, foolish boy."

He walked away, then turned back at the doors to look at them one more time. Freya was leaning on Brennan, glancing up at him with a smile on her lips. And he was engrossed in whatever story she was telling him. Their auras shone brightly, and it was enough to bring tears to his eyes.

Well. I'll be damned.

&&&

In the palace of the gods, Mark stepped to Osiris once more. "A deal is a deal, lord of the Underworld. Have you opened the gates for Thomas?"

Osiris nodded and pointed to the fireplace. In its depths, an image of the elder Wiseman appeared. He was in a meadow, painting a picture of the horizon. He appeared, if not happy, at least calm and at peace. *It will have to be enough.*

"Perfect. And he can visit his grandson, dreamwalk whenever he wishes?"

Osiris headed to the couch and took a seat, resting his chin on his hand. "Indeed."

Mark's next question was harder. "What of Set?"

After the relics had been destroyed, it had been much easier to imprison the god of storms. The image shifted, and fire soon created another window. This time, they could see another cage, surrounded by a barrier of fire and ice.

Mark's eyebrows rose. "Really?"

"Yes," Osiris whispered, as if to avoid Set hearing him. "Isis came up with the idea, and I helped with the implementation."

"And what makes you think this enchantment is enough to keep Set in?"

Osiris chuckled under his breath. "You mistake me, Mark. This cage is not to keep Set *in* – but rather to keep his guardian *out*."

"Guardian?" Mark's surprised expression morphed into a frown.

With a wave of his hand, Osiris showcased the rest of the picture. On the opposite direction of the cave was a column. And wrapped around it was –

"Draykho?" Mark's shocked gasp echoed in the room.

"Like I said," Osiris chuckled, "we are quite sure Set will not risk escaping again."

In the flames, the larger-than-life silvery dragon unfurled its wings and flew to the ground. He paced around Set's cage, snarling and blowing fire. The god moved to a remote corner, turning his back on the display.

Then Draykho spread his wings, and the last thing Mark saw were his blue eyes shining in the flames – a silent warning.

If you liked The Sage's Legacy,[1]
try one of my other series!
For a sneak peek at her fantasy romance
series,
check out The Avalon Chronicles[2]!
If you're in the mood for a different
type
of paranormal romance, the Moonlight
Rogues[3]
are waiting for you ☺

---

1. https://www.alexawhitewolf.com/the-sages-legacy

2. https://www.alexawhitewolf.com/the-avalon-chroni-
cles

3. https://www.alexawhitewolf.com/moonlight-rogues

Preview of Avalon Dreams
(The Avalon Chronicles, Book I)

CHAPTER 1

The wind rushed through her hair, the strength of the horse's back between her legs, the breeze in the air lifting her spirits.

King Adrien's daughter enjoyed freedom a little too much on the sunny day. Riding astride on her faithful steed, Shadow, satin gown billowing in the wind, she was acutely aware her behavior was entirely un-princess like.

The princess joyously opened her arms, welcoming the wind, while the stallion neighed and kept galloping.

"Lady Vivienne!"

Shouts came from behind, and she glimpsed a group of guards following from far away, evidently trying to catch up. The closest one pushed his horse on, heading for the monarch.

Vivienne chuckled at his dishevelled appearance, and threw a mischievous smile his way, emerald green eyes glinting. Shaking her midnight coloured hair loose, she bent over the horse, clutching onto the mane, and laughingly commanded, "Run like lightning, Shadow!"

His sturdy muscles bunched under her legs, picking up speed and leaving the knights in the dust. The royal gleefully giggled along, eyes closed in delight.

&&&

Vivienne was in a half awake fantasy state, fragments of the dream and horse's neigh still around her. The faint glow of a lamp illuminated the bedroom, always on. A sound had woken her up, but she could not identify it immediately.

She blinked, slowly waking up. The faint breeze flowing through immediately shook her – the windows were always, without a fault, locked tight at night.

As quietly as possible, Vivienne tried to reach under the pillow for the dagger always hidden there, but touched only the smooth satin pillowcase. She froze at a sound, mindful there was someone else in the room.

"Looking for this?" The disembodied voice came from the corner next to the closet.

Vivienne could make out the intruder's shape, and tried to hush the beating of her heart, hiding the fear and racing pulse.

She sat up in bed, keeping the covers wrapped tight, and turned to the voice. A glint of metal shone in the dim moonlight, the same one she had religiously kept around a nightstand for ages as a precaution. How ironic that it would be the same weapon endangering her now!

Vivienne distinguished the contours of a male shape, but no discerning marks.

"If it's money you're after, I don't have any," she confessed truthfully, proud to keep her voice firm and unshaken. *I wish Alistair was here right now.*

A crude laugh echoed, brittle and harsh as nails scraping on a chalkboard.

"Oh, well that's too bad. I'm sure we can find another arrangement."

As he spoke, the shape stepped right, and the young woman had confirmation he was male, from the build and outline of the body. She still could not, however, distinguish a visage, as if it was blurred. At his scrappy, sickening voice, her stomach curled in disgust. No exit was possible, due to his nearness to the only door.

Vivienne's senses tingled, fully alert, muscles tensing as she slid towards the opposite edge of the bed, preparing an escape.

"What do you want?" she questioned, in an effort to gain time.

For all response, the man advanced to the bed. His intent to hurt was apparent, but in a split moment, Vivienne's problems doubled – quite literally. Her vision became a confusing fog, and two shapes faced her instead of one.

As it had come many times before, the signs were the same: the bile in the throat, the flare in the stomach, the spinning of the room.

"You've got to be shitting me!" Vivienne muttered out loud, and the man paused for a fraction of a second.

The young woman knew if she passed out, the situation would get out of control. She tried to push the sensation away, but only resulted in making it stronger, whilst the intruder continued his approach.

Vivienne grasped at straws of reality in a last effort.

Close to the bed now, the man went to grab the covers. Vivienne jumped to her feet, already losing grip on the clamoring reality.

The intruder managed to grab her wrist, tugging on it. He breathed on her neck, emanating a foul odour, and she spun around. With a force Vivienne did not recognize possessing, let alone a move she had never learnt, she struck.

When the closed fist connected with his jaw, Vivienne fell, the floor and darkness beckoning.

The last thing she noted before giving in to the blackout, was a luminous bolt shooting towards the intruder... but emerging from her hands.

&&&

Vivienne Du Lac, Viv for all her friends, considered herself a wild twenty five year old, with a mean streak for speaking her mind, and a gift with animals. Though not Snow White by any designation – the jet black hair and rosy lips had often times gotten her the comparison – the small creatures had always connected with her.

Unfortunately, it was a gift the young woman learned to keep under wraps, realizing it set her apart from everyone else.

Another thing differentiating her from fellow humans was what Vivienne called a unique gift – or curse, depending on the day: déjà-vus.

Dictionaries usually define a déjà-vu as a sensation of having experienced a situation already, though it is only happening for the first time. In Vivienne's case, a tornado of flashbacks would hit, sometimes more than once during a day, and she would lose all notion of time and space.

This rather odd ability began manifesting in childhood, when at seven years old, her parents bought a gorgeous white Andalusian foal. The vineyard Vivienne grew up on in Nice, France, was nothing if not fairytale, as were her parents.

The first time she met the foal, the young child jumped for joy. During that first ride, something happened: the nice breeze brought echoes of a different ride, flashes of unfamiliar landscapes, and another horse.

Vivienne could recall, to this day, waking up from the vision on the ground, her parents terrified the horse had thrown her off, and forbidding her to ride again. It did not work out, as the young girl snuck around and formed a bond with the horse. Eventually, they gave in, and returned the riding privileges.

From that first day on, Vivienne's nights were populated by weird imaginations, where she was a pampered monarch in a faraway kingdom. In the morning, she would recount these nightly adventures to her parents, and at first they found it endearing.

As she got older, it became apparent something more was going on, and they decided a shrink would be a good idea. Following the experience, Vivienne promptly realized her uniqueness, and learned to hide the déjà-vus.

To the present day, aside from her best friend, Jennifer, and the faithful Alistair, no one knew what happened whenever she zoned out, or had to leave precariously during a meeting, foreseeing one of the flashes and preferring to avoid passing out in front of strangers.

Luckily, a profession as a historical researcher – and the more than sizeable bank account her parents had set up –

gave Vivienne the freedom to never worry about the secret getting out. Whenever she was on assignment researching papers or books of people contracting her, she was careful.

Her parents still lived in Nice, while Vivienne herself chose to navigate away towards Venice, then London, and finally settled in the ancient city of the popes, Avignon. She rented a small town home in one of the quieter corners, away from tourists, her own little haven of peace to return to from trips abroad.

Rather unfortunately, the déjà-vus followed everywhere, and no amount of therapy could clear them – not that Vivienne needed them gone anymore. They were a part of her life, although rather hazardous at times.

&&&

A kink in the neck woke Vivienne up – a startling pain, followed by the coolness of the hardwood underneath. She awoke slowly off the floor, blinking at the morning's sunrise filtering through the window. The previous night's episode flashed in her psyche, and she jumped up, urgently scanning the surroundings of the bedroom.

She was alone, the bed untouched.

Vivienne ran to the bathroom, taking off the nightgown hurriedly and checking her body in the large vanity mirror: no bruises, no scratches. In fact, there were no marks whatsoever to indicate any struggling.

Confusion was setting in, a nagging doubt now rising. Could she have imagined the entire situation? Yet it had been much too real: the hair at the back of her neck rising, the panic, wishing Alistair had been there...

"You can't have dreamt it!" Vivienne argued with the reflection in the mirror, green eyes sparkling with anger and fear. Once again, she inspected her back for any visible bruises, with no luck.

Had it been all envisaged, a trick of the mind? Sometimes, the reality and fantasy were intertwined with her trances to the point of creating false memories.

Vivienne gave up on the bodily inspection, now sure nothing had happened, and went to shower. Minutes later, exiting the bathroom, she noticed the window open – same as from the so called dream.

Vivienne tip-toed to the bed, lifted her pillow, and frowned in confusion upon noticing the blade missing. She inspected the area around the bed and finally found it near the bedside table, on the floor.

It was still sheathed in leather, but could not have fallen there on its own. To top it off, the dagger was precariously close to where the man had been the last time she had seen him.

All the pieces pointed to one truth only: the intruder was not only real, but had disappeared from last night. Vivienne's first thought was to call the police. The second, quickly following, was, *Who would even believe me?*

Aside from the weird situation, she lived in a rental town home off a private lot, and the neighbors kept to themselves. They generally did not interact, so the chances of them remarking anything odd the previous night were slim. As well, the fences around her own backyard pool kept anyone from getting too close.

The ring of a cell phone snapped Vivienne from her musings.

"Hello?" she breathlessly answered, after rushing to retrieve it from the kitchen.

"I don't know what game you think you're playing, you little witch, but that was some trick you pulled last night!" The angry voice was unmistakably familiar, and Vivienne froze, rooted to the spot, the hairs at the back of her neck rising yet again.

"I don't understand what you're talking about," she tried, but got interrupted.

"We'll see about that."

The line went dead, leaving her even more confused. The call had come from an unknown number.

Almost in a daze, the young woman set the phone away to get dressed. She had barely finished tying her long, inky hair in a ponytail, when the doorbell rang.

Vivienne felt his presence – and annoyance – before even opening the door.

A hundred plus pound of dog jumped up in greeting, large paws reaching for the young woman's shoulders, grey and black hair flying everywhere. Vivienne laughingly embraced him as he licked anywhere he could attain.

"Honestly, I can't fathom how you handle him!" Jennifer, her best friend's voice, penetrated.

Vivienne adjusted Alistair's weight in her arms, to glimpse her standing there, straining with the leash.

Jennifer's blue eyes flashed in annoyance, but the rosy cheeks and blonde hair were still as flawless as the last time they were together. They had been friends for over five years, since Vivienne had first run into her in a café by the house, as though by fate. Even after all this time, there was an unspoken connection between them.

"He's honestly not that bad," Vivienne chuckled, collecting the leash from Jennifer. "Maybe a bit overexcited."

"My childhood cat was overexcited when he ate, Viv. Your dog is a demon."

Alistair, wisely sitting down by his mistress' feet, tilted his head and growled menacingly, causing Vivienne to frown down at him. Big enough to pass her hips, the massive Caucasian Shepherd's body was strung up with anger.

The breed of dog was particularly designed for protection, and they viewed their human as the absolute charge, and anyone else as their enemy. Vivienne had chosen him from a litter of pups based on one stare – as though they were long lost friends.

Although the display of attitude was a daily occurrence between Alistair and Jennifer, she presumed the occasional sleepovers helped smooth out their relationship. After all, her friend had volunteered to care for him whenever Vivienne was out of town doing research for a new contract.

"He's not that bad," the young woman muttered again, moving past the entryway to let them in.

Once Alistair's leash was removed, he bounced around, before settling on his favorite couch to observe them both. Caucasian Shepherds were distinguished for their loyalty and vigilance, and her dog was no exception.

Half shrugging again at his behavior, Vivienne concentrated on Jennifer.

"So, what did I miss?"

"Nuh uh, girl," the young woman giggled, "you first. How was Rome?"

Vivienne grimaced, the recollection of last night still bugging.

"Uh oh," Jennifer's voice interrupted her thoughts. "That bad?"

"No, no, it was alright," Vivienne shook her head, giving an evasive answer. "How about we go get a coffee?"

Despite the casual tone, after one glimpse at her friend, it was apparent Jennifer was not fooled. Perceiving her uneasiness and deciding not to pursue it further, she simply nodded, "Whatever you feel like."

"Great! Alistair can get his walk too!"

Vivienne chuckled at Jennifer's groan, and picked up a small navy messenger bag as they both – with the dog – exited the house.

&&&

A few minutes later, they were seated at a café down the street, a short stroll from Vivienne's house, with Alistair by his mistress' feet as they were enjoying espressos and croissants.

Jennifer accurately interpreted Vivienne's silence as not in the mood to expand on the trip to Rome. Instead, she filled her in on the latest drama in her family's soap-opera life – including the part about a cousin running away with some construction worker, and the parents' indignation.

Vivienne, still fixated on last night's events, was having a hard time focusing. As she scoured around, observing the street, Alistair perked up. She craned her neck in the direction of his stare, immediately drawn to *him*.

The man could not have been more than six feet tall, strolling around in a dark leather jacket and jeans. There was nothing overtly gorgeous about him, rather an implacability which commanded attention. This was someone not ruled by emotions.

He could have passed by, never looked her way, and they would have been none the wiser. But Alistair, quiet up until that moment, stood up and barked his loudest thunder-bark.

Jennifer, unperturbed by the characteristic behavior, rolled her eyes and prattled on. "In the end, it doesn't astonish me. Much. She's been stubborn since the first day I met her."

Having calmed Alistair with a tug on the leash, Vivienne risked a peek in the stranger's direction, and heat instantly flamed her cheeks – he was still there. Furthermore, he was staring back with the most peculiar, shocked expression.

Something about his features was familiar, but the heat in his eyes was an entrancing echo of things past. There was a stirring deep within Vivienne, and a sensation akin to curiosity – or was it a warning? – prickled her skin.

Had his stare not enthralled her, the leather jacket, bruised knuckles, and scar on the side of his jaw would have raised bells of alarm. The onyx eyes, however, were a trap Vivienne could not disengage from.

In a single glance, the man's dismay was apparent, as was her shock at being ogled so openly. As his gaze warmed in recognition, images flowed at the back of Vivienne's head: a swift snippet of a champion bending over a lady's hand, a flash of metal, a chaotic overflow with no heads or tails.

The torrent threatened to consume, when the man stepped in the street, towards her. In that one second beat, an insistent honk – and a car rushing by, narrowly missing him – broke their connection. As swiftly as he had emerged in the field of vision, he broke eye contact, and retreated.

With the man gone, the images evaporated as well. Alistair attempted to get up, but Vivienne yanked on the leash hard enough to instill the command to sit. With a resigned glare, the dog settled back down, grunting heavily in displeasure.

The young woman zoned back into the conversation, in time for the end of Jennifer's tirade about the relative, carefully hiding her uneasiness under a blank mask of neutrality. The day had escalated to full-blown weirdness, as of precisely three minutes earlier.

"Yeah," Vivienne shrugged in response to Jennifer's rant, while massaging the side of her temples to dull the incoming headache.

"What's wrong? Is it another one of those flashbacks?" Jennifer pounced on her friend's vulnerability.

Vivienne was about to deny, pass it off as a normal occurrence – as unlikely as those were – but something stopped her. A nagging voice in the back of her head interrogated, *Why have a friend when you won't even trust her?*

At that exact moment, she peeked at Jennifer, with the uncanny sensation the thought had come from the young woman.

"Not really," Vivienne began, despite an odd reluctance. "More of a connection. It was a man this time."

"Cute?" Jennifer enquired, but despite the gossipy smugness, her attention was centralized.

Vivienne could not help a small smile recalling the eyes, the lips, the strong jaw and Roman nose, all definitive ruggedly handsome good looks. "Yeah, definitely. But, there's something about him..."

Jennifer arched a thin eyebrow – gift of nature – questioningly.

"He brought up stuff," Vivienne continued.

When Jennifer's expression remained blank, Vivienne continued, "Things I've never done: walks in the moonlight, knights, swords..." She stopped with a derisive shake of head. "I'm not sure, Jen, it was weird."

"Coming from you, it must be serious," her friend stated matter of factly, before taking a sip of the espresso. She was avoiding Vivienne's look, now fidgeting with the cup.

Vivienne frowned, both at the words and actions, and murmured, "I guess so..."

"Is there anything else?" Jennifer pointedly enquired, not fooled by the monosyllabic answers. "Anything to suggest he recognized you?"

Again, Vivienne hesitated, before haltingly disclosing, "He stopped, and for the longest time observed me. I thought he was going to come here, but he changed his mind."

She had to wonder at the disappointed tone in her own voice. What was wrong with her – on top of everything else, she now craved a stranger's attention, too?

"Wait," Jennifer interrupted Vivienne's mental tirade. "You're saying he noticed you?"

"Yeah. I was listening to you, when I peeked out the window and saw him pass by. Alistair barked, and he stared straight at me."

Jennifer dropped the usual sarcastic attitude and fidgeting, an assessing gleam in her eyes. "Anything else?"

"Umm..." Vivienne stopped with a cup halfway to her mouth and pondered honestly, with a tilt of the head to the side. "Only that I have a hunch I know him – really know him. Stronger than others."

There was a flash of almost fear in Jennifer's eyes as she recoiled, causing Vivienne to wonder at its reason. The strain in her head – which had previously eased off – returned with a vengeance, causing her to almost drop the coffee cup at the pang of discomfort.

Though her vision blurred, Vivienne noted Jennifer's peering, and distinctly heard her voice asking, *Can it be him already?*

"What did you say?" Vivienne probed, confused. Her friend's lips had not budged, but the question had been as clear as if spoken out loud.

Jennifer froze at Vivienne's words, before forcing a tight-lipped smile. "I forgot, but I have to go." With a nonchalant shake of the head, she got up from the table in a hurry, and spilled the cup. "Damn. I, um," she trailed off, wiping the mess quickly with a napkin, before adding, "I promised Jacques I'd meet him at noon. And it's almost time."

Vivienne raised her eyebrows, beyond surprised at the boyfriend's name. *Didn't she break up with that guy a few nights ago? Or did I dream that, too?*

When she voiced the thought out loud, Jennifer shrugged and explained, "Well, yeah! But I have to get my things from his apartment. I'll call you about tonight. Ciao!"

In a whirlwind, she was gone, and the café's atmosphere dropped a few degrees. Vivienne shivered, and the tension in her head also eased off. Alistair whined low, pleading for attention.

"That was weird," she agreed while petting the pup, having long ago gotten past the bizarreness of speaking to her dog in public.

&&&

As soon as she was out of the café, Jennifer pulled out a cell phone and dialed the pre-programmed number.

When a male voice picked up, she hurriedly conveyed, "Advise him he's here, saw her, and she's remembering things. I'll stand by for instructions."

Hanging up, Jennifer then strode over to her own place.

&&&

The man hung up the cell, and entered back into the church. Situated on the edge of a cemetery, at one point, the religious establishment had been great, a tourist attraction even, but now only an abandoned building remained.

On the outside, the walls were falling apart, overgrown weeds eating into the stone, covering past great architecture. Parts of the building had collapsed, but the main structure still stood the test of time. A few windows had been broken by the elements, and pieces of glass streaked the ground, along with broken bottles and beer cans from teenage rebels.

As the man advanced past the faded brown door hanging on its last hinge, he could barely suppress a disgusted sneer. Inside the building, the remaining oak benches were either painted with graffiti, in pieces, or flat out faded and unusable.

There was only one thing untouched: an altar, with a red tablecloth thrown over it, a few chandeliers, and a large brass cross adorning the opposing wall. A few tiny candles stood in a circle around it, waiting to be lighted in prayer.

"Who was it, Braydon?"

The speaker stood in front of the altar, only his back visible to the one called Braydon. He wore a faded brown cape, with a large hood.

Braydon put away the cellphone – there was no love for such contraptions with his master – and replied, "Jennifer, master. She said he's back. And Vivienne's reminiscing has begun."

The man threw his head back in an almost relieved sigh, lifting both arms up to the ceiling in a V shape.

"Praise the lord!" he sniggered mockingly, before lowering them. "Then it can begin."

He drifted around the altar, picking up some remaining pots, throwing them with such emphasis they shattered, the oil tainting the tablecloth. With a single hand wave, a blazing candle dropped on the material, inflaming it. He stood behind the flames, a cruel sneer playing on his lips, as the last remnants of faith in the building evaporated.

&&&

Having finished the coffee, Vivienne got up and paid, grabbed her jacket and bag – as well as Alistair – and left the little coffee shop to get some air. The dog followed docilely. She only kept the leash on to avoid alarming people, due to his large size, but with or without, the dog's obedience was never in question.

Exiting, she breathed in deeply the autumn air. There had always been something appealing about the multicolored leaves and crisp air, although why, Vivienne could not place it.

Strolling down the street towards her favorite spot in the city, a fountain in the Place des Corps Saints, the stress eased off her shoulders, as if removed by an invisible hand. Her gait became more relaxed, and Alistair trotted silently, enjoying his walk on the cobblestone paths.

Vivienne anticipated a few minutes of peace when they arrived at their destination, as the water always aided reflection. However, as she got to the little roundabout where the fountain was located, her usual spot by the ancient tree was already occupied.

The young woman stopped dead in her tracks, jaw dropping as she recognized the man from earlier. As though alerted by an inaudible alarm, he snapped out of his deep thinking, and turned her way, eyes widening in surprise.

Almost lazily, he straightened from the trunk he was leaning against, and moved forward, eyes locking across the distance. Vivienne advanced before making a conscious decision to do so. She could not break the stare, enthralled.

Before she could step again, he was gone, in two long strides getting into a silver car parked in one of the adjacent alleyways. In a rush – almost a panic attack – she ran towards it, but the car sped away.

As soon as it disappeared, Vivienne became heedful of the weird sensation in her chest, almost as if a hand was squeezing the center. Alistair's bark made her jump, though he was frozen to the ground, also staring after the car.

"What the hell is wrong with me?" she wondered out loud angrily. It was impossible they had met before, of that she was certain. Yet his hold on her was undisputable.

Frowning, Vivienne stepped towards the fountain, sitting down on the ragged edge, still mulling over the unfamiliar man. Alistair settled on the ground, patiently waiting.

His mistress peeked down, exhaling heavily. "If at least I knew his name, maybe I could understand what the hell is going on with me... and him."

The moment the words left her mouth, a breeze picked up, blowing against her flushed cheeks. As it always did around an oncoming flashback, her skin prickled in warning. Alistair whined – a telltale sign the déjà-vu was coming. Vivienne braced for it, but only the wind responded, with a gentle caress as soft as a feather.

Then, so hushed she almost missed it, a name.

"Sébastien."

Startled, Vivienne jumped off the stone, scouring her surroundings to identify where the name had emerged from. *Am I beginning to actually lose it?* she wondered.

The déjà-vu hit before she could prepare, and all that was left to do was submit to its insistent pull.

&&&

Vivienne was in a garden – a vast, filled with ever flower, type of garden. The cold air of the night surrounded, and the full moon was high in the sky. The sand underneath indicated she was somewhere in the desert, yet the encompassing palace was luscious, and not a mirage.

As far as the eye could inspect, were a multitude of flowers and trees. Her gown, of the finest silk, wrapped across her body whimsically, a lover's caress to a heated skin.

He came out of nowhere: leather armour on, weapon in hand; the love of her life. He had always been there, always solid.

The guardian strode towards Vivienne, and the welcoming smile on her lips died at the grieving in his eyes – something was not right. He stepped into the moonlight, and she frowned at the regret in his eyes, heart lurching agonizingly.

"I've failed," he rasped.

"Sébastien..." the name was uttered softly, lovingly. As he got in close proximity, Vivienne detected the sheen of sweat on his face, and the blood oozing from a gut wound.

"No!" she screamed – but it was too late. He crashed at her feet, murmuring words of love, as Vivienne bent over his body, sobbing uncontrollably.

Later, when Sébastien's body had become cold and lifeless, she cried to the moonlight, and begged to be allowed to join him in the afterlife.

&&&

Something wet licked her hand, and Vivienne's eyes fluttered open to notice Alistair. Her head rested on the cold ground, apparently having fallen against the fountain during the recollection – which also explained the irritating soreness around her neck.

It was not a surprising occurrence, considering the weird nature of the flashes assailing her, which more often than not resembled time travel. Normally, a déjà-vu is only a familiar sensation, fading smell or taste.

Vivienne's, on the other hand, were a cross between a déjà-vu, a memory, and getting whacked over the head by something incredibly solid. Whenever they happened, she was literally transported somewhere else, reminiscing, losing complete connection with the current reality. It made the return much more aggravating, and her life even more confusing.

Oddly enough, this particular flash was one of its kind. Previous ones had mostly been centered in a medieval time, but this one was ancient in its environment, as though from a different lifetime. And there was something incredibly familiar about the champion who had died at her feet...

Using the dog's sturdy frame to manoeuver herself up, Vivienne managed to get to a standing position, well-versed now in the art of recovering. Alistair peered at her questioningly.

"I'm fine," she grimaced weakly. "Let's go home, maybe a nap will help."

They took their time getting back to the house, on account of Vivienne still being dizzy. As soon as they cleared the backdoor, she went straight to bed and passed out. Alistair inspected the house quickly, and then joined his dormant mistress, head over his paws, an alert gaze fixated protectively on her.

Vivienne, through restless sleep, was soon dragged into another vision, with Alistair helpless to stop it. This time, she was not in the desert, but in a different recollection, similar to the ones from medieval times.

&&&

"*You summoned me, father,*" Vivienne curtsied in front of the old king, then straightened up and beamed at him.

King Adrien could not help returning it, despite the hour spent attempting to calm down the head of the palace guard, and the guards themselves. They had been beyond furious after Vivienne had, once again, run off with her stubborn horse, and had to give up the chase across the vast plains of the realm Elsior.

Vivienne was his only daughter, and after Vevila's death, Adrien's beloved wife, he had raised her freely – perhaps a bit too much. The young princess was so full of life and laughter, he simply could not restrain her, cringing at the thought of imposing limits. And yet, the challenges awaiting her, especially once he was no longer of this world, would be worse for wear without protection.

Thus, much as the king hated to, he had listened to the reports, and finally given in. Adrien landed a severe stare on his young daughter, to impress the gravity of the situation.

"*Yes, dear daughter,*" he finally acknowledged out loud. "*You are driving your guards quite mad, so I have taken the liberty of hiring a new one. He is knighted, and comes highly recommended from various courts across our land, where he has secured his charges to the satisfaction of his employers. Please, meet Sébastien Dubois.*"

Vivienne tilted her head in the direction king Adrien was pointing to, but the haughty reply died on her lips when their eyes met. Green met midnight, and the instant connection was impossible to miss. The grand throne hall disappeared, the only thing existing was his unflinching stare.

The new guardian was a bit taller than the royal, with broad shoulders that were intimidating, if not enticing at first. The look was completed with hair as sombre as Vivienne's, and eyes of pure onyx, still fixed on her.

Sébastien broke eye contact first, and inched forward. He kept a respectful distance, less than an arm's width, before kneeling at her feet on one knee. "My lady," he began in a deep, hoarse voice, a delicious caress of the senses.

His hand gripped Vivienne's gently, rough pads grazing the skin. When his lips pressed to it in greeting, the princess' knees wobbled. What was it about this man that stirred her to the core, when none had ever managed to before? He had spoken no more than two words, yet she was left without speech.

"Rise," Vivienne rasped, and cleared her throat at the breathless tone, keeping her features as impassable as possible.

Sébastien did as he was bid, and towered over the monarch momentarily, before retreating a few steps. Vivienne tried to ignore the scrumptious new guard, instead glancing back to the king.

"Father, is this truly necessary?"

"Yes, my dear. I appreciate your independence and I do not wish to limit anything from it, but he will be travelling with you during your lessons with your mentor, and anywhere else you wish to go."

"How is it I am supposed to get some time to myself?" Vivienne argued, eyes narrowing.

"You still will... But he has to come everywhere. Please do not push this issue any further, Vivienne."

The princess was about to protest, but the king's tired tone hit her. For the first time discerning it, she frowned at the pallor of his skin, and replied softly. "Father, as you wish," and curtsied again.

She was about to depart, when a shadow emerged from the corner of the throne room and came to her. Everyone present in the throne room gasped at the size of the animal, and Sébastien's hand automatically went to his weapon. When he realized neither the king nor Vivienne were fazed, he remained immobile, observing silently.

The dog, if he could be called such, nuzzled Vivienne's hand, until the royal peered down at him. His head passed her waist, the rest of the body as large as a young bear. The black fur which had permitted him a seamless blend with the shadows, now stood in contrast with the whiteness of the floors.

The dog's eyes travelled to the new guard, whose hand still gripped the sheathed blade. With a dismissive snort, he strode to the king, walking up the stairs to the throne, and set his huge head in the old man's lap. As if preparing to yawn, the massive jaws opened, and a breath came out in puffs of white smoke, which Adrien inhaled.

The king's cheeks regained some colour, eyes now glowing with resolution. Vivienne retained a relieved sigh: Alistair, her familiar, had done it again, invigorating Adrien with life essence, when his was failing.

She could not help but glance towards Sébastien – curious at his opinion of all this – to meet his fixed stare. Before even deciding to, the princess stepped forward, back in his vicinity, drawn to the new knight against all odds.

Alistair retreated from the king, and came to his mistress' side. "Thank you," Vivienne murmured to him, before turning to the king. "You should have told me your health was getting worse," she chastised, half reproachful.

"My dear," he extended a hand out, which Vivienne hastened to grip. "You are aware I will not be long for this world. Old age cannot be avoided, which is why I need you safe, at all costs."

She bit back the tears threatening to escape, before nodding. "If it will bring you happiness and ease your burden, then I shall accept this new guard."

Sébastien knew not what happened – whether the monarch's words, kindness or beauty did it – but his next actions stunned even himself.

He unsheathed his sword, and progressed towards Vivienne, as if incited by an invisible hand. Alistair sharpened his gaze on him, but foreseeing the intent, did not intervene. The princess, however, aimed a confused glance towards him.

Clutching the blade, Sébastien kneeled at her feet once more. He uplifted it, on the flat of the palms, and the words escaped his lips with a rushed intensity. "Lady Vivienne, I swear to you on this day my arm and body to protect you. I will let no harm come to you, and will be there to prevent any perils coming your way. Please accept my oath and bless my sword."

"Interesting," Alistair rumbled in his mistress' head.

Comfortable with his telepathic messages, she did not react visibly. However, Vivienne could not agree more with the assessment. Sébastien had taken a basic oath of allegiance, and transformed it into the promise of a lifetime of defending.

As she extended a hand to graze the metal, some magic seeped into it, without her actively willing. It gleamed, before

being absorbed, the metal shining brighter for a few moments.
"I bless it," she declared, "and accept your oath, Sébastien."

Their eyes met again, and this time the guard's stare did not waver. Something passed among them, and Vivienne became aware of a yearning deep within, as if it had woken up after years of lying dormant. She was the one to break contact, curtsey to the king, and saunter away, Alistair following close behind.

"She is stubborn, but will get attuned to you," king Adrien maintained, noticing the guard's rapt expression.

Sébastien absently agreed, still endeavouring to clear his head. He had come to the castle for duty, but upon contemplating his charge, already control over his emotions was slipping.

The oath was not one the knight had ever given, and it weighed upon his soul now that Vivienne was gone. A sweet citrus perfume assailed his senses, lingering in the air. If he was not careful, this assignment might become more complex than intended.

<u>Continue reading!</u>[1]

Preview of First to Fall
(Moonlight Rogues, Book 1)
∞ 1 – Începuturi ∞

"The <u>beginning</u> is the most important part of the work."
-Plato-

Lucrezia

My feet crunch in the snow, and for the tenth time this morning I thank my lucky stars I invested in my fuzzy warm boots. It may have been money I didn't have, but with the way the winter is acting up, it will only get worse.

Rockland Creek, Wyoming, is renowned for its harsh winters—not that it's the real reason I ended up here. It was the most remote place near the border with Canada and having that quick escape possible eases the tightness in my back somewhat.

Memories of a much darker time linger at the edge of my consciousness, but I shake them off. Distance and months of breathing freely have made it easier to compartmentalize, and I'm determined to get in to work chipper despite the chilly Monday morning.

An icy gust of wind sweeps up, and I huddle in my coat, wishing I had grabbed an extra sweater underneath it.

Almost there. As if to spite me, Mother Nature throws in some nice flurries—and more wind. Gritting my teeth against it, I quicken my step towards Claws Auto Shop, which I see in the distance. I'm one of those lucky few who can walk to work rather than have to drive or bus, which keeps me in an overall nice shape and clears my mind most mornings.

Most times, it only takes me about half an hour to get there. It's a breeze in summer, but not so much in winter. I vaguely consider asking one of my colleagues for a lift for the rest of the season and then dismiss the idea. The last thing I want them to feel is obligated to protect the only girl in their pack.

By the time I finally reach the side door of Claws Auto Shop, where I work as receptionist, my cheeks are frozen and my fingers refuse to cooperate. I fumble with the key, dropping it three times in the snow, before I get the blasted thing open.

After taking off my coat and switching into some comfortable sneakers, I sit down at my small desk and get started on my day. Within the next hour, as I answer calls and confirm appointments, the guys pile in one by one.

Guys, no. These are *men* and so damn gorgeous my heart hurts every time I notice them. Unfortunately, other body parts I've neglected for a while also poke their head out. Normally, I have a tight control on my hormones. These last few weeks, however...

I tear my eyes away from them and focus on my paperwork, going through the previous week's sales and amounts for collection. Having studied accounting and business while in university, numbers always fascinated me. They make sense, more so than people ever do—to me, at least. But this time around, not even the dry accounts payable booklet is enough to keep me focused. With every ring of the bell announcing someone's presence, I glance up.

First Finn McConnell shows up, his mischievous green eyes twinkling already. With his mop of unruly dark hair and the lithe body of an athlete, he could easily be an actor or model. The lilt in his voice hints at his Irish background, and yeah it's sexy as hell. You would never peg him for a lawyer, but he once dabbled in the trade before leaving Ireland for the States—a long, long time ago like he says.

Next comes Tristan Cayne, brooding about another sleepless night, if the circles under his eyes are any indication. He's a war vet, honorably discharged from the Marines with PTSD—post-traumatic stress disorder. He lost his entire unit in an ambush in the desert and still has the nightmares about it. His skin is tanned even in winter, due to his Brazilian blood, but the man knows how to pull off jeans and a simple shirt like no other. With his shaved head, gentle hazel gaze and square jaw, he's the most aloof of the four.

Third in is Dominic Kosta, with blue eyes that capture me every time and the sinful body of Apollo. Dark blonde hair, clean-cut jaw and muscular build, he's the gentlest of the bunch. At first he told me he was born and bred here, but after many late evening conversations, he revealed he was adopted from a Romanian orphanage by an American couple who couldn't have children of their own.

The story answered a lot of questions about him, and it gave me more insight into this gentle giant who I've seen break more than one heart with all his womanizing. Despite it, there's a quiet confidence in him I respond to, and he puts me at ease in a way no other man has. I've been working here for the last year, but it's Dominic I connected with more than all the others.

His grin lights his face when he sees me, and he moves in for a hug. I squeal out of his grip, shivering at the wind drafting in with him. "Get away, you're ice cold!"

Dom picks me up snorting and twirls me around, before putting me back down. I'm still recovering from the closeness, when the last of them walks in.

"Already wasting time, I see?" Lucas Bianchi's remark would have stung, had it not been delivered with his side-smirk and glittering onyx eyes. The man is Italian to the bone, and his commanding presence tends to leave me shaking at the knees.

Lately, it's morphed into more than that. Whenever he's around, I lose my words—and I haven't crushed on anyone since high school.

"Morning, Lucrezia," he murmurs in his gravelly voice, and I smile feebly in return. To this day, Lucas is the only one who calls me by my full name, all the others having picked up on the nickname Dom gave me: Luz, for light.

As can be guessed, the mixed nationalities have definitely increased my vocab, at least where swearing is concerned. Both Tristan and Lucas lose it in their respective native tongues, and it's almost fun watching them when it happens.

With a nod to Dominic, Lucas heads to the back, already barking orders to Finn and Tristan. Two other guys help around the store in summer, but they're only teenagers from high school, learning the trade. Mostly, it's just us five: me on the paperwork and phones, and the guys tinkering and fixing the cars of Rockland Creek—and of the people passing through.

And I was the lucky one who got to work with them every week, day in and day out.

"Why the long sigh?"

Oops. I'm uncannily aware of Dom's steady gaze on me—and his keen sense of observation.

"Bah, it's Monday," I try to joke, but even I don't fall for it. I peek towards Lucas, who's now opening the doors of the garage—a tell-tale sign announcing they're ready for work.

The inside of their working environment has heat blasting so even with the cool air wafting in, they're comfortable. Not that it seems to matter to these four—they're so hot-blooded a hug from them will have you sweating in no time!

Thankfully for me, a transparent window and well-insulated door separates me from the garage area, and I get to stay indoors and enjoy the warmth.

My gaze is drawn to the two cars already driving in, one of which is a sporty red Mustang convertible. The other is a pickup truck that has seen better days. It's no surprise when Lucas walks over to the Mustang, with Tristan heading to the other car to greet the clients.

"Who the hell drives a car like that in winter?" My eyes narrow in annoyance.

The answer soon makes itself known. A leggy brunette steps out of the car, dressed in dark leggings, thigh-high boots with six-inch stilettos and a white fur coat. Even from afar, I notice her makeup is done to perfection.

Though I'm confident in my flaming locks and exotic features, I don't tend to flaunt my looks. Working with the guys gives me the perfect excuse for casual dress and flying under the radar in jeans and t-shirts.

It's better this way, the reasonable voice in my mind warns. *Remember what happened last time?*

A snort from Dom has me focus back on him, in time to see his grimace.

"What?"

"The girl," he rolls his eyes. "She'll be a handful. I better go, Lucas might need help."

I watch him go, trying to stifle an exasperated sigh—and failing. "You sure it's not *her* you want to get a closer look at?"

Dom turns around at that, a flash of surprise crossing his features. It's gone so quick I might have imagined it. He grins instead and winks. "Not with you around, Luz."

He's gone before I can figure out what he means, and I turn my attention to my regular tasks. At least until the brunette comes for payment. "I was told to come here to pay for the services," she says huskily, and I wonder for a second if she fakes that voice.

I force a polite smile, realizing how mean my thoughts are turning. "Of course. May I see their quote?" She hands me the paper—perfectly manicured nails, I notice—and I plug it into the computer and issue her a formal invoice.

Once she pays I staple a receipt to the invoice and hand it back to her. Eliza Porting is her name, and if it didn't fit her so classically I would laugh about it. She sounds so posh, dresses to a T, yet here she is in the middle of nowhere with a car that broke down.

You once ended up here in a similar way... I try to ignore the reasonable voice nagging me. A lecture would be bad right about now.

Oddly put off, I hand Eliza back the card and return to my computer. I figure this will be it and she'll go wait in the seating area, but she sees fit to hang around.

"How do you work with all that man candy around?" An annoying giggle follows her whispered words.

I track her gaze to the guys, for a moment detracted when Lucas bends down to check under the car, giving us both a perfect view of his, err, assets. Eliza's practically panting in delight, eyes glued to him solely now.

Mine, I want to growl, and hold back. This possessive nature is new for me, as is the jealousy. I have no right, but Lucas is that kind of man. The type you want to lock up and have your way with, day and night... *especially* night.

"Not sure what you mean," I mutter, focusing on papers that need no more organizing.

She turns to peer at me then—really looks at me, assessing me from head to toe—and smirks knowingly. "Oh, I get it. It's ok; I have nothing against people who play for the other team."

The diva goes back to ogling the guys lasciviously, dismissing me in the process. "More for me."

My palm itches, consumed by an almost insane urge to slap her. Just because I dress a certain way, she needs to label me already? *Bitch.*

I'm about to comment, when her next words hit me hard. "So, seen Tommy lately?" Her lips turn upwards into a sneer at my shocked expression, but those eyes are emotionless.

Shit. I thought I escaped this.

Dominic

I stare at Luz for who knows how long this particular time. At first, I tried to keep my distance. She was new, different, and mortal. But something in her calls to me as sure as the full moon, and the more I've known her these last months, the more I want her.

Unfortunately, she only has eyes for Lucas. She doesn't understand the reason for her attraction is linked to his status as chieftain of our pack. Nor that he officially took the lead as alpha in the summer, causing a hell of a lot of hormonal changes in his scent over the last weeks that affect even the most hardened females.

Then again, Luz also has no idea she's living and working in the midst of a town ruled by werewolves.

Some secret, huh?

We've kept it on the down low from the uninitiated—basically, people like Luz who think the world is normal. Her working for us was a complication at first. We were so used to joking around and acting like mutts in heat that needing to censor ourselves seemed like chaining.

It would have built resentment, were it not for Luz's open perspective on life. She quickly—and bossily—got us all in check, ordering us to treat her like one of the guys. It established a certain professional relationship.

Which is why I'm loath to break it. That, and there was something wounded about her when she first appeared in town. I still remember the day she got off the bus with nothing but a backpack, looking lost and so damn vulnerable it tore at my heart. I was in wolf form, and her scent acted like an aphrodisiac I had a hard time letting go of.

Not many humans are supposed to affect us this way. Not many *do*.

Except Luz.

Back then, despite morphing into my human form, I'd still struggled to quiet my wolf down. I can recall, even to this day, the anxiety in her expression when I first asked if she was new to town. After a few moments of awkward talk, I offered to show her around.

It might have been the loneliness or her quick assessment of me, but Luz agreed. Within the day, we ended up at a diner. No matter how much I tried to probe back then—and since then—the only information I got was that she recently moved to Rockland Creek and was searching for a job.

Before I thought things through, I was already telling her our mechanic's shop direly needed a receptionist. Lucas had been none too happy when I showed up with her in tow, but after some discussion, he relented. Luz was hired the next day, and Lucas has admitted on more than one occasion since that it was the best decision he ever made.

My thoughts of Luz must have intruded on my senses because my wolf is growling. *Danger.*

And no, I don't make a habit of hearing voices, at least not in the losing-my-mind way. But I do have a second facet to my personality, and that's my wolf.

He lives within me, like a subconscious part of me, not an alter ego but more... a voice of reasoning. On a regular basis, he pokes his head out only when strong emotions control me, luring me away from my more human side.

But this time...

I listen to the warning and look towards the reception desk where Luz's anger reverberates across the distance. The high-maintenance gal who's with her irks me, and she annoys my wolf.

"Don't," Finn mutters next to me.

I glance at my buddy, surprised he read me so easily. Then again, with Finn, you're an open book more often than not. That's the thing when you're around werewolves with special *gifts*, like I call them.

"You know she has feelings for Lucas." His eyes narrow in disapproval, darting from Luz back to me.

"And you know *why* she has them," I retort, going back to what I'm supposed to be doing— hammering back into shape a beat-up bumper.

Finn follows me to the long table meant for the task, not dropping the conversation. "You're assuming," he accuses, and I hammer the metal a little too hard.

My back muscles tense, and my wolf jumps to defense when I turn to him. "Back off, Finn."

He notices my glare, because after a few tense moments of staring at each other he steps away, hands held up in the air. "I'm only saying, mate. Keep in mind, Luz may have real feelings and more than a crush on our boss."

I don't believe that. *Won't* believe it, is more like it. And as I sense Luz's annoyance go up a notch, my wolf whines. *We can't sit by and do nothing.*

"Need a coffee." My mutter is barely audible, but I don't wait for an answer, instead storming toward the doors. I step through, and the gal from the city moves towards me like a cat pouncing on her favorite toy. Her overwhelming perfume makes me cough and I take a step sideways.

"Aw, poor baby's got a cold?"

I don't know what my face conveys at her idiotic question, but she backs away so fast she almost trips over her heels. "No, just allergic to perfumes, *miss.*" I stress the term for professionalism's sake, before dismissing her and turning to Luz.

Luz's eyes flash towards the client and the scent of anger hits me again, something I seldom see in her. It makes the gold stand out against the green of her eyes, and the image of a cat superimposes itself for a moment in my imagination.

Cats and dogs don't mix, my wolf points out. I stifle a smile at that, and Luz stops glaring at the fake Barbie long enough to spare me a concerned look. "You ok, Dom?"

I fake cough this time and force a sheepish grin. "On second thought, I may be coming down with something. Want to make me one of your special teas?"

Whenever any of us is sick, we go to Luz. She has an insane knowledge of herbal teas and their best properties, which comes in handy. My eyes roam over her as she moves from behind the desk, noticing the jeans and long-sleeved purple top she's wearing. She's shorter than me by a head at least, but damn those curves have my mind wandering in a not-so-innocent way, one too many times a day.

Then Luz grins at my words, and it's quick and bright like the sun appearing after a morning of clouds. I swallow past everything else I want to add—this is not the time. Instead, I pout in supplication, hoping the ruse will work.

Luz glances over at the client, undecided and unwilling to slack on the job. "I'll watch her." My promise comes in a mutter, as I'm none too pleased about spending alone time with the snotty client.

After a moment, Luz bites her lip, but relents and moves to the back. "Her name's Eliza."

I'm staring in confusion after her. Why would she give me the useless piece of information? It's not like I'm planning to ask this girl out. Still, once Luz disappears around the corner, I turn to Eliza. "I'm not sure where you think you've landed, miss, but I would loathe rejecting your business because you're upsetting our staff."

She gapes, evidently used to getting her way. *Spoiled*, my wolf snorts, and I can't help but agree when she yells, "Upset your staff? How dare you!?"

The urge to roll my eyes is strong, but I hold back—barely. "In case you haven't noticed, we're a quiet town here. Tight-knit group of people. We notice when someone upsets one of us."

Eliza continues to scowl, but now there's a stubborn lift to her chin as if she's thinking of disputing my words. "Not my fault your girl can't take a joke."

A growl slips past my clenched teeth then, and she widens her eyes.

"Leave. Now."

"You can't do that, I already paid!"

"There is such a thing as a refund," I drawl, crossing my arms over my chest.

"I didn't even *do* anything!" She stomps her foot at that—I wish I was joking, trust me.

"Either you keep your mouth shut around Luz, or I kick you out." When I move towards her, she gives up and sits on the far couch. "Thank you. Now stay there until your car is ready."

I turn away, ignoring her glare, and follow Luz to the kitchen, determined to make sure she's ok.

Lucrezia

Dom's a sweetheart, and his actions warm my heart. Even if he offered to stick around so he could chat up little Miss Princess.

I'm aggravated with myself for caring, and even more so for not being able to let it go. Dom fools around, I know this. He's not a player per se, but he dates enough. In a small town like ours, he's known as a catch—in bed. But never for good.

Enough.

I go about making the honey and cinnamon mixture in the small kitchenette, adding some of the ginger root I keep in the fridge here. Once it steeps enough, I pour it all in a cup and am about to return to the reception area.

I almost smack into Dom, who apparently snuck up behind me and was watching me work.

"Easy," he cups my hands, grabbing the mug from them before it spills and burns me everywhere.

After placing it on the side cabinet, he turns his attention back to me. "You ok?"

I want to answer him, really I do. But I'm struck dumb by his proximity, now in my internal bubble, as I call it. Have I never been this close to him? Or have I only been blind to his charm until today? And why in the hell does it feel like I'm left staring at a real-life Apollo, instead of my best friend?

The broadness of his back seems to dwarf me, and every nerve in my body is aware of our secluded presence. *He could do anything...* My brain tries to backtrack, memories pushing forth, and I half-expect a panic attack.

Yet nothing happens, and that scares me more than the opposite. Either I've lost my mind, or there is something about Dom that makes me feel safe. *Maybe it's because I've known him for so long.*

If I was to reach out, I could touch the muscles of his chest. Even from where I am, heat radiates off him, and something in my stomach unfurls in response.

My breath turns shaky, and this time I can't tell if it's a panic attack, or emotions...or something else.

"Luz, you ok?"

I glance up at his worried tone and manage a nod that's too stiff. "Yeah, fine. Just...out of breath. Sorry."

He frowns then, those beautiful blue eyes warm and scanning me up and down. My skin tingles, and I take a minute to realize he's holding my elbow, as though afraid I'll topple over.

"You sure?"

"Mhm," is my only intelligent answer. Then, like a coward, I side-step him. "Your tea is getting cold," I mutter over my shoulder, and take off the minute he releases his grip.

Dominic

After the morning incident, the day goes by fairly smooth. Eliza leaves with her damn Mustang, and we get no more high class maintenance clients, only our regular clientele. Finn keeps his mouth shut, and I stay busy with as many things as I can take.

Despite my best efforts, I can't stop watching Luz. I see her blush when Lucas asks her out to lunch to go over the sales reports—which they end up doing on the couch in the reception area. I can smell the waves of arousal off her and want to rip his throat out.

Finn steps in at that point, not fooled in the least by my resenting silence. "He's our alpha, Dom."

I ignore how in my face he is, trying to keep my tone curt as I continue to fiddle with the timing belt. "I'm well aware."

"We promised him loyalty."

I throw the piece on the table, ignoring the clank of metal on metal that echoes. I face Finn, failing to appear calm. "He's still new as alpha. And if I recall correctly, I promised him my obedience as his beta, but not my allegiance—and not forever."

Finn glances towards Luz and Lucas, then back at me. "Pack law is clear, mate."

"He hasn't made a claim." The words are more than a growl, but enough to quiet even my wolf.

Then Lucas gets up to go in his office, and Luz watches him with longing. A thought strikes me and before I have time to reason it through, I'm already moving.

This is a terrible idea.

Or so I keep telling myself, even as my feet inch towards Luz. Before I know it, my mouth is running off again—without me. "I can help."

Luz turns those otherworldly eyes to me, the gold more clear up close, and I gulp. I've never had an issue with women, but hell, this one will be the death of me.

"Dom?"

I snap back to with a very unintelligent, "Huh?"

Luz laughs, and I rub the back of my neck.

"Help me with what?" Again, her eyes slide to where Lucas disappeared to.

"With him."

She turns so fast I'm afraid she got whiplash. "What are you talking about?"

"I can help you with Lucas." I drop on the couch, ignoring her stunned expression and those lips I want to kiss so bad my mouth tingles. "You like him, right?"

Her face falls as she whispers, "Am I that obvious?"

"Only to me," I answer truthfully. "But you *do* like him?"

She nods, her eyes big pools of uncertainty.

"Let me help. I know Lucas, we've been buds forever. If he has feelings for you, he may let rules get in the way. Guy always had a thing for not breaking them."

"What rules?"

I want to smack myself—the reference to our werewolf life slipped too quickly. "Dating work colleagues." I save face and change the subject before she inquires further. "Either way, nothing like dating someone to get him to make a move if he's interested."

"I'm not good at dating," she whispers, looking away.

My wolf points its head, sniffing her scent, which changed in a few seconds. *Fear.* I sense it, too. But of what? *Surely it can't be me.* Either way, this is a chance to find out more.

"It won't really be dating. We'll fake it for his benefit. If it makes you more comfortable, we can even put a time limit on it. A week, two weeks, whatever you want."

She glances back again towards Lucas as he steps out of his office and back into the garage. The longing in her expression crushes my heart, but I promise myself to rein it in.

"And what's in it for you?" Her gaze is wary when it meets mine.

I shrug. "A chance to annoy him." *And make you happy. And show you he's not the one for you.* That last part, I don't say out loud.

Luz is silent for so long, I'm sure she'll end up saying no. Besides, what am I thinking? Nothing except selfish thoughts. I want her first kiss, and I want her to at least have the memory of my lips imprinted in her mind before she ends up with Lucas. I want to stake my claim even if it won't be permanent.

"Ok," she surprises me by saying. "How will this work?"

I'm too stunned for a moment to react, but already my wolf is roaring in victory and a grin spreads on my face.

"Leave it to me. Meet me tonight for drinks at The Cave, eight o'clock sharp."

When she nods, I lean forward and kiss her cheek, not even surprised when she jumps at the contact. "It'll be fun, you'll see."

And no kidding, I walk away whistling. Yup, like a poor sap who won the girl—not the one who promised to help her get the man of her dreams.

Bite me.

Continue reading![1]

Did you love *Relics of the Underworld*? Then you should read *First to Fall* by Alexa Whitewolf!

*He was given a new life, a new choice, a new path...*Once upon a time, Dominic Kosta didn't have a last name. In fact, he had nothing growing up in a secluded orphanage in the mountains of Transylvania. Then an American couple adopted him, and life changed. He left behind the old legends, the myths, the hunger within him.***He threw it all behind, choosing seclusion and a little town....***Rockland Creek may be a hole in the middle of nowhere, but Dom's happy there. Life has its perks between fixing cars and seducing women. And best of all? There are no rules, other than Lucas'.Then Lucrezia San Marco walks in, and draws him in like a moth to a flame. Only, she only has eyes for Lucas, his boss - and alpha of the pack. *...filled with were-wolves.* There's nothing normal about Rockland Creek - or Dominic's existence there. But things are about to get worse, and not just because he sees the girl he loves slipping through his fingers. *A war is brewing, eclipsing their romance and dragging old ghosts into town...*As Dominic navigates the murky waters of romance and obedience to his leader, his feelings for Lucrezia can no longer be tamed. But not every-one supports their relationship - and the Reapers have a word or two to say against it. As does Lucrezia's ex, and the demons he brings with him.Fire and ice, cold and hot, wolf and human. Dom and Luz will have to combine their differ-ences and learn to compromise, or risk being torn apart by the wave of change unfurling onto Rockland Creek.*Book I in a new series of sizzling werewolves, forgotten folklore and untamed legends.*

Read more at https://www.alexawhitewolf.com.

About the Author

Alexa Whitewolf is a dog-loving, caffeine-addicted, all-around traveling enthusiast. Author of three series of fantasy, paranormal and young adult, she spends her nights dreaming up new stories and her days fighting reality. She lives in Ottawa, Canada, with her husband and two mischievous furballs- Zeus and Achilles. Check out her website at www.alexawhitewolf.com !

Read more at https://www.alexawhitewolf.com.

ALSO BY THE AUTHOR

The Avalon Chronicles series
Avalon Dreams
Avalon Wishes
Avalon Nightmares
Atrox - A Novella

The Sage's Legacy – YA series
The Dragon Medallion
The Dragon Manuscript
Relics of the Underworld

Moonlight Rogues series
First to Fall
Second to Surrender
Third to Tumble
Last to Love
Moonlight Rogues: Origins

Standalone novels
Blood Ties, Love Binds
Unconditional Love
Blazing in a Storm of Ashes (Coming Soon)
More novels coming soon!

Sign up for my readers' group **at
www.alexawhitewolf.com/contact** and receive
a copy of *Unconditional Love* for **FREE,** as
well as first dibs on cover reveals, discounts,
giveaways, prizes **and more**!